Blue

The Birdie

Alison Craig is an award-winning radio and TV
presenter from Scotland. She was a presenter on
The One Show and hosted many other programmes
on BBC and independent radio and TV when a
health issue stopped her in her tracks

Since then, she has concentrated on writing the result
of which is *New Beginnings at The Birdie and Bramble*,
her first novel.

Alison's married and lives with her husband David
and sausage dog Charlie in Edinburgh. She has one
grown-up son Louis, who can found in his own flat
or in Alison's fridge inhaling the contents.

Twitter: @Alisonsdiary
Instagram: @Alisonsdiary
Facebook.com/Alisonsdiary

Also by Alison

New Beginnings at The Birdie and Bramble
Snowdrops at The Birdie and Bramble

Blue Skies at
The Birdie and Bramble

Alison Craig

First published in Great Britain in 2021 by Orion Dash,
an imprint of The Orion Publishing Group Ltd.,
Carmelite House, 50 Victoria Embankment,
London EC4Y 0DZ

An Hachette UK Company

1 3 5 7 9 10 8 6 4 2

A CIP catalogue record for this book is
available from the British Library.

ISBN (Paperback) 978 1 3987 0891 4
ISBN (eBook) 978 1 4091 9556 6

Typeset at The Spartan Press Ltd,
Lymington, Hants

www.orionbooks.co.uk

For my lovely Mum – Patricia Mary Craig
who left this world for a better place, April 2021

Prologue

Waking up in Jack's arms was a dream.

His strong warm presence, his arms encircling my waist, his mouth slightly open, his lips, warm and soft, on mine as I leant in and …

'Yip!'

My eyes sprang open to an alarmed dog, dying to get out of my grasp. 'Frank!'

Waking up in Jack's arms was a dream.

Chapter 1

The one thing I love about the restaurant business is that it is never dull. In fact, it is so challenging and unpredictable that when I roll out of bed in the morning, I have no idea what to expect.

Just last week we found ourselves holding The Great Birdie and Bramble Sausage Challenge, a competition thought up on a whim to settle an impasse between Claude, our head chef, and Javier, our head waiter.

It had all the hallmarks of a very entertaining day, so I made sure to be in the restaurant early, a good half an hour before the others arrived. First to pitch up was the diminutive and brilliant Claude who continues steering our ship to bigger and better things, his reputation growing, his talent in the kitchen bringing customers from all over the country to taste his amazing food. It recently earned him a red rosette from the AA, which has really put us on the map.

Five minutes behind him was Mouse, just a year ago a desperately shy goth Art student and part-time dishwasher who had recently undergone a literal metamorphosis, her confidence now soaring under the tutelage of Claude, and not just in the kitchen.

Claude initially appeared to be a scary bossy man in whites but had, over time, revealed underneath his cool exterior a heart of gold as he slowly nurtured Mouse, bringing out the very best of her. With his strict rules – no piercings, hair tied back, no painted nails – gradually she'd emerged as a very natural, confident woman no longer feeling the need to hide behind her curtain of black hair and swathes of inky clothing. But it's not all Claude's doing, of course, my daft cousin Hamish is madly in love with her too and in his eyes, she can do no wrong.

It is the love and support of these two very different men in her life that has given her the confidence to relinquish her role in the kitchen, to follow her dream of becoming a full-time artist. This confident decision is tempered only slightly by her insisting she works on the floor, at least two nights a week, in case she sells none of her work and starves to death. Of course, I am delighted, firstly because we have such fun working out front together, and secondly because if she hadn't stepped back from the hot plate, we would never have discovered that Javier is an absolute whizz in the kitchen, too.

Luck was on our side the day he walked in off the street having read a hastily scrawled note in our window, amidst one of many crises, which simply read, 'Help needed, apply within.' Three hours later he did a trial shift and since then the charming Spaniard has become an integral and in-dispensable part of the team. Having been born and brought up in a hotel and restaurant business in Spain, catering runs in his veins, so he can turn his hand to most things and is more than happy to do so.

Javier was last to arrive, holding a cardboard box that looked heavy but, as there was a dishtowel over the top, we couldn't see the contents. He was grinning like a Cheshire cat as he grabbed a coffee and disappeared into the kitchen.

Managing chefs' egos is an acknowledged downside of running a food business and Claude was no exception.

Classically trained and French, he was very particular about his kitchen and who had access to it. When Mouse announced her plans and he was informed that Javier was stepping into her shoes, initially his long pointy hooter was slightly out of joint. Our maestro of the hotplate acknowledged Javier was a fabulous front man but voiced serious doubts that his skills would transfer to the kitchen, so naturally things came to a head.

One day as we sat eating our staff meal after a busy lunch service, Claude and Javier, our two Alpha males, got into a very animated discussion about sausages, the way only two food-obsessed blokes can. They went on and on about size, shape, consistency, length and were quite oblivious to Mouse and I doubled up trying not to snort with laughter at this almost chimp-like standoff, testosterone flying. So, I threw down the gauntlet.

'Right, you two. The only way to settle this is for you both to make your best sausage, then we can have a blind tasting for customers and amongst ourselves. So, we will find out, fair and square, whose sausage is the best.'

There was a bit of grimacing and foot shuffling as both men, convinced they were right, were reluctant to be put to the test.

'Come on,' said Mouse. 'It's just a bit of fun.'

'Fun!' said Claude, giving Javier a sideways look.

Javier's response was a gentle smile and a shrug. 'Sure. Porque, no?'

This left Claude with little choice but to join in, so it was decided they each had forty eight hours to produce their supreme sausage. Both men committed to the challenge, and determined to win, began making notes, checking ingredients, and furtively squirrelling themselves away at either end of the workbench in the kitchen scribbling notes.

Individually they visited Uncle Fraser, who was also sworn to secrecy, at his butcher shop across the road to discuss their meaty requirements. Neither gave anything away to each other or to the rest of us.

As Sausagegate loomed, tension was mounting. Claude and Javier were ultimately polite to one another but aware that the clock was ticking on who would be declared the winner. During this ridiculous display of macho nonsense, Mouse and I fought to keep our hysteria at bay, the basis of which were the impressively high number of sausage-related innuendos we had come up with to amuse ourselves.

The day of the tasting arrived.

We all agreed to adhere to certain rules; after all, there was a lot at stake.

1. We were all banished from the kitchen as Claude and Javier cooked and prepared lunch.

2. Customers were asked when they arrived if they would like to take part in the Great Birdie and Bramble Sausage Challenge.

Almost without exception, when we explained what was going on, our customers were suitably intrigued and didn't hesitate. Just after we took their drinks order, each diner got a small plate with two slices of the sausages in contention. I observed a great deal of discussion between them before they declared their favourite, with results duly noted. The fact they had to discuss it proved both sausages had merit, thank goodness. I was already planning my runner-up speech, fearing the result would almost certainly bruise someone's ego. The kitchen was taking the whole thing very seriously indeed.

The first customer I presented the plates to declined, which I reported to Claude when he slipped into the dining room to check the bookings.

'Why she say no?' he asked, desperate for feedback and clearly taking it very personally, as if she had just insulted his very being.

'She's a vegetarian,' I answered.

'Oh, OK,' he said, returning to the kitchen slightly less put off.

Mouse sniggered.

And so, it went on.

At the end of the lunch service, it was our turn to taste. Mouse went over to retrieve Uncle Fraser from the butcher's shop. His son, Hamish, came shambling in grinning, and removed his muddy boots at the door. Being a vegetarian, he wasn't going to taste, but he wasn't going to miss out either. Even Noel closed his antique shop for twenty minutes to take part and so, troops gathered, we settled down for the blind tasting.

Once we were seated, Claude and Javier, in a rather gladiatorial fashion, whipped out of the kitchen, chests puffed out, and sat at opposite ends of the table. An Ennio Morricone soundtrack played in my head whilst Claude took the floor and explained that the remainder of the sausages had been cooked, sliced, and placed on identical dishes. There was a saucer covering each contender to hide any discrepancy in colour which might give the game away. We had no idea which was which, and neither did Claude and Javier, but just to add to the drama, they both whipped out linen dishcloths and asked me to blindfold them, ensuring absolute impartiality.

'If we do this, we do it properly,' said Claude, tightening his napkin around his head, which made his already very prominent nose look enormous. Mouse and I stared intently at the table, deliberately avoiding one another's eyes. There was no doubt a huge guffaw would go down very badly at this juncture.

The tension was thick as the tasting began.

To be honest, and I'm not just saying this, they were both stoating sausages. Meaty, moist and delicious, but in my opinion, there was one which offered a depth of flavour – a rich smoky paprika undertone, with caraway seeds and spicy black peppercorns throughout – that was so moreish I could have scoffed the lot. The other had sage, tiny flecks of red pepper, and a slight fennel aftertaste. Silence reigned as we masticated and made notes, the odd groan of pleasure escaping unchecked. Tasting over, blindfolds removed. I gathered everyone's notes and removed myself to another table to count the results as the others sat with bated breath.

'OK,' I said, standing up and turning to face them. 'First, the customers' votes. There were a total of fifty-two customers—'

'Gosh, that's good for a Tuesday,' said Hamish, rewarded with a nudge from Mouse.

'Sorry,' he said, looking down as Claude nodded for me to continue.

'It's very close,' I said. 'Of the fifty-two, twenty-four preferred Sausage B and twenty-eight Sausage A, and I can reveal sausage A is ... Javier's sausage!'

A cursory round of applause and a pat on the back for Javier. Claude's lips pursed as I continued.

'Next, the professionals' vote – that's us, by the way,' I clarified. 'OK, everybody, except one, preferred Sausage A, Javier's sausage, including you, Claude!' I grinned, which caused great hilarity and broke the ice. Claude nodded.

'Not me!' said Javier, standing up. 'I prefer Sausage B.'

I watched him deliver this news directly to Claude. Despite overwhelming evidence that his sausage was the outright winner, he insisted the Frenchman's attempt was superior, ever the charming diplomat. Initially Claude was a little miffed, and we all stayed silent, sensitive to his feelings and unsure of how he and his ego would react. We watched as he reached forward, plucked another morsel of Javier's sausage off the plate, scrutinising it with his eyes before popping it into his mouth. Hardly daring to breathe, we watched as his snout twitched and he rolled it back and forth in his mouth, chewing it and finally swallowing it before pronouncing, 'It is true! Javier's sausage is the superior product. A worthy winner, monsieur. Congratulations!' He stood and walked over to Javier, who leapt out of his chair to accept the hand of sausage supremacy and friendship.

And from that day to this? The two of them are inseparable. Really.

The other interesting result of this debacle was Uncle Fraser, who was so impressed with the taste of Javier's sausage, he asked him to come over to the shop and show him how to make it so he could sell the Birdie and Bramble Banger in his butcher shop.

'Cross promotion,' he declared, looking at Hamish, who had been trying to drag his father into the new millennium in regard to his business for years.

So Sausagegate was over. It had been a risk and could have gone terribly wrong, but I am thrilled to report that since then Claude has become a mentor to Javier, who is in turn a willing sous chef, eager and keen to learn everything from Claude.

So here we are, remarkably steady and busy with Mouse and I out front together one or two nights a week. A further three nights a week, I work with one of our three student part-timers, Ruby, Erin and Prue, and when William comes back from his honeymoon, he intends to work five days a week.

The only day we are closed is Sunday, opening again on Monday night for dinner.

At last, a perfect balance and a happy team.

Well, it was until I buggered things up.

Recap Jack

I've been relishing my job, motivating staff, chatting to customers and keeping suppliers happy whilst dealing with all the marketing and social media too. It has been relentless which is just the way I like it; it means I have no time to think about my, frankly catastrophic, personal life.

I am not one of these women who thinks that life is not complete unless there is a man involved. Since I decided to return to St Andrews and commit to running the business, I have felt loved and supported by my new family. I swear on Frank, my wee dachshund's life, this statement is logical and true during the hours I am upright and awake.

But as I drift off to sleep, absolutely puggled at the end of every day, I have no choice but to relinquish control, and nine times out of ten Jack MacPherson, the Merchant of Venison, is there.

I can lock him out during the hours of daylight with a million other things to distract me, but the battle with my subconscious leaves me wanting, and too early most mornings I wake to the reality that Jack and I, despite our visceral connection, are only together in my dreams.

Jack. It's as if the fates conspire to keep us apart. The moment we met in rather inauspicious circumstances, in Uncle Fraser's shop, he took my breath away. I was grieving for my dad and was only back in St Andrews to sell his restaurant, planning to return to my life in London ASAP.

The last thing on my mind was love but love, doesn't consult the people involved, it just does its damnedest. Be it chemistry or kismet, I was hooked. That first sojourn back in St Andrews ended in a magical night. Jack and I shared just one kiss and yet as I travelled the globe, expanding my horizons and trying to decide what I wanted out of life, that kiss remained like a tattoo on my heart. No matter where I travelled, the need I felt to return to St Andrews, to run the Birdie and Bramble, surprised me more than anyone. Though my decision to move back was not led by my feelings for Jack, I would be lying if I said that the hope we might pick up where we left off hadn't crossed my mind. Which we eventually did.

It was a slow burner. When I first returned from my travels, my business partner William was in crisis, so I had to hit the ground running and was at the restaurant every day and night trying to steady the ship. When Jack and I saw each other again, it was clear that visceral connection was still there, stronger than ever. But the combination of his job and mine meant for those first few weeks all we managed were a series of snatched moments, the sexual tension building to a ridiculous level. Then one day, Jack took things to the next level, picking me up and taking me to his cottage for what I thought was going to be a beans-on-toast impromptu supper, only to realise not only had he had spent hours cooking and preparing the most delicious meal, but he had set a table for two that could not fail to make a girl swoon. And swoon I did. After months of fantasising about this man, it felt like a dream when we finally sealed the deal, did the beast with two backs, danced the horizontal mambo aka shared the most extraordinary night. The following morning every cell of my body was tingling, my head racing, believing, ridiculous as it sounds, that Jack really was the person I was destined to be with. For a woman like me, who has never believed a man was that big a deal, this was a shock on many levels.

It was barely daybreak the following morning when we were woken by the dogs going mad. I was totally disoriented as Jack went off to investigate the kerfuffle, leaving me lying on the bed, grinning, like some sort of deranged satiated lovesick teenager.

Ten minutes later, impatient for him to come back to bed, I went off downstairs to rectify the situation, only to come face to face with a complete stranger. Meet Jody, an Australian girl he had a one-night stand with a year ago, when he was in Australia for a wedding. And if you thought things couldn't get worse … You're wrong! Swaddled against this woman was a silken-haired wee baby Scarlett, whom she claimed was Jack's. It completely sideswiped him and us, if there ever really was an us. Both in shock as he drove me back to St Andrews, he promised he would sort things out, and as I looked at his squished sleepy face, and unruly hair framing that look of utter shock as we said goodbye, my heart went out to him, and to be honest me, too.

the Birdie, as ever, was busy as hell, so I worked every hour as Jack went to ground for a few days. My imagination running riot about him, her and the baby holed up in his cottage together, there was a lot of gnashing of teeth. When we finally caught up, he explained that when he met Jody, she was in a fragile state as her marriage had just broken down, and they had a fling, simple as that. Jody was adamant that Jack was the only guy she had slept with, so she was convinced Scarlett was his baby. Of course, I encouraged him to get a DNA test but he said no, at this point it would be like calling Jody a liar, and if he did that, then what hope would there be of building some sort of relationship for the sake of the child?

At this point I went slightly bonkers and decided I would do a DNA test without Jack's consent or knowledge. It was a knee-jerk reaction to the arrival of this baby in his life. It was all very well if he wanted to believe Jody but a one-night stand? In Australia? I was very dubious indeed. When I told William my plan, he was horrified at the mere suggestion, but Sarah, my oldest pal and partner-in-crime, agreed to help me. But once I had snagged a DNA sample from Scarlett and nicked Jack's toothbrush, I had to forge Jack's signature, which was when Sarah had second thoughts and backed out of the plan. I understood completely – after all, it was a criminal act. But I was like a runaway train and so bagged, tagged, signed the forms, and sent them off. I felt sick doing it but my curiosity and desire to protect this honourable man won the day.

However, before the result came back, the biggest shock of all was when Jack got up one morning to find Jody had packed her bags and disappeared. Leaving the baby behind.

This all happened on the days running up to William and Noel's wedding. I was up to my oxters in getting the restaurant ready for the big day. My goal was to make it the best day William and Noel had ever had, so the wedding preparations were thorough, extreme and as a result, rather tiring. I had no option at this stage but to leave Jack to it. We texted every day, but I was as much use as a chocolate fireguard; I knew less about babies than nuclear physics and I knew bugger all about that.

The DNA test result arrived at the bothy on the morning of William and Noel's wedding. As the best woman, I had a million things to do, the most challenging of them was to keep over-excited William away from the champagne until at least 11.00 a.m., so I stuffed the envelope in my bag to open later. After a wonderful day, after Jack had scooped up Scarlett and left early, as it was all about her these days, full of booze and remorse for my underhanded behaviour, in a fit of conscience, alone in the ladies' loo, I rashly decided not to open it at all, and binned it only after I had ripped it into bits.

Please don't think I'm making excuses, but I thought at least if I gave you a bit of background it might go some way to explaining what happened next.

Chapter 2

We all know weddings can get messy – it goes with the territory. Everything starts glittering fresh, upright and bright and then as the day slides into night, the lines become a little blurred. Well, mine do.

William and Noel's wedding was joyful, from the start to the moment they were waved off on their honeymoon and as their wee car disappeared out of sight it was Uncle Fraser who clapped his hands and shouted, 'Okey dokey, my round!'

The boys had made it clear they wanted everyone to continue the party, which we did, rather excessively in some cases, namely mine.

After Jack left abruptly halfway through the evening with baby Scarlett, I ended up at the bar, like Oliver Reed, necking coops of champagne with Javier.

Over the past few months Javier had become a valuable member of the team. He had a heart of gold, was an enthusiastic hard worker and, I am not sure if I mentioned it or not, devastatingly handsome. When he first rocked up to the Birdie, I was so in love with Jack, the Merchant of Venison, I was the only one that didn't react the way the majority of red-blooded women and some men seemed to i.e. stammering, giggling, and, when his back was turned, staring. His kindness and support over what had been a difficult few months meant I had come to rely on him less as an employee and more as a friend and confidant, so it was just as well I was immune to his manly wiles.

I am just telling you this as it's important to know that after we waved William and Noel off and piled back inside to carry on the party, I was feeling a little drunk, a lot vulnerable and very alone. Standing at the bar, it seemed like love was all around. Cousin Hamish and Mouse clamped together, swaying in the gloaming, in time to the music, the boys in love and away on their honeymoon. My best friend Sarah stayed for a while, long enough for her and I to dance and for me to tell her I loved her more than chocolate, before her husband Phil whispered it was time to go. Hugging me back, Sarah told me she loved me, too, but not as much as prosecco, as she scooped up a sleeping baby Tilda. Phil heaved my very tired wee godson Charlie into a fireman's lift before wandering off home to bed. Uncle Fraser and Auntie Mary, married for nearly forty years, danced the night away. Claude, who had never batted an eyelid in the direction of anyone at all, talked to Jeannie the Kelso Lodge housekeeper all night, his arms flapping, occasionally whapping his hand off the table. And of course, Jack had already left with his new love, Scarlett, his pudgy wee baby, and that's how I came to be propping up the bar with Javier.

The cold fizz of champagne was like a drug; the more I drank, the less it hurt, and with the attention of a gorgeous man, life didn't look so bad after all. Until the next morning.

I woke up with a mouth like the inside of a budgie's cage, and a deep thumping buzz in my head. I tried to open my eyes but shut them again fast, the bright morning light like a razor slicing through my brain. I groaned. Then my heart stopped.

Light? There was only the smallest window in my little bothy as it looked out onto the wall of the postage stamp garden at the back of Noel's antique shop. The bothy didn't do light. So, where the hell was I?

My eyes flew open. All I could see was a door, a nasty-looking carpet and garish wallpaper. I was Marty McFly and someone had beamed me back to the 70s, I thought, and then, moving the heaviest head in Europe, I turned round. Javier.

My heart rate was already high due to the surfeit of booze but now I wondered if it might just stop altogether. First things first, I looked down. Yup, I was naked as the day I was born. Rolling back onto my side, facing away from Javier, I kept going until I dropped out of my side of the bed and onto the carpet on all fours, pausing briefly to tamp down the nausea rolling over me, before crawling round the bottom of the bed looking for my clothes. No sign, until I inched round to Javier's side of the bed, and there they were. My dress, knickers and bra were in a clump on the floor right beside him. The swirly carpet was not helping matters as I swallowed. As quietly as I could, I stretched my arm out, grabbed the wrangled clump of clothes, and dragged them back along the floor towards me, my heart thumping in my ears.

Mission accomplished, I stayed on the floor as I crawled to the door and was just reaching up to touch the handle when I heard him.

'Hola.'

I dropped back on all fours and froze, wishing I had an invisibility cloak. Turning slowly, I clocked Javier still lying in bed, his head hanging off the edge, watching me with an amused expression.

'Morning,' I said, turning away again, and then realising he was addressing my bare-naked arse. I twisted around, attempting unsuccessfully to cover myself up with the skimpy dress that I had balled up in my fist.

'Here,' he said, jumping out of bed stark naked, casually retrieving his boxers from the floor and slipping them on before walking over and handing me his robe. Dropping my dress, for the second time in twelve hours, I grabbed it gratefully. Sitting up on my hurdies to put it on, I came dangerously close to Javier's not insubstantial groin, which was at eye level as I shrugged the dressing gown on. FFS. Averting my eyes, I jumped to my feet, hitting my head off his thigh and grabbing the wall to steady myself as the blood rushed to my head. Seemingly unfazed he wandered off, found himself a towel and wrapped it around his waist. Thank God.

'Coffee?'

I just looked at him because I was unable to form words in my budgie cage mouth.

'Tea?' he tried again.

I nodded.

He smiled as I stood to the side, tying the dressing gown cord so tightly round my waist my liver threatened to fly out of my mouth.

As the door closed behind him, I spotted my clutch bag and my vertiginous heels poking out from under a chair. Opening it I saw a packet of fags, and a disposable lighter, always a sign of appalling behaviour as I had given up smoking years ago, a lipstick without a top and my mobile.

Thank God I still had my phone, I thought, as I dressed as fast as my shaky limbs allowed and began mentally preparing for the walk of shame.

Living in St Andrews, I was unaccustomed to dressing in anything other than working clothes, when in the Birdie and Bramble, and jeans and a t-shirt when I was not. Everyone dressed like a student around these parts, primarily because a lot of the people were students.

Javier had been living out here at Kelso Lodge for a few weeks which made this already embarrassing situation potentially ten times worse. Kelso Lodge was Jack's family home and the place where he was brought up. He hadn't lived here since he was a child but that wasn't the point, it felt like a violation of him to have committed this heinous act under this roof, if indeed we had committed a heinous act. After all, Jack was the man, I was in love with, which was why I could not quite work out in my fucked-up head why I had thrown away my caution and my knickers to the wind and just spent the night with Javier.

My instinct was to run for the hills, but I couldn't. Kelso Lodge was five miles outside St Andrews, I didn't have a car, and neither did Javier, so I was completely reliant on someone driving me home. My phone was nearly dead. My reputation shot. My behaviour unconscionable.

Gagging on my cup of tea, I decided to put the dressing gown back on over my shantung blue silk strapless dress and stuffed my mobile into the pocket before heading along to the kitchen, my feet enjoying the cool feeling of the stone floor; I was feeling rough as hell. It was risky wandering about given that Claude was living there at the moment too. I knew Jeannie the housekeeper didn't work Sundays so I was pretty sure at 7.00 a.m. on a Sunday morning I wouldn't bump into anyone else, plus I might just keel over if I didn't get some liquid into my dehydrated body.

As I neared the kitchen, the door opened and Javier came out carrying a large mug of tea that I was just about to take, when I heard a car rumbling over the gravel of the drive coming to a halt outside.

'Shit!' I hissed. 'Who's that?'

Which was irrelevant as whoever it was, I didn't want to see them. Looking at the front door, I wheezed, 'I've got to go ...' and before he could say a thing, I turned and tore along to the other end of the corridor to the back door, which I unbolted and ran out of, closing it behind me. Pinned up against it on the outside, my heart hammering in my chest, I felt like Jason Bourne. I was on the run.

Somehow, I had to get back to St Andrews without being seen.

'Sarah.'

Digging my mobile out of the dressing gown pocket, it showed one bar of signal and one bar of battery.

Please God don't die on me, I thought, as my trembling fingers typed.

Help. At Kelso Lodge. In the shit. Will be at the end of the drive. I'm wearing a white dressing gown. Send.

A text pinged straight back.

Can't wait to hear this. Will be there in 20.

My phone went dead.
Thank God.

After a Bear Grylls style exercise through the woods travelling parallel to the drive, I made my way barefoot, swearing under my breath as my feet met sticks, jaggers, and nettles. A bloody great pheasant squawked up, flapping in front of me, which damn near finished me off, and eventually I almost cried when I saw that the end of the drive was in sight. Back on my haunches I hid behind the stump of a huge, felled tree and waited. Hearing a car slow down as it approached the opening to the drive I was just about to jump out when I realised the noise was familiar; that sputtering, farty engine wasn't Sarah's car, it was Jack's. Cringing down into the smallest ball possible, my heart in my mouth, I watched as he turned into the drive. Scarlett's child seat was strapped into the front seat, Duke and Gaston the deerhounds in the back, their heads lolling out of the windows, eyes honed for anything smelly and interesting. As they passed, Duke's eyes settled on where I was lurking, his eyebrows lifted. I scooched down further as he did a double take and barked.

'Duke,' I heard Jack hiss, admonishing the dog who refrained from making any more noise, though he craned his head round to where I quivered in the wood, keeping his eyes on the same spot, until the Land Rover was out of sight. Before I had the chance to process that terrifying encounter, another car approached; the third one of the morning! It was like bloody King's Cross Station, I thought, peeking out, but this time it was Sarah pulling over onto the verge of the main road. I burst out of the wood and grabbed the back door, opening it, shouting, 'Go, go, go!'

Sarah burst out laughing.

'Auntie Maddy!' squealed Charlie as I very unexpectedly landed in the back seat next to him.

'Shit!'

'Ooooooooooooo,' he said.

'Sorry, I didn't mean that. I just got a surprise. I didn't see you there,' I said, reaching out and tickling his pyjama-clad leg.

He giggled.

'Yes, I didn't think it was prudent to leave my two small children alone in the house, so they're both here,' she said, indicating Tilda was in her car seat in front, too.

'Oh God, sorry,' I said. 'Where's Phil?'

'Sunday morning? Golfing.'

'Sorry,' I said.

'No, don't worry, we've been up since 5.00 a.m. with Tilda and her teeth. It's nice to have an outing,' she said in a Mary Poppins voice, giving me 'the look' in the rear-view mirror. 'I cannot wait to hear this,' she said, grinning.

'It's not funny.'

'I think that's a matter of opinion,' she said, accelerating away from the scene of the crime at last.

With the kids in the car, it was neither the time nor the place to talk; plus, I couldn't be sure that if I opened my mouth, I wouldn't be sick. She looked at me in the rear-view mirror, her eyebrows aloft in an expression that meant, 'come on then, spill the beans'. I eyeballed her back, shaking my head and drawing my hand across my throat.

The next obstacle was getting past Noel at the shop, I thought, and then remembered that of course the boys were on their honeymoon! They'd gone straight from the reception to the airport and would be about to arrive in Zanzibar. At least they weren't here to witness this latest carry on.

Sarah pulled up right outside the shop. Looking right and left I got ready to dash to the front door, my key clasped in my sweaty hand, ready to run.

'Come round later,' she said. 'I will literally combust if you don't tell me exactly what's going on.'

'OK,' I said. 'Coast is clear, I'm off.'

Thank God it was Sunday and I didn't have anything to do. I felt so grotty I went for a shower, turning the water up so hot, it damn near skinned me. I needed to cleanse my soul which would take more than a loofah and some shower gel, I thought, as the steam rose. Shaky but improved, I decided to go back to bed.

Frank was livid. I had been out all night and he had been on his own. The one life other than my own that I was responsible for and I had failed him. He had been at the wedding, being a social sort of sausage, but I had walked him around and fed him as the dancing had started because I didn't want him being stood on by some whirling Scotsman doing the Eightsome Reel. I had only left him on his own all night once before and that was when Jack and I had been snowed in whilst out in the hills, caught unaware, which was completely beyond my control. Frank had been OK then, but this time, it was as if he knew about my appalling behaviour. I couldn't bear the way he was looking at me, and despite apologising with an extra big dinner and even a few dog biscuits, he was having none of it. I was in disgrace and lying there under his forensic gaze it was clear I was not going to go back to sleep, my brain in a loop piecing together the shenanigans of the previous night.

Flashback to me dancing with Jack, that unmistakable electricity sparking between us. Him dropping me like a hot potato when Scarlett began to cry, scooping her up and heading off into the night. Then me in the loos freshening up when I found the letter from the DNA company. After a moment or two of looking at it I shredded it into a hundred pieces. Having seen the way he looked at the baby, it was not going to make any difference whether she was his or not. That really was a love match. The deed was done when I exited the loo and went straight up to the bar and joined Javier who poured me a glass of fizz.

Javier was looking devastating in his white shirt, the V of tanned flesh at the neck, attentive and laughing at my jokes, the biggest aphrodisiac of all.

Cut to me, stumbling around behind the bar, grabbing another bottle of champagne, opening it, slugging it like water.

Cringe. Cut to me … opening yet another one, making a bit of a mess of it, Javier putting his hand over mine, removing the bottle and opening it for me. As I watched him, I pulled my bar stool closer to his. Thanking him, my hand lingering on his back like a predatory booze hound. I was his boss. I shuddered. I couldn't lie here all day – this was torture.

Chapter 3

So, I did what I always did when I needed a distraction: I walked. The beach at St Andrews consisted of miles of pristine sand and no matter what the weather was doing, with a hairy bonnet, a cosy jacket and a pair of good stomping shoes I was good to go. I seriously credited walking miles and miles up and down this beach and sand dunes with keeping me sane over the past twelve months, and despite feeling awful I needed to do something until five o'clock rolled around and I could go to Sarah's. The mere thought of Javier now made me feel sick. Excessive boozing had been a very effective method of blocking out thoughts of the Merchant of Venison, but it had resulted in me losing all control and ending up in bed with another man.

'You're a bloody fool,' I said out loud, upping my pace. I wouldn't be surprised if he was in the process of packing his bags and going back to Spain. What appalling behaviour. I shook my head to block out the flashbacks. Jack and I had experienced inevitable change in the dynamic of our relationship since Scarlett arrived. Prior to that fateful moment we had been seeing more and more of each other, spending quality time together. The sweet anticipation of what for both of us felt inescapable was delicious; there was no rush. Yes, we were madly attracted to one another, a connection unlike any we'd felt, which had led to an unspoken understanding that we were feeling our way through the beginnings of what we instinctively knew would be a very significant relationship. Which was why the night we finally got together had felt so right on every level, a feeling of certainty, of coming home.

During the early days, après Jody, we met in St Andrews for coffee now and again. He would pop into the restaurant where I was spending most of my days and nights. On the occasions he did have Scarlett with him, it was clear I was a fat lot of use. I didn't have a clue. Being an only child, I had no real experience of kids, unlike Sarah, my oldest friend who has two great kids; Charlie aged four and baby Tilda whom I love dearly, especially Charlie who was old enough to chat back and laugh at my jokes. Tilda, like Scarlett, was still titchy, and to be honest tiny kids scared me; their wobbly heads, and unnerving way of staring right at you, as if they sensed, like horses, that you were terrified of them. So it was Sarah who became Jack's support in terms of the practicalities of looking after a three-month-old baby, whilst Hamish, Mouse, and I stepped back and got on with our own lives, giving him space and time to come to terms with things and work out what to do next. I knew Sarah was the only one who could advise me on how to handle this latest escapade. After all, she could speak to him normally without that dry-throated chemical kick which rendered me speechless every time I clapped eyes on him.

Chapter 4

Standing on the doorstep, Sarah opened the door as Charlie ran past screeching, naked as the day he was born, still wet from his bath as Phil chased him about trying to catch him with a towel.

'Come in,' she said, smiling radiantly, not even acknowledging the cacophony.

'Thanks,' I said, stepping in, handing her a hastily grabbed bottle of wine.

Following her into the kitchen, she closed the door and leant against it.

'Bedtime with Phil is the highlight of Charlie's day,' she smiled.

'Where's Tilda?'

She pointed behind me. There she sat in her highchair smearing banana all over the tray with one hand and spreading it liberally over her face and downy blonde hair with the other.

I laughed. 'Has anyone told her she's supposed to put it in her mouth?'

'Honestly? At this time on a Sunday, anything goes, the end goal is at least a few minutes peace and quiet,' Sarah said.

Watching the baby intently concentrating on her banana art, I settled myself down at the kitchen table.

'Drink?' said Sarah.

'I'm never drinking again.'

'I've heard that before,' she said.

'I mean it this time.'

'Really?'

'Yes ... I ran amok at the wedding and still feel bloody awful. What about you? Aren't you hungover?'

'No ... I'm not drinking.'

'Since when?' I asked, surprised to say the least.

'Since about a week ago?'

'God, you're not pregnant again, are you?' I snorted.

She laughed and looked at me.

'You're not?' I stared at her.

'I bloody am,' she said.

'Oh my God!' I said, standing up and giving her a hug. 'How long have you known?'

'Just a few days.'

'Sarah, that's amazing ... was it planned?'

'Erm ...' she looked at me. 'With a four-month-old baby? Erm, no.'

'So how are you feeling about it?'

'Initially stunned and now ... well, actually really excited.'

'And Phil?'

'Cock of the North.'

I laughed. 'That's wonderful news, I'm so happy for you both, really. OK then, I will have a drink to celebrate!' I said, celebrating, commiserating, anything really to have a drink.

'You sure, Maddy? I'm happy with a chamomile tea,' she said.

'Just the one,' I said, watching as a flicker of something crossed her face.

'What?' I said defensively.

'Nothing?'

'Sarah. What?'

'Well, I know you won't want to hear this but when you said you had stopped drinking, I thought…' she hesitated.

'Yes?' I said.

'That's not a bad idea.'

I looked at her.

'I don't have a drink problem,' I declared.

'No, of course,' she said unconvincingly.

'I don't!' I snapped.

'Sorry, Maddy. I don't want to fall out with you. Just ignore me, my hormones are rampaging. I'm probably just jealous because I can't have a glass of wine for another nine months!' she said, standing up and preparing our drinks, at which point Phil swept in.

'Right, my little banana pudding, you're coming with me!' he said, picking up the sticky wee girl who giggled as he blew a raspberry on her cheek. Once secure in his arms, he turned to us. 'Hey Maddy, how you doing?'

'Am I safe?'

'What?'

'Well, it seems you just need to look at Sarah and she gets pregnant… the most fertile man in St Andrews. I'm afraid to get too close.'

He guffawed. 'I know, it's great, isn't it?'

'Yes, it is,' I enthused. 'I'm over the moon for you all.'

'Thanks,' he said as Tilda began to wriggle to escape his grip to get back to her banana squishy highchair. 'Oh no you don't,' he said, hoisting her high, much to her delight. 'Right! I'm going to have to love you and leave you and get this one into the bath. See you soon, Mads, and wish me luck!'

The door closed and, peace restored, Sarah looked at me.

'OK, come on, spill the beans, I cannot wait to hear what you were doing ferreting around in the undergrowth at eight o'clock on a Sunday morning.'

Sarah's face was a picture, her eyes bulging. The shrieks that emanated from her caused Phil to put his head round the door and tell us to pipe down as the kids were wondering what the hell was going on. The irony. By the time I finished the story, we were both sore from laughing. I felt worn out, and a quick glance at Sarah confirmed she was done in too.

'You OK?' I asked.

'Just a bit tired.'

'Me, too. It's been a long day.'

She burst out laughing again. 'Sorry, I'm just having a flashback to you in that dressing gown in the bushes ...!'

I sighed. 'God, what a bloody mess.'

On a more serious note she added, 'Have you any idea what you're going to do now, Maddy?'

'To be honest, I was hoping you might be able to help me with that. I mean, you've been seeing more of Jack than I have recently. How is he doing, really?'

'Between you and I, he's struggling,' she said.

'Really?'

'Yes, he's trying to do the right thing, but Jody up and leaving like that has been a nightmare for him. He's tried everything to track her down, he's been in touch with his pal Gordon whose wedding he met her at. He even put out the feelers in Australia, but with no luck – she's just disappeared into thin air. So, he's counting on her maternal instincts.'

I snorted.

She acknowledged my scepticism. 'Such as they are, to lead her back to her baby. Otherwise ...'

'Otherwise?'

'Well, who knows, it's impossible to second-guess what the hell is going to happen.'

'God, it's hard to get your head round the enormity of it.'

'It surely is,' said Sarah, subconsciously patting her tum.

'What would you do if you were me?'

'Just be there for him, all this is life changing stuff, and he needs time to try and work his way through it all. Be in touch but don't expect too much. You know how he feels about you.'

'Well, I thought I did, but I do wonder if maybe I imagined it.'

'I don't talk to him about you, he's quite a private guy.'

'Yeah, I know,' I said. 'Annoyingly.'

'Discretion is the better part of valour,' she added.

I smiled. Thinking about him gave me that warm feeling again …

'And not wanting to burst your bubble, what about Javier?'

'Ah Javier, I am so fond of him, he really is a lovely bloke but he's not …' I trailed off, searching for the right word.

'Jack,' said Sarah, hitting the nail on the head.

'Jack,' I said, putting my cheek down on the table and closing my eyes.

Sarah put her arm around me and said, 'Maddy, I think you need a good night's kip, it will all seem better in the morning. You look shattered.'

I opened my eyes and looked at her, head still on the table, 'You, too.'

'Yeah. Me, too,' she smiled, crinkles around her eyes making her seem older all of a sudden.

'OK,' I pushed my chair back and launched upwards. 'I'm off.'

Chapter 5

Early the next morning I was up, showered and looking like shit having had a sleepless night. I felt sick to the pit of my stomach.

Despite my bravado the previous evening at the situation, in the cold light of day things seemed infinitely worse. I had gone over it all in my head a thousand times until full paranoia had kicked in and I was hunched, grumpy and desperately in need of a coffee. So, I clipped Frank onto his lead, and rocked up to the Birdie.

One coffee down, I was still feeling nauseous as I eyed up the croissant I had bought on the way but before I had time to sink my teeth into it, the door opened and in flew Mouse, pink and fit to burst.

'What?' I said.

'Remember that guy that was in for supper the other night, the bean pole Child Catcher?'

I smiled. We always had names for our customers, it made them easy to identify as we swapped tables during a busy service. And easy to identify in circumstances such as this.

'Yes.'

'Well, he's only a bloody art dealer from Edinburgh.'

'Ooh, really?'

'Yes, and he only bloody loves my stuff.'

'Oh my God.'

'And he only wants to meet me and talk about the possibility of doing an exhibition in Edinburgh!'

'OH MY GOD!' I squealed, jumping up and grabbing her hands, and we did an impromptu dance.

'Mouse, this is it! You've made it!' I said, stopping dead and retrieving a bottle of champagne from behind the bar.

'Maddy, it's ten in the morning.'

'So what? We have to celebrate!'

She looked slightly unsure and then succumbed. 'Yeah, what the hell?' she said, as she grabbed two champagne flutes and I popped the cork. Standing grinning, glasses aloft, we chinked them together as the door flew open.

'It's a bit early for that, no?' said Claude, his chin visibly puckering under his goatee in disapproval.

'No!' I said. 'Mouse is being courted by the Edinburgh art world to do an exhibition!' I blurted and then realised I had just revealed her big news. 'Oh God, sorry, I'm just so excited for you,' I said.

She giggled. 'Maddy, you have been my biggest supporter and—'

'Biggest mouth,' I butted in and then slapped my hand over my mouth again. 'Shit, I'm sorry.'

Mouse smiled. 'Don't be, I need someone to shout about it. That's the one side of this whole thing that terrifies me, even more than showing my work.'

I squeezed her arm. 'Glad to be of service,' I said, taking a sip of my drink before putting it down. The fizzing booze was not going down well at all. 'So, what does Hamish think?'

'He's out doing his deliveries; I haven't had a chance to tell him. You know him and his bloody mobile, he never picks up.'

I rolled my eyes. 'Yeah. So anyway, tell me what this guy said ... first, who is he?'

'His name is—' she flicked through her messages. 'Adrian De Witt.'

'Oooooh.'

'I know! He wants to come up here, meet me, talk me through his proposal and we will take it from there.'

'When?'

'Tomorrow!'

'Shit, he is serious.'

Suddenly she retreated slightly.

'What?' I asked.

'Putting myself out there in the big wide world,' she said 'I don't know if I can do it.'

'You can! Listen, you've got me and Hamish and, well, everyone,' I said, flapping my arm round.

'And me,' said Claude, standing up to his full height and looking at her with an intense serious stare.

'See?' I said. 'Nothing to worry about, we've got your back.'

She exhaled, a shy smile in place. 'Thanks, guys.'

After a little encouragement she texted Mr De Witt back and agreed to meet him.

'Where?'

'The Old Course Hotel.'

The Old Course was THE hotel in St Andrews. Five-star unadulterated luxury. World famous, it sat on the side of St Andrews Old Course, a location that could render a golfer weak at the knees. Panoramic views of the world's most famous golf course, the beach, and the east coast. It was beyond jaw dropping. Everyone who was anyone had stayed there, from Clint Eastwood to Obama ... and it wasn't the sort of place we went to on a regular basis, unfortunately.

'Well, he sounds like a class act' I said as Mouse began to smooth her fringe down repeatedly, trying to make it as long as possible to hide behind it, a nervous tic I hadn't seen in a long time.

'What will I wear?'

'Anything, daaahling, you're an artist!' I said.

She giggled nervously, patting her fringe again.

'Whatever you're comfortable in.' I smiled at her.

'In there?' She pointed over her shoulder in the direction of the hotel, which was two hundred yards from the restaurant.

'Yes,' I grinned.

Mouse turned back to me, a look of anxiety on her face.

'Maddy, will you come with me?'

'Me? What about Hamish?'

'Well, you're a bit more ... business-like,' she said. 'Plus, nothing might come of it and I don't want to get him all excited.'

'Of course, I will,' I said. 'Just tell me where and when.'

'Thanks, Maddy.' She smiled, the colour coming back into her cheeks.

The door flew open. 'Delivery!' shouted Jimmy the Fish.

'Right, I better be off,' said Mouse, recognising this was the beginning of another hectic day at the Birdie.

'Keep me posted,' I said, signing the delivery note as she slipped out.

Chapter 6

Before I had time to draw breath, the door opened again and in came Javier, fresh-faced and lively as ever, making me cringe as I recalled the shock of seeing my jaggy bunnet in the mirror not an hour earlier.

'Hola!'

'Morning,' I said, hoisting my chops to a smiling formation, avoiding his eye.

'You been at the booze already?' he said, laughing as I picked up the two glasses and put them behind the bar to wash later. Laughing nervously, I told him Mouse's news.

'The best news,' he said. 'She is a very talented artiste.'

He was so nice. 'Yes, she is.'

Claude had retreated to the kitchen as Javier took off his jacket.

'Coffee?' I asked, turning my back to him and feeling unsure about how this was going to play out.

'Yes, please,' he said, pulling out a barstool and sitting down facing me. Hoping he couldn't smell shame on me, I shakily made an espresso, with one sugar, and handed it to him, the cup clattering on the saucer.

'You OK?' he asked, looking right into me.

'Yes,' I said, reddening up. 'Listen, I wanted to apologise.'

'Apologise? For why?'

'Well ... for the other night ...'

'There is no need,' he said matter-of-factly. 'We are both adults, no harm was done. End of story.' He sipped his coffee.

He sensed I was mortified and a bit stuck.

'Listen, Maddy, we are good friends, no?'

'Yes.'

'And you trust me, no?'

'Yes.'

'So,' he shrugged his shoulders. 'Is fine.'

Phew. What a lovely guy. Man enough to talk about these things, no games or acting the goat. I could do with taking a leaf out of his book.

'So, it is OK between us?' I checked.

'Of course, why would it not be?' he said, standing up. 'Now I better get to work, or Claude will be hot.'

'You mean angry?' I smiled, tension dispersing.

He laughed. 'Yes.'

And with that amiable exchange, off he went.

What had started as a dreaded day was already turning into a much better one than I expected. That is until my mobile buzzed. Picking it up, my anxiety kicked back in tenfold. It was Jack.

Just dropped off Scarlett, time for a coffee?

Shit, I couldn't face him yet. I texted back,

Am at the Birdie.

Great there in 5.

Oh, that hadn't been what I had meant. I meant busy working but it had come across as sitting waiting for him. Getting to my feet I ran into the loo and attempted some damage control. The only thing that would fix this was a balaclava, which I didn't have to hand.

Well, thank God it was sunny, I thought, opening my bag and taking out my sunglasses. With a slick of lipstick and a spray of perfume, I was as ready as I would ever be. The dread of Jack and Javier coming face to face was giving me the heebie-jeebies, so I decided to wait outside in the doorway and head him off at the pass.

'Why don't we sit outside? It's a lovely morning,' I shouted as he locked the Land Rover and headed my way.

'Great idea,' he said, squinting into the sun as he gave me a crooked smile.

'Coffee?'

'Lovely. A cappuccino, and put in an extra shot, will you? I've had about three minutes of sleep.'

I knew how he felt.

'OK, just be a minute,' I said, disappearing back inside and hurriedly making coffee for two, unable to get out of my head that slightly dazed rumpled look he was sporting; it just made me want to snog the face off him.

God, was this an age thing?

I knew in my heart – and various other parts of my body – I adored Jack and yet I had woken up naked in Javier's bed.

I felt so awful about what had happened, like a two-timing low down dirty dog. And about the fact that Javier and I knew what had happened and Jack hadn't a clue. Suddenly I felt nauseous, and I just about made it to the loo.

Five minutes later, feeling goppingly awful but upright and faking being a woman in control, I arrived outside with the coffee.

'I thought you'd run off with another man,' he joked.

The shrieky snort that came out of me startled us both.

'Sorry, you know whats it's like in there ... there's always someone—I mean, something to do ...'

'Yeah sure,' he said, taking his coffee from me. 'Thanks.'

Jack and I sat in companionable silence, my heart rate slowing down to less than potentially fatal as seabirds wheeled above us, and the typical noises of the town waking up surrounded us.

Chapter 7

The gentle hum of early morning St Andrews shattered as Barclay MacPherson, Jack's estranged father's decrepit Willies Jeep rumbled around the corner, spewing exhaust fumes as the bald front left tyre mounted the pavement, missing us by inches. Automatically Jack launched to his feet.

'Hey! Watch it!' he shouted, scooping Frank up with one hand and stopping the sausage in his tracks as he was clearly determined to protect us from the puffing metallic dragon that had just arrived. Ignoring Jack's protestations, Barclay came barrelling out of the vehicle towards us with a face like fizz, causing Frank to break free and start snapping at his heels. Barclay shook his leg as if he was going to kick him.

'Don't you dare!' I shouted, grabbing the dog by the hurdies and lifting him up out of the way of this runaway train.

'What the hell's going on?' barked the buffoon.

Jack looked at him, rage palpable as he bristled silently.

'I've had your mother on the phone,' he went on.

Despite Jack's practiced ability to rise above his father's antics, this news elicited an unmistakable intake of breath. This was remarkable news.

His mother and father had had nothing to say to each other for years. In fact, they studiously avoided being in the same place at the same time and they never ever agreed on anything. The marriage had ended twenty years previously, and to say it was not an amicable relationship was an under-statement.

Barclay was off. 'She tells me some floozy has pitched up from the other side of the world with a little bastard claim-ing it's yours! And you have accepted it as fact and haven't even had the common sense to get a DNA test.'

'It's got nothing to do with you,' Jack growled.

'Nothing to do with me? I'm your father! Don't be a fool, man. From what your mother tells me, you know nothing about this girl. For God's sake, she could be anyone. And why on earth would you believe for a moment *you* are the father?'

'Because I had sex with her,' said Jack, which caused me to step back. Jesus, these two were brutal.

'Listen, why don't you go inside and discuss this?' I dared to say, breaking the death stare between the two, as a few locals were casually slowing down to catch more of this St Andrews soap opera playing out in front of them. But neither of them acknowledged me, and Barclay was roaring now.

'For all you know, she's had sex with half of bloody Australia. Grow up, for God's sake, man. This is not just about you,' he blustered. 'Think about it. This child will stand to inherit the whole of Kelso Estate.' His fat yellow-veined eyeballs expanding as he stared at Jack.

'Huh! Kelso Estate! You mean that rambling old money pit over half a million pounds in debt and counting, thanks to you,' Jack batted back.

Barclay harrumphed. He loved the idea of being the laird, the lord and master of the manor, never failing to use his title at the drop of a hat, ignoring the fact that his list of debtors stretched from Land's End to John O' Groats. It was a well-known fact locally that the disastrous state of the estate's finances sat firmly at his door.

By now, quite a crowd had gathered including Uncle Fraser, who was blatantly standing outside his butcher's shop, arms crossed, nudging Jono, the butcher's boy who stood next to him, eyes out on stalks.

This moment's grace was just long enough for Barclay to register the crowd gathering.

'What the hell are you lot looking at?' He turned his back on the bystanders, marching back to the Jeep and shouting at Jack, 'And you! You better get your house in order, my boy, you have not heard the end of this!' He got in, slamming the door behind him, bumped back off the pavement and was off.

'Well,' I said, rather stuck for words.

'Cheeky bastard,' Jack said, clearly using all his skills to calm down.

'Well, he has got a point,' I blurted.

He turned on me now. 'I'm sorry?'

'Well, he does,' I mumbled, realising this may not have been the best time to broach the subject, but it was out now. 'And your mum agrees ...'

'And so do you, apparently,' he said, digging about in his pocket and dropping a couple of pound coins on the table.

'You don't need to pay for that!' I said as he zipped up his jacket and said a rather cursory, 'I better be off' and left.

'Jack!' I shouted after him, as he marched down the road and out of sight.

This stramash caused a real divide between us. I understood he wanted my support, but he surely also wanted me to be honest. I cringed at a flashback to Javier. Well, honest when it suited me ... I was a bad person.

I was in a no-win situation. I had brought up the whole DNA thing when Scarlett and Jody first arrived, and it had gone down like a lead balloon. By the time I got my oar in, Jody had convinced him he was, without a doubt, Scarlett's dad. And the fact they looked like clones didn't help my case.

I couldn't believe he was being so pig-headed. Despite becoming a single parent overnight, he really had stepped up to the role of caring for the wee baby, and whether they shared the same DNA or not, it didn't change the way he felt about her.

And from the way he had just stomped off and left me standing on the side of the road, things were not going to change any time soon. He needs some space, I thought, realising the humiliation of the public run-in he had just had with his father. It would take some time to distil and maybe when he calmed down, he would realise all I wanted was to protect him.

Chapter 8

Next morning, tidy, smartly dressed and looking very unlike ourselves we met in the foyer of St Andrews' Old Course. It was 11.00 a.m. sharp.

Mouse was already changing her mind.

'I'm not sure about this.'

'Listen, you don't need to do anything, it is just a meeting to hear what he's got to say, no commitment at all. OK?'

She smiled at me. 'OK.'

Ordering a glass of water each, we sat watching as people streamed through the revolving door, out of lifts and wandered in from the breakfast room. Our eyes were peeled not knowing where he would appear from.

Then a man, tall and thin, came in and looked around. I almost expected to hear his bones crack together, his angles and juts were so sharp as he walked towards us. His features were indiscernible with the light behind him.

'It's him,' hissed Mouse as we both jumped to our feet.

'Dorcas Pratt?' he said.

'Yes,' Mouse squeaked.

'Adrian De Witt,' he said, extending his spidery hand to Mouse, before turning to me. 'And you are?'

'Oh, erm, Madeleine Campbell,' I said, grabbing his hand and inadvertently crushing it. 'Oops, sorry,' I added as he winced. Stepping back, he slipped off his jacket, folding it meticulously and placing it on the arm of the sofa.

'Coffee?' he asked, his arm already up waving a member of staff over.

'Yes, please,' said Mouse, as I nodded coolly, or at least tried to.

Once the coffee was ordered and the niceties were over, we got down to business.

Sitting back, he crossed one endless leg over the other, revealing a shin bone you could sharpen a knife on and a patch of milk-white, hair-free skin between his sock and the hitched-up leg of his impeccable trouser. I shuddered.

'So, tell me about yourself, Dorcas,' he said, pinkie aloft as he sipped his espresso, intense black eyes focused on my friend through circular black glasses that made him look like an emaciated bee.

'Oh well, there's not much to say really,' she said, about to launch into her self-effacing modesty routine as I knew she would.

'Mouse – sorry, Dorcas – is too modest,' I said, butting in.

The laser gaze switched to me; a flicker of irritation crossed his eyes as I took the floor.

'Dorcas graduated last year from Edinburgh Art School with a First class degree in Fine Art,' I said. 'The Graduates Exhibition was held in July last year. She had three pieces in the final show, all of which sold well. Her work was reviewed in the *Artist* saying she was a huge new talent and one to watch.'

Mouse reddened.

'I know,' he said. 'I saw it.'

'Oh, OK, good,' I said. Not the most intelligent thing to say, but the best I could manage under such scrutiny from this man spider.

'I mean why don't you tell me about you, Dorcas?' he oozed, swivelling his body toward her. 'It's all part of the story, that's what people buy into. Where are you from? Tell me about your background.'

Not wanting to come over as her stroppy minder I sat back and let her answer. To be honest I was intrigued to hear what she said.

When I first met Mouse just under a year ago, she had been a goth, her face and feelings hidden behind a mask of white face paint, black baggy clothes, piercings all over her ears, lips, and nose. I was no psychologist, but I took these to be signs that there may well be things in her past she preferred to leave unspoken. She had never offered up the details, and I never asked.

I remember when Dad died, she was terribly upset and blurted out that she had thought of him as the dad she never had, which at the time I felt was rather over the top. She had started working part-time at the Birdie just after I left to work in London, and I remember Dad clearly him telling me about her, saying she walked in the day after looking for a job and though he didn't really have one he took her on because he had a girl-shaped hole in his life, and she looked like she needed a break.

'Well ... I ... erm,' said Mouse, bringing me back to the present and looking at me for encouragement.

I nodded, egging her on.

'I was adopted.'

My eyebrows shot up. I had no idea.

'As a baby?' he probed.

'Yes, I was ...' she hesitated, looking towards me as she stammered, 'abandoned.'

De Witt moved in his seat.

'Abandoned? How aaaawful,' he said, placing his cup down in its saucer and putting it on the table as I grasped her hand.

'Oh, Mouse, I'm sorry, I had no idea.'

'Where?' asked De Witt.

'In a bag, in a bus station.'

My heart broke for her. Sitting in this plush hotel, with a man who suddenly resembled a vulture, picking over the bones of her past for his own benefit.

'I am not sure we need to go any further down that line,' I said, squeezing Mouse's hand in mine. She squeezed it back.

'So, before we go any further with this, can you give us an idea of what it is that you are proposing?' I said, meeting his beady eye.

'Of course. I would like to launch Dorcas onto the art scene in Scotland with a bang!' he said, his arms unravelled and flapping about. 'Her work is extraordinary, wild, vibrant and with a sense of desolation, a loneliness, a—' He stopped. 'She is a fresh new talent.' I coughed. 'You are a fresh new talent,' he said, addressing her directly once again.

'So, I would propose we do an exhibition at the Edinburgh Festival, for three weeks in August. The great and good from the world gather in the city. There is a film festival, jazz festival, arts festival, TV festival, and fringe festival. It brings in millions of pounds and people all focused in the city for one month. It's perfect timing for Dorcas, maximum exposure and a lot of potential buyers.'

'Gosh,' said Mouse.

'OK, and how would this work for Dorcas?' I asked.

'Well, I would like her to come to Edinburgh to see the space and if she is happy, she can begin to work towards a solo exhibition.'

Here came the rub. This was no charity event. He didn't get those bumblebee glasses in Boots, I thought, as he delicately pincered them off the bridge of his nose between his thumb and forefinger and polished them methodically with a small cloth that seemed to appear from nowhere.

'OK,' I said. 'So, what's in it for you?'

'You're quite direct,' he said, baulking for a moment, before popping the glasses back onto his nose, an almost smile playing round his lips. 'But it does save time. OK well, the established galleries usually take between forty and fifty per cent.'

'Bloody hell,' I said. 'That is outrageous.'

'Well, yes and no,' he said. 'They have the list, the venue, the reputation, the location and when you consider the number of artists there are who would give their eye teeth for an opportunity like this, it's actually quite reasonable.'

'Well, that's a matter of opinion,' I said, bristling. If he thought he was going to get half of Mouse's money for her work he was very much mistaken. He continued, 'As Dorcas is an unknown artist, a new face if you like, to some extent one might say exhibiting such a person's work in a high-profile gallery during the biggest art festival in the world is a huge risk.' Mouse deflated slightly and sat back.

'And do you have your own gallery?' she asked.

'No,' he said with a smile, revealing small sharp-looking teeth. 'I'm an art impresario, if you like.' He licked his lips. 'A facilitator.'

I didn't like the sound of this one little bit, but I let him go on.

'I know all the gallery owners, the buyers and have a client list which I also bring to the party. After twenty-five years in the business, I have a reputation.'

Silence as he bent forward, his eyes fixed on Mouse.

'So, I have a proposition for you.'

Mouse sat up, eyes wide as he lounged back. She sat forward, not exactly playing it cool. 'Oooh,' she said. 'What?'

His eyes flickered over me, realising I was bad cop in this particular scenario.

'OK, if you are agreeable to the idea in principle, I will approach the best galleries in Edinburgh about hosting your inaugural exhibition, your coming out as it were to the art world, and broker a deal for you.'

'What's to stop Mouse doing it direct?'

'Nothing, of course,' he said, baring those teeth again as he slid his jacket off the arm of the couch, slipping it on whilst raising his hand to call a member of staff over.

I wondered if he was going to order some Chianti and some fava bean for a moment, but no, thank God he was after the bill.

'Some food for thought,' he said. 'Of course I have several other artists to talk to.' I sensed Mouse shuck forward another inch to the edge of the sofa, liable to jump up and do something stupid, as I exerted pressure on her leg with mine as a sign to keep her cool. 'So I'll be in touch by end of play tomorrow, then we can move forward, one way or the other,' he said as the bill arrived. He swiped his card without even reading it, leaving a cash tip of ten pounds on the saucer as he stood to leave.

We said goodbye and waited until he had disappeared through the revolving doors before following him out. The moment we were off the premises, Mouse had me by the forearm.

'He's going to see other artists. Shit. I've blown it. I should have said yes. Fuck.'

'Don't panic, it's part of the game,' I said.

She smoothed her fringe down again a few times, as we walked. 'Phone him, Maddy, I want to say yes.'

'OK, do you want to wait just a wee while, at least make him think you are considering it?'

'No. Phone him now.'

'Sure?'

'Sure.'

'OK,' I said, and standing there not one hundred yards from the entrance to the hotel, Mouse passed me her phone and I called him.

'Hello, Adrian?'

'Yes.'

'It's Madeleine Campbell, Mouse – I mean Dorcas's – associate.'

'Ah yes,' he said.

'Mouse and I have discussed it and, in principle, would like to proceed.'

'Excellent,' he said, sounding remarkably enthusiastic. 'I shall put a few things in place and be in touch.'

'Excellent.' I imitated his tone. 'And when do you—'

Click. He ended the call.

'Well?' said Mouse.

'It's a goer... he's going to give you a shout when he's set something up.'

'Brilliant.'

As we walked back into St Andrews, Mouse rattled on about her studio or lack of it, her canvases or lack of them and started working out in her mind the scale of what she had just taken on. 'Oh my God, I have to tell Hamish!'

'Well, off you go and see him now. I've got to get to the Birdie, lunch has already started,' I said, waving her off.

The restaurant was busy and after we'd had our staff meal, I had loads of things I had to do but just felt wiped out. Putting my chores off, I headed back to the bothy for a cup of tea and to put my feet up, and went out like a light.

Waking up in the half-light, it was cold. The bothy was entirely made of stone with little natural light or flow of air.

Everything felt damp, I thought, as I patted Frank's head and went off back to work.

Fast forward five hours and I was back. Frank was in the same position but in a state of high dudgeon that I had had the audacity to leave him on his own again, but with a biscuit and the promise of a quick walk, he came around.

Walking the streets of St Andrews at night was like taking a step into a Dickens book. Stone houses, cheek by jowl, deep-set windows from which the warm glow of lights and open fires emanated. So inviting, so homely, I suddenly realised how much I missed having my own home. The boys had been so generous letting me stay in the bothy and I was so grateful, but if I was here to stay, I needed to put down these roots I kept talking about and find my own place. And Frank, my hairy baby, needed somewhere to call home, too.

Calling it a night, I curled up in bed with the fairy lights Mouse had dangled round my wee room twinkling in the darkness. I was asleep in a flash.

Chapter 9

I was up with the lark the following morning. William and Noel were due back and I wanted to fill their fridge with goodies and get some fresh flowers before I had to go to work. The last time they had come back from a trip it was to a very spick and span cottage, but the smell of bleach was strong, as for one reason or another – OK, mainly drama with Jack – I had been living mainly on their couch subsisting on crisps and wine. It looked OK on the surface, but I could tell by Noel's face he suspected I had been up to something.

So, this time I wanted them to open the door and feel a real welcome home with all the bells and whistles.

As usual I had no food in my own mini fridge, so I was feeling distinctly wobbly by the time I had done a supermarket sweep and arrived at the cottage.

Scooping the mail off the mat, I heaved the groaning shopping bags onto the kitchen table and set about putting it all away.

Suddenly ravenous, I grabbed a banana and stuffed that into my chops whilst arranging a huge bunch of daffys – well, when I say arrange, I cut the elastic bands and plonked them in a jug, but fair's fair, they looked right at home, as did Frank who had taken up residence in the wee chair by the Aga.

Looking at him there I decided to leave him where he

was so when they came in, they got a lovely waggy welcome from their sausage-shaped friend, who I knew they would love.

I wrote a note which I propped against the jug, and explained to Frank he was staying put because William and Noel were coming back, then I was off.

Feeling rather pleased with myself, I walked around to the restaurant.

I was off tonight and wondered if Sarah might be able to get out for a couple of hours. I needed to fill her in on the whole Jack and Barclay thing. I was still smarting from our last encounter and as Jack's baby information station I wanted her take on things. After finishing lunch service, I was making my way back to the bothy when suddenly a hairy Exocet headed along the pavement at speed, jumping up and into my arms.

'Frank!' I laughed and then, looking up, was thrilled to see William and Noel tanned, smiling and home.

'You're back! I screeched, walking into their outstretched arms. 'Welcome home,' I added tearing up.

'Thanks for all the goodies,' said William.

'And the welcoming committee,' added Noel, smiling down at the joyful dog who had his three most favourite people in the world within reach of his wee snout.

'You're welcome. God, you look fantastic! How was it?'

'Amazing,' mooned William, smiling at Noel who smiled back.

'Oh God, love's young dream,' I laughed.

'Listen, we thought we'd book a table for tonight at the Birdie.'

'Oh, it's my night off.'

'Well, why don't you join us? Or would you rather come to us?'

'No, the restaurant is a great idea, the last thing you will feel like doing is cooking. OK, what time?'

'Early if you don't mind, we have the jet lag droop,' said Will.

'Suits me,' I said. 'OK, half six?'

'Perfect.'

'Right, let me nip in and sort that now,' I said and then looked at the pair of them. 'God, it is so good to see you both.' I beamed. 'I can't wait to hear all about it.'

'You may live to regret that,' said Noel.

'See you later!' I grinned.

At 6.30 a.m., the boys arrived looking fresh, ironed, and fabulous.

I had dug out a less crumpled selection of clothes and done my best, but not owning an iron, I was far below their standard of personal hygiene and grooming – not that they noticed, or if they did, they didn't say anything; they were so full of it. I listened rapt as they told me all about Zanzibar. Descriptions of spices, colour, heat. They had loved every second of it. After the first couple of days, Noel tried to get William to lie on the beach and relax but of course that was easier said than done. Will was happiest ferreting around in every food market, kitchen and restaurant picking up recipes, ingredients and ideas for the Birdie.

On the run up to the wedding, William had been recovering from a breakdown, but now his energy and exuberance were back, recent months of stress and exhaustion a distant memory.

William and I had enjoyed a see-saw relationship since we first met. If he was up, I was down, and vice versa. We'd been through a lot together in a very short space of time, so to see him back on top of the world warmed the cockles of my heart. And much as I loved running the restaurant, it had

54

been hard on my own. I was so relieved to have him back. We were both up, both loving it, and it felt great.

I was happy to sit back and let them take the floor. All their adventures were wonderful to hear, and the evening went by in a flash.

'Oh God, we haven't asked one thing about you!' said Noel.

'You see it all,' I said, waving my arms round.

'The place looks great,' said William, his eyes twinkling. He loved the Birdie almost as much as I did.

'It is, and depending on how you're feeling about work,' I broached, 'it would be fantastic to have you back.'

William reached out and put his hand over mine. 'I thought you'd never ask.'

It was still early, so after walking the boys back to their cottage, I clipped Frank on the lead and went on a fact-finding mission. I was interested to see how other restaurants were doing at this time of year, so I criss-crossed my way through the centre of the town, feeling quite buoyed by what I saw. The Birdie was one of the busiest eateries in town which gave me a deep feeling of satisfaction, tempered only by the snapshot I was getting into other people's lives. For some reason, people in this part of the world didn't close their curtains as the night drew in. So, it was impossible to resist gazing in windows at the roaring fires, flickering TVs, kids hunched up doing homework, people talking on phones, lying on rugs; a glimpse of lives lived in a real home. It made me acknowledge how much I would love a home of my own, though I would definitely be closing my curtains at nightfall.

Chapter 10

That brief window into the world of settled domesticity had sown some sort of seed in my head and so a restless night ensued as I dreamt of giant squishy armchairs, open fires, tartan rugs and laughter. It was blissful and made the contrast all the starker as I opened my eyes, back down to earth with a bump to the bothy.

Harrumphing, I turned over, rolling back into the duvet, as Frank tried to get back under the covers. It was bloody freezing.

It was my own fault.

When the boys went off on their honeymoon, they offered me their cottage to live in, but I knew the more comfortable I was the less likely I would get my shit together and find somewhere proper to live. So, I had stayed put in the bothy which was all very well but a little basic. When I first came back, Noel had said I could stay in this tiny stone house in the garden behind his antique shop. I spent six weeks in it the previous summer, but as Noel and William had done their best to warn me, it was a very different proposition in the winter. God, I wish I had listened. There was no heating and, not to put too fine a point on it, it was bloody freezing. There was a window, but it faced the perimeter wall of the garden so there was no natural light. Lying there this morning, I was just steeling myself for the dreaded moment when I had to leap out of bed, when there was a knock at the door.

I squeaked, pulling the duvet up to my chin. Who the hell was that?

'Maddy, it's me,' said Will.

'For God's sake, it's eight in the morning. You nearly gave me a heart attack.'

'Sorry, I texted. It's the jet lag, I was up at the crack of dawn. Thought I'd go out for a walk so I was going to take Frank with me.'

'Hang on, I'm still in my jammies.'

'Don't worry, I've seen worse,' he said.

Tiptoeing over the stone floor, I unlocked the door before diving back into bed and scooching the duvet up to my chin.

'Morning,' said my sunshiny friend. 'Oat milk latte?'

'Oh yum, thanks,' I said, extending my arm out from under the covers to take it.

He sat on the edge of the bed and looked at me. 'Maddy, you don't sleep with that on, do you?'

'If you are referring to my bobble hat, well, then, yes I do,' I said in high dudgeon. 'Why?'

'Nothing,' he said, grinning and patting Frank's head which had just poked out of the top of the duvet to greet him.

'It is bloody freezing in here. And what is that?' he exclaimed, walking over and scrutinising the wall beside the door. I watched him as I sipped the hot milky coffee, enjoying the warming sensation as it slid down my throat. 'Spores!' he blustered.

'What?'

'Spores! Fungi! Mushrooms. Whatever you want to call them, this place must be damp as hell.'

'Och, it's fine ...'

57

He looked at me, incredulous.

'Maddy, it is not fine. Fungus the bogeyman would snap this up if it was on Rightmove,' he said, continuing his investigation of blotches, and speckles on the ceiling, too. 'Noel would have a fit. There is no way he would have let you stay in here if he realised it was as bad as this. This air can't be good for you ... it was supposed to be short-term, so what's happened to the flat hunting?'

Initially the theory of flat hunting on my own was rather disheartening so I sort of went off the boil with it and stopped looking. I wasn't ready to accept my fate as a one without a plus one, so hadn't bothered to make an appointment to see my bank manager to find out if I could even get a mortgage.

Taking that step felt like an admission of long-term singledom, so rather than address all that it was a lot easier to live like a student. But rather than burble all that out I simply said, 'Haven't had time.'

'Well, you can't stay here. God knows what extinct species are lurking in the corners. I'm going to walk Frank now and I will meet you in St Andrews property centre at nine and we can see what's on the market. OK?'

I knew that look, that determined face – this was not a question but an order.

'OK,' I said, sitting up and, curse my nostrils, sneezing.

'See!' he said. 'OK, Frank, walkies.'

As the door closed behind them, I lay there for another minute or two looking at the spores on the wall, the speckles of damp in the corner, and inhaling the unmistakably fusty smell. I conceded that William had a point: it was time to move on.

★

By 9.00 a.m. I was outside the property centre with William waiting to get in.

As the girl opened the door she looked down.

'You can't bring him in here.'

'Please?' I said. 'He's just got back from his honeymoon and he's desperate.'

'Ha ha,' said William, as the girl relaxed a little and said under her breath, 'OK, shove him up your jumper but don't let anyone see him or I'll get a bollocking.'

'Thanks,' said William, beaming,

No sooner had we sat down, with a few property particulars, a cup of tea and a scone, than Sarah walked past with the buggy. I knocked on the window and she jumped and, seeing I was with William, did an about turn. After parking the pram outside, she scooped up the baby and came in to join us.

'Hi, what are you two up to?'

'House hunting,' grinned William.

A small squeak emanated from her . . . 'For you?' She pointed at me.

I nodded. 'Yes.'

'Oh my God, give me a minute,' she said, plopping the baby on my knee and marching off to order herself a coffee before swooping back and joining us. 'So where are we looking?'

'We?' I grinned.

And there we sat, discussing budgets, locations, what I needed, and what Frank needed. Despite being rather unconvinced to begin with, the idea really began to grow on me.

After half an hour William said his fond farewells and left Sarah and me with the now snoozing baby.

'Exciting times,' she grinned, looking at me rather strangely.

'Yes?' I said, not quite sure what she was getting at.

'I'm going to get myself another coffee, want one?'

'No thanks, I'm off coffee. I'll have a hot chocolate though, and a cake.'

She looked at me. 'You just ate my croissant.'

'Did I?'

'Yes, you did!' she laughed.

'Oh, I'm still hungry,' I said as she pulled a face and made her way back to the counter, leaving me sitting stock-still holding Tilda, afraid to move in case she woke up.

Plopping a cake down in front of me, Sarah sat down again.

'Thanks,' I grinned.

'So, what's the chat?' she said.

'Just running around like a headless chicken as usual, there's always so much to do. I don't know where the time goes. More to the point, how are you doing?'

'Good. I am a bit knackered and starving 24/7 but that's no surprise. What about you?'

'Yeah it's been a bit of a week,' I said. 'I was out last night for an early supper with William and Noel – just on mineral water, no boozing – but I had a crap night's sleep and this morning felt like I could have stayed in bed for a week.'

'Tell me about it,' she said.

As if to illustrate the point, my mobile rang. Glancing down, I saw it was the Birdie. 'Sorry, I have to get this,' I said.

She put her hands up. 'No problem.'

It was Claude. 'The accountant is here.' Short and sweet as usual.

'Oh shit, sorry, I forgot. OK, I'll be there in a minute…

Sorry,' I said to Sarah and Claude at the same time, hanging up. 'I'm sorry, I've buggered up again, I have to go.'

'No hassle,' she said. 'When's your next night off?'

'Sunday.'

'Perfect, Phil's working away so wine o'clock about six?' She laughed as I gathered my bits and pieces.

'Great, I'm looking forward to it already. Bye Tilda,' I whispered to the wee dozing baby. 'See you then!'

Rushing round the corner, I stopped. I had forgotten to pay the bill. I started up again. Sarah would understand. I would sort her out when I saw her. I had so much going on, I was forever forgetting things, I thought, skidding to a halt at the door of the restaurant and rushing in.

Chapter 11

Jeffy, our bookkeeper, was sitting at the bar chatting to Javier who was polishing glasses.

'God, Jeffy, I am sorry to keep you waiting,' I puffed.

'Don't worry, I've been well entertained,' she said, smiling at Javier who smiled back at her, and then to me, causing my entire body to go beetroot.

Oblivious to my discomfort she chatted on as we sat down, giving me an update of how the business was doing.

'Good news,' she said, 'you are well above the projected cashflow.'

'Oh, that's good,' I said.

'Yes, indeed. In fact, I am pleased to say you really have this place going like a fair,' she surmised.

I grinned.

We were running at such speed I never had time to sit back and take stock. Never a numbers girl, I just knew we had more coming in than going out, which had to be good. 'Play to your strengths,' was one of my dad's favourite expressions so as soon as the Birdie began to busy up, I asked around and Jeffy was recommended, an old pal of Hamish's, as a freelance accountant to look after the books for us.

All I had to do was remember not to throw out receipts and count on everyone else to do the same, and cash up at the end of the night. Claude and I hoped William, now that he was back, would deal with the rest of it, so all in all it ticked over very nicely.

There is so much more to this business than I had ever imagined and my flabby brain literally throbbed some days as I tried to assimilate how to understand the figures, the GP, the bare bones of whether or not we could break even, and how the smallest move one way or the other would determine whether or not we would make money. The investment of time and energy required building relationships with suppliers, customers, staff, trying to keep up to speed with the dazzling amount of red tape every restaurant in the country must adhere to, and gazillions of other things; all of which left me little time for anything else, so I was more than happy that Jeffy was in control of the finances.

A small ring binder was all Dad needed back in the day, all the rules of food preparation easily fitting onto one piece of A4 paper which he sellotaped to the wall as a reminder for everyone to see. And Now Wash your Hands. But these days it was more like a forty-two gigabyte hard drive of ever-changing rules and regs we had to adhere to, to keep Scotland, UK, Europe then EEC Brexit rules and guidelines up to date.

Some of the rules were ludicrous. For instance, Jimmy the Fish had been supplying Dad since he started over forty years ago. Jimmy still runs his own boat out of St Andrews harbour and whatever he catches is what we buy. But the powers that be don't understand this rural, traditional way to do business, the way it has always been done here. Their highfalutin rules may be relevant to large landlocked city-based establishments, serving huge amounts of diners, but not a small family place like ours. Now every piece of shellfish and seafood that is sold must have the time and date it was caught labelled on it. This didn't go down well with the old guard, Jimmy the Fish being the case in point.

'Ye whit?' he said, incredulous, when I told him what he would be required to do.

I went over it again as, jaw set, he lifted his cold box up and plopped it on a table. Opening it up there was a great array of haddock, cod, two lobsters, a crab, and some hand-dived scallops.

Claude the chef was out of the kitchen in a flash, the highlight of his day.

'Bon, bon, bon,' he said, picking things up and examining them.

'And the piece de resistance,' announced Jimmy in a shockingly bad French accent, lifting a lobster out of the way and revealing something underneath. 'Pour vous chef, as requested.'

'Ahhhhh aliboot,' said Claude, taking it as if it were a gold bar and smelling it. 'Parfait.'

'Halibut,' said Jimmy, clocking my expression of confusion.

Once Claude had gleefully returned to the kitchen clutching the halibut, I reiterated with Jimmy the new rules and the cheeky bugger laughed in my face.

'I'm serious, Jimmy, I need to be able to prove to the Health and Hygiene lot when and where it was caught.'

Picking up a lobster he turned to it and asked, 'So, son, when did I catch you?'

In response the large clacking claw clamped onto his white fishmonger's coat.

'Aye,' he said, turning to me, 'about an hour ago and as you can see he's afa' pissed off about it.'

I couldn't help but laugh. 'I'm sorry, Jimmy, you know if it was up to me ...'

He harrumphed and made a show of taking each item

out, one by one, all of which had that salty, fish-slick, sea smell, abundantly fresher than anything, and told me when and where he had snagged them. After a cup of tea and a couple of Claude's extraordinary madeleines he capitulated. Most people did.

So, there were challenges, keeping everyone on board with some of the nonsense we had to adhere to, but all food businesses were in the same position, so we just got on with it. We rubbed along quite nicely, buoyed up by the folk who live and work in St Andrews itself. It turns out one of the intangible things about being a part of the virtual fabric of a small town is that, almost without exception, the locals are right behind us, which is a very comforting feeling, a feeling of belonging and being supported which was not so much about me, but the restaurant itself. After all, the Birdie is really an institution in these parts, having been part of the landscape for over forty years.

Forty years! And every single one of them with Dad at the helm until I, aka Johnny Come Lately arrived on the scene, and despite a rocky start, I have been shocked at how much I love it! I really do. It seems like all the things that made me feel trapped and determined to get the hell out of Scotland and St Andrews as an ambitious young graduate have now become the very reasons that drew me back. The penny dropped when I went travelling and was afforded the luxury of time, distance and perspective. I'd loved my time in London, living the big city life, but what the ups and downs of the past year had made me realise are the important things in life: family, friends, love, security and hopefully soon, a home.

Chapter 12

During lunch service I reflected on my meeting with Jeffy, during which she emphasised, several times, how well the Birdie was doing, By the time I bade farewell to our last customer I had already decided to take the first step to becoming a property owner and made an appointment to see my bank manager. The sooner I found out if he would support me or laugh me out of the building, the better.

I called Gordon Ferguson straight after lunch hoping to see him that afternoon, but I was informed by a rather amused-sounding secretary that he was a very busy man and he didn't have any appointments until the following week, which rather took the wind out of my sails. In all fairness, when she heard me go from over-excited to droopy in a heartbeat, she apologised that the earliest appointment she could give me was for the following Thursday.

Thanking her, I hung up. I would just err on the side of optimistic and hope that he would agree to giving me a mortgage and keep looking anyway. Now that I had the idea in my head I was determined not to rest until it was in my own bed, in my own room, in my own home.

Just as I arrived back, there was a knock on the door. It was Mouse.

'I've agreed to go to Edinburgh tomorrow to meet Adrian De Witt.'

'Brilliant!' I enthused.

'Will you come with me?'

I looked at her.

'Pleeeeeease,' she said, giving me her head-tilting smile.

'Well,' I said, taking my phone out as it rang, interrupting our conversation.

'Maddy, Jeanette Stuart, Gordon's secretary from the bank. As luck would have it, I have a cancellation for tomorrow afternoon. I know it's short notice but it's yours if you would like it?'

'Oh yes, please,' I said.

'Great. Four pm tomorrow afternoon?'

'Perfect,' I said. 'See you then.' I was grinning as the call clicked off and then realised Mouse was still standing waiting for my answer.

When I explained my predicament, she understood but looked terrified at the prospect of meeting De Witt alone.

'Even if I could come, Mouse, I honestly think you would be better off without me.'

'What makes you think that?' she said, sounding horrified at the prospect.

'Well, try as I might, I cannot stop butting in and taking over and that's not going to do you any good. I mean, come on, you could see I was getting up his nose last time ...'

'I think I'll cancel,' she said rather abruptly.

'No! Don't.'

'I can't do this on my own.'

'You can.'

'I can't.'

'You can, Mouse,' I said, holding her by the shoulders and looking into her anxious eyes.

She looked away, nerves apparent. 'Well, maybe I should see if Hamish can go then ...'

'Honestly, Mouse, I think you should do this on your own. You are the artist, De Witt is the one that needs to impress you, not the other way round. He loves your work, and you haven't signed anything, so you are under no obligation. Go and see what he's all about. If, once you get there, you don't like anything about it, just get on the next train home.'

She wiggled her fringe out of her eyes, re-establishing eye contact.

'You can do this. I know you can,' I said confidently.

She nodded silently, mulling over what I had said and a few moments later, her face broke into a tentative smile.

'You're absolutely right,' she said, 'I can do this.'

'Yeah!' I said, giving her a squeeze.

'Come on, let's get out of here and talk tactics.'

I clipped Frank's lead on and the three of us went for a windy walk along the beach. Tripping along in the wee dog's wake as he skittered over the sand towards the sea spray hunting for a stick, the bracing air filled us both with energy. I delivered a pep walk, shouting over the buffeting wind until, suitably buoyed up by my words, Mouse and I began to jog, in an almost Rocky Bilboa-like formation. By the time we arrived breathless back at the bothy forty-five minutes later, we were practically punching the air as the long shadows of the winter sun stretched out before us. Coming to a halt, I looked at my pink-cheeked, bright-eyed friend.

'Now you look like a woman in control,' I said.

'I am. I really am!' she said, grinning back at me. 'Thanks, Maddy.'

Chapter 13

The following morning, I confess I expected a call from Mouse from the train or the station, or from a loo somewhere or all three, to give me an update, so I kept my phone on and in my pocket the whole time, but by the time lunch service started at twelve, I hadn't heard a word.

I texted Hamish. *Any word from Mouse?*

He didn't respond as usual. Infuriating man.

I was gagging to know how she was getting on, checking my phone for the umpteenth time that day, but I would just have to wait.

By the end of lunch service, with still no word from Mouse I headed off to the beach with Frank, where I bumped into Jack along with Duke and Gaston. It was the first time I had seen him since his outburst outside the Birdie and I wasn't sure what to expect.

As Frank rushed up to his giant Scottish Deerhound pals, Jack waved, a smile in place.

'Hi!' I said, relieved there looked like no hard feelings from the bust up the other day.

'Hi,' he said. 'How are you doing? I was hoping to bump into you.'

'Oh, were you?' I asked. 'Why?'

'Well, I wanted to say sorry for going off on one the other day. My father just has the knack of turning me from calm to rabid in three seconds flat and I shouldn't have taken it out on you, Madeline.' My Sunday name. He always used it. It always had the same effect. My heart swelled as he took my hands in his. 'Forgive me?'

'Of course,' I said. 'There's nothing to forgive, really, it had nothing to do with me. I had no right...'

He looked at me. 'But you do,' he said gently. 'I mean, this whole thing has kind of blown everything out of the water for us, just when we had—'

I blushed and held his gaze.

'Yes, we had,' I said, my voice dropping into a dry croak.

'So anyway,' he said. 'It's my birthday next week and I wondered...' He hesitated. 'Will you come out for dinner with me?'

'Yes, please,' I said with undue haste, and then rolled my eyes, adding, 'Playing it cool as usual.'

His eyes crinkled as he smiled. 'You don't need to play it cool with me, Madeline, we are well past that.' He took a step towards me and kissed me.

'Just as well,' I said. 'If you kiss me like that again, I won't be responsible for my actions.'

His response was to take a step closer, so the toes of our boots touched, and he kissed me again, more deeply this time, setting my every nerve jangling, erasing any doubt I had that exaggerated our connection. There was no question we were stronger than ever. God, I would have dragged him into the dunes right then and there if we hadn't been interrupted.

'Break it up, break it up, there are children present,' a familiar voice boomed.

It was Sarah and Phil with Tilda in a papoose strapped to his front, walking towards us, Charlie running ahead and about to bowl into my legs.

'Maddddddddyyyyyyy, from London!' he shouted, bumping into me.

'My God, with a rugby tackle like that, you'll be playing for the first fifteen before you're five,' joked Jack.

'What's that?' he asked.

'I'll tell you later,' said Phil as they caught up. 'Now let Maddy go!'

'Yes sir,' said Jack.

'Not you,' he said, still in parental mode and then burst out laughing as both Jack and Charlie released me.

'Well, did she say yes?' said Sarah.

'Yes, she did,' Jack grinned.

'Told you.'

'Hey, what are you two up to?' I asked, looking at Sarah.

'Nothing, I was just telling Jack that you're not as scary as you look and that I thought you might just be up for a night out.'

'Bubble bubble, toil and trouble,' I said, grinning at her. 'Well, you were right!'

Frank chose that moment to jump up and steal the half-eaten biscuit out of Charlie's hand which broke the moment.

'Hey, sausage dog,' the excited boy shouted, chasing Frank who was off like the clappers, swallowing, chewing and ducking and diving at top speed all at the same time.

We all began to wander along the beach together, Charlie chasing Frank, Duke and Gaston wading out into the sea chasing each other, Phil, Sarah, Jack and I walking and talking. I had never been happier.

Chapter 14

After our protracted walk I was in danger of being late for the appointment at the bank. Wrestling my sandy clothes off and into a heap before slipping on my tidiest of ensembles, hair tamped down with a series of bands and clips for the occasion, I arrived with moments to spare for my meeting with the bank manager, Gordon Ferguson.

I had sent him the Birdie's up-to-date accounts the previous night, which he was familiarising himself with when I was shown through to his office.

'Ah, Maddy,' he said, smiling and standing up. 'Come away in and have a seat. Cup of tea?'

That bodes well, a free hot drink, I thought.

'Yes please,' I replied.

'OK,' he said, making his way to the sideboard and pouring two very dainty cups of tea from a stainless-steel teapot, placing one in front of each of us and retrieving a wee jug and sugar bowl which he placed between us before he sat back down. It was so St Andrews, I thought with a wave of affection.

'Thanks,' I said, smiling and taking a sip, eyeing him over the rim of the cup.

'My pleasure. Now, first things first, thank you for sending all this information over. I just want to clarify these figures are for the last six months?'

'Yes,' I said, clenching my knees together as his eyebrows knotted together in a clump on his wee shiny bald head.

'OK.' He nodded, scrutinising them, before raising his eyes to me once again. 'So, what is it I can do for you?'

'Well, I'm thinking of buying a flat.'

'Oh,' he said, nodding at me.

'And I was wondering what the chances would be of me getting a mortgage,' I said, my face burning hot, so unaccustomed to talking about such things and feeling like he may laugh me out of the place.

'I see,' he said, looking back at the figures in front of him.

The silence was deafening, as he contemplated my future.

'I mean, there is no rush, I just thought it was something I might be able to think about...'

Sitting back, his eyebrows aloft, he said, 'OK, I have to say I was quite taken aback by these.' He tapped the paper with his finger. 'I mean, if you can generate this sort of money in six months with one restaurant, I'm surprised you're not thinking of opening another one. Have you considered it?'

'To be honest, no.'

'Well, maybe you should,' he said, the knot of eyebrows relaxing as he smiled and passed me a plate of Rich Tea biscuits.

Taking one, I held his gaze, breaking it only to dunk in my tea a few times, before placing the soggy biscuit in my mouth, crumbs frittering down and clinging to my jumper and hair. Synapses firing, good lord. Expanding the business hadn't even crossed my mind until the second he said it and then BANG, the idea of buying a flat dropped off my list instantly, and it was replaced by the extraordinarily exciting prospect of the Birdie and Bramble two.

'Oh my God! What a brilliant idea!' I said, unable to hide

my enthusiasm. 'Are you saying if I did, you would consider supporting me?'

'Well, if you find the right place, and the figures stack up, then I don't see why not? After all, investing in local business is what we do.'

I stared at him. 'Where on earth would I start?'

'Well,' he said, fiddling about in his desk drawer for a moment before producing a business card. 'Take this. Mackie Scott is a long-term client of mine, commercial estate agent, and a very successful one at that. He lives in St Andrews and works in Edinburgh. He's a good sounding board, he played golf with your dad and I am sure he would be delighted to have a chat with you.'

'Th... thank you,' I said, taking the card and scrutinising it.

After popping the second half of the Rich Tea in my mouth, I realised I had a hundred questions to ask so, surreptitiously ditching the biscuit into my napkin, I started firing them at Gordon.

'Have you got a bit of paper and a pen? I need to write this all down.'

Laughing, he produced an A4-lined pad and Bank of Scotland pencil and allowed himself to be interrogated, as I asked the ABCs of what I needed to do first.

The next fifteen minutes were spent firing random questions at the poor man as he jotted things down for me to do in order to move things along before his next appointment arrived. When his secretary knocked to announce my time was up, I stood up and was still talking as he ushered me out, handing me the piece of paper he had been jotting notes on and telling me to stay in touch.

I backed out of the bank and practically skipped onto the street. Geez. My head was spinning with possibilities. Emerging into the daylight I practically ran round to the restaurant where William and Javier were getting set for dinner.

They looked up at me as I burst in gagging to tell them what had just happened, but it would have to wait, as the door flew open behind me with the early diners of the evening arriving at five sharp.

During dinner service it was all I could think about. On automatic pilot, smiling and serving customers, I was thinking about expanding the business. I would need to decide on location, size, timescale, and name! Then calming myself down, I needed to speak to an expert to help me work out my next move and so I decided to keep it under my hat rather than blurting out a half-baked scheme. Keeping secrets was hard enough in St Andrews without me bumping my gums prematurely.

The Birdie and Bramble two, my baby.

At the end of the shift, we cleared down and Will emerged from the kitchen with bowls of venison stew for the staff dinner.

'Any news?' asked Will.

'Sorry?' I said, wondering if he was a mind reader.

'Mouse?' he said, looking at me as if I had lost it. 'Anything from Mouse?'

Checking my phone for the first time in a couple of hours, guilt washed over me. I'm some friend, so self-absorbed I had completely forgotten about Mouse.

'Yes!' I said, reading it out.

Sorry not been in touch, had an amazing day.

'Well, that bodes well,' said Will.

'Thank God,' I said as the door flew open and in came Hamish, looking around to see if there were any customers left so he could gauge how much of his current attire he had to cover up, change and hide. Relieved to see it was just Will and me, he asked,

'Is Claude here?'

'Yes, he's in the kitchen.'

'Any word from Mouse?' I've not heard a peep since I dropped her at the station this morning,' he said, anxiously digging his mobile out of his pocket, his face dropping. 'Oh, it's run out of charge.'

I rolled my eyes. Typical bloody Hamish.

I passed my phone over to him so he could read her text.

'Oh, great,' he said as the colour began to seep back into his face. 'Do you mind texting her to say my phone's dead, but I'll be there to collect her at the station?'

'No problem,' I said as William stood up. 'Do you want something to eat, Hamish?'

He eyed the casserole hungrily. 'Och, that would be great, I am due to collect her off the train in twenty minutes so that gives me plenty of time,' he said, pulling up a chair.

'I can't wait to hear how it's all gone...' He smiled at William as he placed a bowl of delicious stew in front of him before picking up his fork and getting stuck right in. 'You lot have a good night?'

William began talking him through the usual tales of any evening in the restaurant. Of course, I was gagging to tell them about the exciting possibility of expanding the business, but I decided to keep my powder dry and not blurt out a half-baked plan, which was my speciality, so I stayed relatively quiet as the rest chatted on.

'Oh, I meant to say, anyone want a car?' Hamish piped up.

'What?' said William, a look of incredulity on his face. It was very Hamish, issuing a random question apropos of nothing. I smiled at him as he went on.

'It's this guy who owes Dad big time, he kept putting stuff

on the slate and didn't pay for months and when Dad asked him to cough up, he said he didn't have any cash so offered him this car. He's had it sitting on the farm for years. Dad just said yes. He's known the guy for years, and you know what he's like, doesn't like to make life difficult for folk.'

'Oh,' I said. 'I could do with a car. How much?'

'Five hundred pounds.'

'Five hundred pounds! I'll have that,' I said, thinking about my impending property hunt and need for independence.

William dropped his fork. 'You can't be serious?'

'I can and I am,' I said. 'Business is good, I need transport and, well … it's fate, isn't it?'

'Yeah.' Hamish grinned.

'What kind of car is it?' asked William.

'Yellow,' said Hamish.

William rolled his eyes and chose not to get involved with this juvenile exchange, realising it would just egg us on further.

'OK, Mads, I'll get all the chat and let you know,' Hamish said, wiping his face with a napkin and pushing his chair back, still chewing his final mouthful.

'Thanks.' I grinned, delighted with myself.

'Right. I better be off,' he said, launching himself up. 'Thanks for dinner, guys. Claude, that venison is a triumph,' he said, as the French chef exited the kitchen and joined us at the table.

Claude nodded at him, smiling. 'Merci.'

'Hamish, tell Mouse I am dying to hear everything!' I said.

'Will do,' he said, waving and disappearing out the door.

'Right,' I said. 'I'm going to make a move.'

'Me, too,' said Will. 'Come on, I will walk around the corner with you.'

'Claude?'

'I'll just check orders for tomorrow and then lock up. I will see you in the morning.'

Will and I enjoyed a wrapped up walk round to the bothy, so I dived in and got Frank and walked him back to his place, where he bid me goodnight with a hug. Fifteen minutes later I was scrambling into bed, tired but unable to sleep, so I Googled late into the night, getting an overview of possible sites for my expansion plan. I started with small commercial properties in some of the smaller east coast villages south of St Andrews and ended up looking at a 250-seater behemoth of a place in central Glasgow. It was 2.50 a.m. when I switched off the light.

Chapter 15

After a fitful sleep, I awoke bleary-eyed the next morning, walked the sausage and made my way round to the Birdie where I continued Googling commercial property when a text pinged in from Hamish.

Am just around the corner, got some stuff for you, is the coast clear?

By the coast he meant Claude. Claude was a stickler for cleanliness and had put some much-needed restrictions on what acceptable attire was for Hamish and his rather haphazard delivery style. A hairnet, wellington boots and a white overall, which worked well for the first few days but since then, the overall was either yirded or in the wash, the hairnet on the floor of the van and the wellington boots encrusted with dung.

Claude is here, beware, I texted back, smiling to myself. There was no getting away from the fact that every time Hamish dropped in to make a delivery we needed to hoover and wipe down after him; but despite this, I could not deny the growing admiration I had for him.

Up until Hamish's newfound passion as a green-fingered guru, I had always thought of winter as a time when everything stopped growing, shrivelled up and died. But my big daft cousin was bucking the trend, as his hothouse hobby in the wee lean-to greenhouse in the postage stamp garden behind the Birdie and Bramble continued to flourish. So much so that he had outgrown our wee patch and had taken over his mum and dad's window boxes on the first floor above the butcher shop across the road, before expanding into their garden at the back of the shop. Uncle Fraser was far more interested in golfing than gardening and Auntie Mary just used it to hang out washing and occasionally sit in on a sunny day. Of course, Hamish's folks adored the very bones of their only son and loved watching as he rooted about, and good old Hamish always had time for a chat. The quantity and quality of herbs and vegetables he had managed to produce over the past few months were outstanding. The excess vegetables from what we needed at the Birdie were enjoyed by family and friends. And it didn't stop there. His propagating passion was reaping the benefits, too. With so many pots with newly visible curls of green bursting out all around, he had erected a little stand outside Fraser's butcher's shop selling growing herbs for ninety pence each, a successful wee addition to Hamish's burgeoning business. Mouse had even done a logo for him. It read HH and looked very classy, a little like HRH but rather than His Royal Highness it stood for the slightly less grand, Hamish's Herbs.

The transformation of my previously nomadic cousin in one year was extraordinary. He had gone from occasional plant waterer to green-fingered obsessive gardener and supplier. He was still toeing the line and helping Uncle Fraser in the butcher's, but his heart was in the soil. The second he finished work, he would rush upstairs to his parents' flat where he was still officially living and change into his gardening stuff. In reality, he was more or less living with Mouse in her bedsit, which was tiny, and his bedroom at home was now a 'dumping ground for all his crap' as his long-suffering mum described it. Having said that, she loved having him back in St Andrews and her wee face lit up when he was around, on the surface always complaining about his untidiness but in reality, doing his washing, ironing and she was more than content the great hairy galloot was back.

When he just had the wee bit of ground outside the back of the Birdie to tend, he would march through Claude's pristine kitchen, which caused a great deal of friction until the meticulous chef put some strict rules in place, which Hamish agreed to. So, we were now used to seeing him slipping through the restaurant with even his shoes covered, a hairnet keeping his unruly mop from flying around the place, in a zip-up white boiler suit with whatever gubbins he carried in a huge ziplock sack. What had started as a hobby had proved to really be his 'thing'. Every spare minute he had he would appear with a sheepish grin, tiptoeing through the kitchen past Claude whose beady eye followed him and his paraphernalia carefully.

Over time he began to reap seeds and send them off to other growers across the length and breadth of the country, receiving others in return. It was like a great big vegetable love-in, the idea being that no one should buy seeds as they came free with every fruit and vegetable naturally. His green credentials had always been a passion but now even more so as he sourced many heritage and heirloom varieties of vegetables and fruit. His topic of conversation these days was an infomercial on the world of vegetables – parsnips, carrots, turnips, kale, rocket, spinach, tomatoes, onions, and potatoes. He was a man with a mission. Celeriac, fennel, cabbage, garlic, radish, chillies. He was always chuntering on about his newfound passion and his latest dream was of starting a commercial growing business for profit whilst spreading the love in order to feed those who needed it most. My eco warrior cousin was now no longer chaining himself to whalers in Japan, but he was equally motivated and passionate about caring for the planet but happily a lot closer to home.

★

Suddenly the door flew open, held in place by a muddy welly as Hamish heaved a large armful of produce in.

'Hamish!' I shouted. 'Did you not get my message? Claude is here and you're dropping mud and weevils all over the floor.'

'Oh, sorry,' he said, stopping in his tracks, as Javier, hearing the commotion, popped his head out of the kitchen and without hesitation retrieved a huge empty basket which he plopped down in front of Worzel Gummidge.

'Thanks,' said Hamish, opening his arms and letting the great clump of produce fall into it. Cue Claude bustling out of the kitchen. Taking one look at Hamish, he shook his head, took a deep breath, walked over to the basket and hauled it onto a table to begin inspecting.

Hamish, Javier and I watched silently as Claude picked up each item, examined it closely, gave it a stroke and the professional sniff, nodded his approval and placed it back.

We awaited his verdict.

'Yes,' he said and then pointed at Hamish's feet.

'Sorry, man,' said Hamish. 'It's pouring out there, but if I can just remind you all that stuff is fresh from the ground to your gaff in under thirty minutes.'

Claude looked at him. 'OK,' he said and turned and looked at Javier who took the cue, picked up the basket and followed him through to the kitchen.

'Phew!' said Hamish, grinning and pulling up a seat. 'I think I got away with that.'

'Yes,' I said, returning his smile. 'But please,' I brushed some earth off the tablecloth, 'sort yourself out. It's driving me mad, too.'

'OK,' he said, accepting he was in the wrong, 'I'm really sorry I haven't got my stuff on.' He flapped his arm around indicating he was wearing neither his hairnet nor hazmat suit. 'But I had a really, really, late night. By the time Mouse got back from Edinburgh ...'

'Of course! How did she get on?' I said, forgetting my irritation in an instant.

'Well, really well,' he said nodding, his internal dialogue as ever more engaging to him than spilling the beans.

'Well?'

'Well, yeah, it went really well,' he said. 'She's so up for it, she was, like, totally inspired when she came back and so we sat up planning and well ... yeah,' he said, smiling and staring off into the middle distance.

Hardly a mine of information, but I was used to him and it was loud and clear that Mouse was happy, it had gone well and things were progressing with her foray into the art world of our capital city.

'Oh yeah and the car ...'

'Oh yes, the car!' I said, having completely forgotten.

'If you're still up for it, I will bring it round later.'

'Brilliant. Thanks, Hamish.'

'No probs, cuz. Well, I better get on, Napoleon wants me in the shop by eleven and I'm cutting things fine,' he said as he waved and backed out the way he had come in, leaving a trail of earth behind him. I rolled my eyes at Claude, who was lovingly stroking the produce in the basket as he smiled at me, in love with a celeriac. I wish I was as easily pleased. Getting any clear info about Mouse from Hamish was impossible – he was a complete space cadet. I'd have to get the details straight from the horse's mouth, so I dropped her a quick text. After lunch service I was heading off into town on a rare shopping trip, the perfect opportunity to catch up.

By the time we waved our last customer off, there was still no word from her, and as I got togged up and ready to go

Claude marched into the dining room, holding aloft a dish of something delicious.

'What is it?' I said, putting my bag down whilst I assessed what I might be missing if I was too hasty running off.

'Macaroni cheese,' he announced.

I took off my coat immediately.

'Well, there is no way I'm going to miss this,' I said, settling down with Javier, Claude, and Lyle to enjoy it.

Just a few days before, Claude and I had had a rather heated conversation about the merits of macaroni cheese. Me pro, him anti, which ended rather abruptly when I informed him it was so popular in these parts that if he cared to walk into any bakery in St Andrews, he could purchase a macaroni pie. His face was a picture, his Gallic culinary sensibilities shocked to the core.

'A pie full of macaroni cheese?' he said, incredulous. 'No!'

He had returned to the kitchen rather disillusioned and had obviously had a long hard think about it and the fact he had gone to the effort to make this was a true mark of the man: despite an ego the size of Peru, admitting he was wrong and seeking acceptance. And bless him, he didn't do things by halves. It was absolutely delicious, bubbly, cheesy and it had the unmistakable luxury of homemade macaroni.

'Claude, that is a triumph!' I concluded, breaking the silence of the assembled macaroni cheese fans.

'We should put this on the menu,' Lyle said through his last mouthful of a very generous portion.

'I agree,' said Javier. 'It is perfect.' His eyes closed as he savoured the flavours.

'Well, Claude, you have well and truly kicked the macaroni pie into a cocked hat,' I stated.

'A cocked hat?' he repeated suspiciously.

'Erm … what I meant is … this is the ultimate macaroni

cheese, the pinnacle of the fromage de macaroni, the best one I have ever tasted.' I grinned at him.

Claude visibly relaxed and rewarded us with a tiny nod and an almost smile, which we now understood was his way of saying thank you.

Peace restored, it was the perfect time for me to disappear.

'Right guys, I'm off, back at five.'

Chapter 16

Rushing along the road, I was surprised at how excited I was to be going shopping. The last time I had got dolled up was for the wedding and although I loved the shantung blue silk dress I had worn for the occasion, I had no intention of wearing that ever again. The mere thought of it elicited a shiver of horror, as an image of me squatting in a hedge in the offending article the morning after the wedding flashed through my mind. Marching on at speed, I shook my head to rid the image from my brain.

When I lived in London, I was constantly on Oxford Street swanning about, spending my hard-earned cash on the latest trend, but I was so out of the loop now and I didn't know where to start, so I was just standing looking vacant on the High Street when I saw Mouse.

'Mouse!'

'Maddy, hi!' she said, turning round.

'I texted you earlier… how did it go yesterday?' I asked, looking at her as I tried to detect what was different about her.

'Great, it wasn't nearly as scary as I thought,' she said. 'Adrian introduced me to so many people, and we went to all these galleries and he took me for lunch to this amazing restaurant and…'

I know what it was! She was wearing makeup for the first time in months and when I say makeup I don't mean lipstick and eyeliner, I mean a very pared down version of the white face makeup she used to wear when I first met her, a sort of diluted goth resurgence. Slightly worrying, so I decided not to mention it. 'Where are you off to?' she asked.

'To buy something for tomorrow night. Jack is taking me out for dinner,' I grinned.

'God, I'm only away one day and it's all happening. I've got to go and order up some canvases but that won't take long. Have you got time for a coffee?'

'Yeah, give me thirty minutes and I'll meet you in Northpoint?'

'Fab. See you then,' said Mouse, heading off along the road.

I watched her for a second. That white makeup thing could be interpreted as a step backwards in terms of her recent transformation. Maybe it was just me being dramatic, but I would monitor it carefully nonetheless, I thought, stopping outside Sam Brown and seeing what looked like the perfect outfit displayed in the window.

Entering the shop, I asked to try it on, only to be told, 'No, that is not right for your shape,' by the proprietor who offered to line up some options for me to try on. Thanking her and relieved because she knew what she was doing, I retreated into the changing room and waited. Stripping down to my bra and knickers I was rather disheartened to find I'd clearly put on a few pounds. The downside of being in the restaurant business was constantly tasting food, though to be fair the number of steps I walked during a shift on any given day usually meant I worked it off. Clearly, I was doing less steps and eating more food, I thought, as my tummy gurgled, reminding me of the vast plate of cheesy macaroni that lay in there, digesting slowly. After I started with size twelves, reluctantly I agreed to go up a size. But Sam knew her stuff, she knew what she was doing, and within ten minutes I had settled on a khaki shirt dress, white linen jacket and espadrilles all of which fitted perfectly.

'But a size fourteen...' I said.

'Och, don't worry about that,' she said. 'Clothes these days are made small.'

'You're good at this!' I enthused as I turned round, admiring her choice in the mirror. Quite understated and I hoped not too safari, but all the colours and styles she had picked made me feel confident and, despite sizegate, quite slim.

'I hope so. I've been doing it for years,' she laughed.

Thanks to her speedy styling I was five minutes early to meet Mouse, who was already settled and scoffing a trusty carrot cake and hot chocolate when I arrived.

'Oops.' She smiled, wiping the marshmallowy whipped cream from her face. 'Caught!'

I hesitated briefly but there was no way I was resisting that, so I ordered the same, and then we settled down.

'So ... tell me all,' I said, settling back to hear her chat.

'Well, Adrian met me off the train. He was so lovely, honestly. Much nicer than the other day.'

'Good.'

'The first thing he did was take me to Harvey Nichols! Up to the fifth floor where we had coffee. It's amazing up there, you can see right across Edinburgh to the castle,' she said, eyes wide.

'Nice,' I said, sipping my coffee, thinking he was obviously out to impress.

'And Adrian knows ... well, just everyone!' she enthused. 'He even had an itinerary for the whole day.' She dug about in her bag and produced a folded piece of A4, which she handed to me.

10.00 a.m. Harvey Nichols. Coffee
11.00 a.m. Meet Guy Peploe, The Scottish Gallery
11.30 a.m. The Dundas Gallery
Midday The Open Eye Gallery
1.00 p.m. Lunch at the National Gallery and a wander round
2.00 p.m. Meet Avery Stewart, Patron of the Arts
3.00 p.m. Cocktails at Bramble
4.00 p.m. Meet Gordon Lannister, Art Critic
5.00 p.m. Meet Fiona Duff, Publicity Agent
7.00 p.m. Supper at Howies Restaurant on Waterloo Place
9.00 p.m. Train back to St Andrews

'Bloody hell. You must be absolutely exhausted! That's some itinerary.'

'Yes, that's what I thought, but Adrian said he knew he had one day to get me over the line, as he put it,' she said, sounding quite unlike herself.

'And did he?'

She nodded. 'Yes.'

'So?'

'All of these galleries were amazing and the people so lovely and the most amazing thing was they all spoke to me like I was a real artist.'

'You are!' I laughed.

'I know but you know what I mean. They treated me ...'

'With respect?'

She blushed. 'Yeah'.

'Well, you deserve it. So where is it going to be held?'

'The Table Gallery.'

'Which is where?'

'On Dundas Street, right in the heart of the Edinburgh art scene. It's a brand new concept. Essentially, it's a massive bare room in a Georgian flat. All that's in the room is a huge chandelier and loads of tables. Their plan is to invite a well-known chef up from down south to create a menu to complement the art, so the food and art work together, which is why he thought it would be such a great fit, having seen my stuff in the Birdie.'

'Oh God, what a great idea,' I said.

'Yeah, that's what I thought, and when he showed me round it, well ... It's perfect.' She practically swooned.

'Mouse, that is fantastic!' She grinned, as I forged ahead. 'And what about the deal? Only if you want to discuss it, of course,' I added, not wanting to appear too nosy.

'Well, that was interesting, too. He explained in detail why he takes such a big cut. You see, he has this list, which he has collected over twenty years, and he literally knows the world and his wife – well, the art world and his wife, really, collectors and enthusiasts and the hoi polloi of Scotland as he called them. I know without him I would have no chance of getting my foot in the door,' she said.

'So?'

'So over dinner, he produced a contract which he had had drawn up and I said I would get my lawyer to look over it before signing it.'

I exhaled. 'Good,' I said.

She looked a little uncomfortable.

'What?' I asked.

'Well, we had such an amazing day, and honestly, he was so nice, like a different man to the one we met the other day, and by then I had made my mind up and had a couple of glasses of wine, so thought, bugger it, I will just sign it there and then, so I did.'

'And do you have a copy?'

'Well no, he only had the original with him.' Seeing my face, she changed tack. 'Don't worry, Maddy, he's said he would send it over to me today or tomorrow.' She smoothed her fringe down with her hand looking at me, her eyes nervous, and as big as saucers. She knew what I was thinking so pre-empted me. 'I know, I know, Maddy. I just got a bit carried away.'

'Och, I'm sure it will all be fine,' I said, sounding more confident than I felt, and not wanting to vocalise the alarm bells that this scenario had set off. My gut feeling was that Adrian De Witt had planned the whole thing to get her on her own, out of her comfort zone, turn her head, bamboozle her and get what he wanted. Like a cheetah hoving off the weakest of the herd, his prey.

'Well, if you want a real grown up to look over it for you, I could ask my lawyer, Gerald. I'm sure he would do it as a favour, or for an invitation to the launch of the exhibition,' I grinned, trying to keep things calm.

'That would be great, Maddy, thanks,' she said, looking relieved as she picked up her teaspoon and set about scooping the last chocolatey remnants from her mug.

The awkward conversation over, the next twenty minutes were taken up with her recounting details of the breathless whirlwind of her day in the capital. Give him his due, De Witt had certainly pulled out all the stops. Watching Mouse so confident and animated I dearly hoped he was the honourable man he was intent on painting himself to be, and that this really was the big break Mouse so richly deserved. When she finally drew breath, a text pinged in.

'Oh my God, is that the time? I'm supposed to be meeting Hamish right now!' she said, apologising profusely, waving for the bill and slipping her big black coat on whilst still talking, 'God, Maddy, I'm so sorry, that was so bad of me. We didn't even talk about you and Jack!'

'Oh, don't you worry, there's plenty of time for all that.

Now take care of yourself and don't forget to ping over that contract when you can,' I said, hugging her as she dug out some cash and plopped it on the table.

'OK.' She smiled and was off.

Chapter 17

Sitting there going over our conversation, I took out my purse to pay and found the business card of the commercial property guy Gordon Ferguson had recommended. No time like the present, I thought, pulling out my mobile and calling him. He picked up immediately and quite wrong-footed me when he said Gordon had dropped him an email introducing me and, though he usually worked in Edinburgh, he happened to be in St Andrews that very afternoon. He suggested we meet in the bar at Malmaison at four pm. So, of course, I said yes.

This gave me time to go back to the bothy, dump my stuff, and collect Frank before my meeting. Dogs were allowed in Malmaison, so I just took the sausage with me and was rather pleased with myself to note I was five minutes early. I ordered a black coffee in the hope it would give me a much-needed boost of energy and make me look business-like. The coffee arrived at exactly the same time as a sharp-suited, hyperactive individual at four on the dot.

'Maddy Campbell?' he said, flashing a big-toothed grin at me.

'Yes,' I said, standing up, as he shook my hand and ordered a black coffee for himself before sitting down. The man was a whirlwind.

'Lovely to meet you. Knew your father. Lovely man.

Condolences. Hear you're doing a grand job at the Birdie. Chip off the old block, eh?'

I smiled at him and failed to get a word in edgeways as he fired a few questions at me.

'So, what are you looking for? Location? Size? Budget? Timescale?' As I ummed and stammered, making no sense whatsoever, he realised pretty quickly I had no idea, which didn't deter him one bit. He was off like a runaway train and boy, could he talk. We were there for just under an hour during which he bamboozled me with facts and figures about commercial property in Scotland. He knew every restaurateur in town and beyond. I just sat back and listened intently to him, my head fit to burst. Fifty minutes later, he stood up to say goodbye, shook my hand and then almost as an afterthought, opened his briefcase and handed me an A4 envelope.

'Just a random selection of what's on the market in Scotland,' he said. 'I didn't know what you had in mind but having a look at this lot might help you decide.'

'Thank you so much,' I said, taking it from him.

'You have my card?' I nodded. 'Call me when your thoughts crystallise, and don't hesitate if you have any questions about any of it or want to view anything.'

'OK,' I said, and with that he was off.

A man who lived his life at a very different pace to mine, I thought, watching as he marched up to the bar, paid the bill, put on his jacket and made a call simultaneously. 'Bloody hell,' I said to Frank as we ambled along the road to the bothy. I looked at my phone and realised I would have to be quick if I wanted a shower before I was due back at the Birdie for evening service. At that moment, I spotted Hamish waving like a loon from the other side of the road.

94

'Hey, what are you up to?' I shouted, waving back, which was when he stood up, very obviously leaning on a car.

'Your transport, madam,' he grinned.

'Oh my God,' I said, rushing across the road, all thoughts of showers and changing out of the window. So, the big news is, I have transport! Yes, it is an absolute rust bucket of an ancient Citroen Dyane, yellow, brown and black. The black is Hammerite paint that someone decided was the best way to shore it up as it became rickety. Apparently it leaks when it rains, but it's mine for the princely sum of bugger all.

'What? I thought you said five hundred pounds,' I said when Hamish told me.

'I did but when Dad took me out to get it, the guy had to start it with jump leads and then we pointed out there was straw and mouse shit all over the back seat. But the final straw was when Dad asked him about an MOT and once he found it, realised it runs out in about five weeks. He felt so guilty he finally decided we were actually doing him a favour taking it away.'

'I love it,' I said, stroking its lumpy roof. I was thrilled. I had never had my own car before.

'The roof comes down,' he said, loping in and unclipping something before manually pushing the roof back in an accordion style before wrenching it back into position and reattaching it, his demonstration complete.

'What do you think?' he asked.

'A convertible,' I said, clapping my hands and jumping into the passenger seat as Hamish turned the key. It spluttered to life and we wheezed it around the corner towards the Birdie. As luck would have it, William was sweeping the pavement outside in preparation for opening as we approached.

'That is a death trap,' said William as it juddered to a halt outside the restaurant.

'Oh, come on, William, it's not that bad,' I said defensively.

'Yeah admit it, it's so cool,' cajoled Hamish.

'Sorry?' said Will, unable to hide his disdain.

'The number plate! It's MRS 151 W,' said Hamish, as if this would make any difference.

'Oooh, I didn't notice that,' I enthused.

'For God's sake, it's practically an antique,' said William, leering at it.

'Och, it will do the job and the roof comes off so I can lug big things about in it, too. Like you,' I said, poking my hand into Hamish's oxter.

'Very good,' said Hamish, snorting.

'Has it even got an MOT?' asked Will.

'Yes,' said Hamish.

'Just under two months to run,' I chipped in, exaggerating slightly.

William looked at me. 'I give up,' he said, turning and going back into the restaurant.

Hamish and I grinned at each other conspiratorially. I was no Jeremy Clarkson but there was little doubt in my mind it would most likely be heading to the scrappie in five weeks. But for now, it was perfect. Reluctant as I was to let it go, Hamish reminded me I needed to get it taxed and insured before I hit the road. 'Fair enough,' I said, hugging and thanking him and watching as it huffed and lurched along the road before I entered the restaurant. What a day!

Dinner went by in a flash. It was the A team. I was manning the bar, William was out front, Claude and Javier in the kitchen. Forty-two covers and we barely drew breath until we gathered for our nightly meal and post-mortem.

'You OK?' asked William.

'Yes, why?' I said.

'It's not that car, is it?'

'No,' I said. 'It's nothing.'

'It's just you seem a bit ... distracted.'

He knew me so well.

'Well, I am going out with Jack tomorrow for dinner,' I said casually.

'Oh, so that's what it is.' He smiled.

'And ...' I said.

'What?' he asked, eyes narrowing, waiting for the truth as Claude and Javier burst through the kitchen door carrying plates full of delicious food for our supper. I winked at him. He would have to wait.

'I will tell you tomorrow.'

He pulled a face. 'Maddy! What?'

'Tomorrow, I promise,' I said as I took a plate from Javier's outstretched hand. 'Mmmmm, that looks great, guys, thanks.'

Finishing off less than fifteen minutes later, I shivered. In less than twenty-four hours I would be sitting opposite Jack MacPherson, at the St Andrews Seafood Restaurant celebrating his thirtieth birthday. I felt sick with excitement as I relived, for the hundredth time, the moment he kissed me on the beach. I was jelly. Although I saw Jack most days, the excitement I felt at the prospect of going out with him for dinner, just the two of us, was undeniable. After saying goodnight to the guys, I walked briskly back to the bothy, preparing for a sleepless night.

Chapter 18

Amazingly I went out like a light, waking up to a text from William.

Coffee?

I grinned. He knew something was up, and his instinct was right. I was looking forward to talking everything through with him. After all, he was my business partner and a safe pair of hands, plus I still wasn't sure whether opening another restaurant was really a good idea or whether my ego was out of control after hearing so many compliments about my business acumen from my bank manager. Maybe I was just believing my own press, always a fatal mistake. Yes, it was time to spill the beans.

See you at Northpoint in an hour, I texted back and jumped out of bed.

First things first I wanted to insure the car so I could start using it ASAP.

A quick shower later I clipped Frank on the lead and marched off to walk him and call the insurance broker. I used the same broker as we did for the restaurant, and after the usual niceties, I began to furnish him with the details and he laughed when I gave him the number plate, MRS 151 W, thinking I was joking. He soon realised I wasn't and was rather embarrassed when he had to reel in his hilarity and find me a policy, albeit for a measly five weeks. But he did and was full of apologies as we said goodbye. I admit even I was surprised to learn she was forty years old but what the hell, she was all mine. A quick text to Hamish to ask him where to pick up the keys and I was off to meet Will.

He was like a cat on a hot tin roof.

'I knew there was something, Maddy,' he said, grinning at me as I shucked off my jacket and took a seat opposite him. So, I just blurted it all out, the meeting with the bank manager, the tentative mortgage enquiry, and the fact it was him that put the notion in my head to expand the business.

'Oh my God,' said Will, putting his hands up to his face, eyes wide.

'What do you think?'

'I think it's bloody genius,' he said.

'You do?'

'Yes, I do!'

'Ha!' I exclaimed as we sat grinning at each other across the table. 'I do, too!'

We sat staring and silent for another few seconds.

'Wow,' he said.

'Yeah. One thing, though, what about Noel?' I asked.

William looked at me. 'Yes, good point. We will have to tread carefully there.'

After I had handed half the business to William and rather irresponsibility buggered off to the other side of the world, leaving him to look after things, he had got himself so wrapped up, determined to look after it for me whilst making it a huge success, he ran himself into the ground and had become seriously ill as a result. It was only a matter of weeks since he had come back to work, on the condition that he would now work to live and not the other way round. His husband Noel was understandably hugely protective, and we would need to tread very carefully indeed in order to convince him expanding the business would be in William's best interests.

William smiled. 'OK, I say we keep it between us and then if and when we find the right place, well, that's when I'll talk to Noel.'

'Good plan. I mean it, might take ages and there's no point in worrying him at this stage.'

'Oh my God … this is too exciting!' said Will.

'I know! Now if you promise not to scream, I will give you this,' I said, wheeching the envelope of commercial properties Mackie Scott had given me and holding it out in front of him.

His face was a picture. 'What is it?' he asked.

I told him and he put his glasses on and began leafing through them immediately.

'I am so happy you're up for it, Will. I wondered if it was too soon, or whether I had just got carried away,' I smiled.

'That's why I love you,' he said. 'You just go for it! If it was up to me, I would just sit tight, safe as houses for the rest of time. You are a force of nature.'

I hugged him.

'OK, let's catch up tomorrow. I have to go. I have a lot to do. It's my hot date with Jack tonight,' I said, my face heating up at the mere thought of it.

'Of course!' he said, looking up briefly from his homework. 'Have a wonderful time, Maddy.'

'I will,' I said, giving him another hug and heading off.

As a real treat I had made an appointment to get my hair done for the first time in an eon. It needed it. A great messy tangled mass of curls and frizz, which was the bane of my life. As I approached the hairdresser I had to rein myself in as I realised I was practically skipping along the road, the fizzy feeling of optimism bubbling up as to what the future might herald.

Taking a deep breath, I stopped for a second before opening the door and sauntering in casually. Arriving like a burst mattress and leaving with my hair dried straight and God knows how, but Derek the hairdresser had made it shinier than glass. I gawped at myself when I looked up from my phone as he announced it was done.

'Bloody hell!' I said.

He grinned. 'Your hair is in fantastic condition.'

'Really? God knows how,' I said.

'Well, it is, and you look fabulous!' He grinned at me in the mirror.

'Well, my hair certainly does. Thank you,' I said, leaving him a generous tip and acknowledging, though not cheap, how it had elevated my confidence considerably as I headed back to the bothy to get ready.

Chapter 19

Just before seven a text pinged in from Jack.

Am outside. I'm a little early, take your time, no rush.

No rush! I had been perched on the edge of the bed, determined not to get covered in dog hairs or smudge my lipstick for over twenty minutes. Taking a deep breath, I gave Frank a biscuit, told him I loved him, and channelling serenity, went out to meet Jack.

Emerging onto the street, there he stood. His hair was swept back, giving him the look of an Italian count, I decided, admiring his dark denim blue eyes that were exactly the same colour as the jacket he was wearing. He leant forward and kissed me gently on the lips. My knees nearly gave out. Jack MacPherson was too bloody good-looking, I couldn't handle myself at all, I thought, considering dragging him straight into the bothy, to hell with dinner. And then, remembering Frank and the piles of clothes that I hadn't quite managed to elevate into my laundry bag splayed over the floor, I thought better of it.

'You're beautiful,' he whispered into my ear.

Good Lord, I wasn't used to this sort of chat, especially when completely sober, so I reverted to type. 'It only took me three hours to get ready.'

He smiled. 'Right, shall we go?'

Looking round for his Land Rover, I asked, 'No car?'

'No, it's a celebration! And I can feel some champagne

coming on.' He grinned, taking my hand and gently pulling me along beside him.

'Who's looking after Scarlett?'

'Duke and Gaston.'

I stopped dead in my tracks. 'What?' I screeched.

He chuckled. 'Sarah.'

God, I loved that girl, I thought, as my stomach did a full three-sixty. This meant Jack was free for the night, we had the whole evening and glorious night ahead. I shivered, focusing on not buckling at the knees, tucking my arm into his and heading in the direction of the seafood restaurant. My tongue thick, for once I remained silent as we fell into our natural rhythm – it was just so easy with him.

'This must be your first night off in how long?' he asked.

'Honestly, this is the first Friday night I've been out since … Nope, can't remember. It feels quite weird being out and about in the real world.' I grinned. 'And what about you?'

'God yes, looking after a baby is exhausting. The thought of an uninterrupted sleep …' He glanced at me, and as our eyes met, an electric shock shot between us. There was little to no chance of having an uninterrupted sleep if this evening went the way I hoped it would. I blushed. Without verbalising, it was clear we were on the same page. We finally found ourselves outside the restaurant.

'Here we are,' said Jack.

'I've walked past this place a hundred times, but I've never eaten in it,' I confessed.

'You'll love it,' he said. 'It's the perfect spot for a special occasion, apart from the Birdie, of course.'

The St Andrews Seafood Restaurant is a glass cube sitting perched on a bluff overlooking the West Sands. Clear minimalist design, twinkling lights, sharply dressed staff gliding between the elegantly white linen set tables. Entering, we were welcomed by the smiling maitre d', who greeted Jack like an old friend.

'Best seat in the house as requested, Mr MacPherson,' he said, whipping away our jackets seamlessly and showing us to a corner table. Glass walls surrounded us and as we sat down, looking round, it almost felt like being on a ship on the sea, the grey churning waves of the North Sea below us and vast open sky above.

'Wow,' I managed as I gazed at it.

I turned and grinned at Jack as a waiter arrived at the table with a champagne bucket and bottle of Veuve Clicquot, expertly pouring each of us a glass before discreetly disappearing as Jack and I sat forward, eyes locked on each other.

'Happy birthday, Jack,' I said.

'Thank you. And thanks for coming tonight, Madeline,' he said.

'Well, it was a hard decision,' I joked as my brain joined the party. 'Running round the restaurant like a blue-arsed fly or this.' I gestured at the twinkling crystal glasses, impeccably turned out staff, and smiling chefs whose skills were on display as the kitchen sat open plan in the heart of the restaurant. Culinary theatre, I thought, appreciating more than ever the effort and professionalism it took to make it look so easy. I couldn't help but smile at the idea of Claude in the Birdie's cramped, vintage kitchen being open to our clientele with shelves stacked, things hanging from hooks, a cacophony of clattering and banter being de rigeur. Jack smiled and handed me a glass of champagne.

'This is the life,' I acknowledged as we clinked glasses.

'To you,' he said.

'To you!' I said.

'To us,' we said in unison.

Blushing from my hair down, I glugged a large mouthful of fizz, savouring the effect it had chilling my parched throat and instilling an instant giggly high.

'So, tell me, how is life in Lilliput?' he asked, shifting the knee-knocking sexual tension by referring to the nickname I had coined for my small bijou accommodation.

'Well, it would be fair to say the novelty has worn off, so much so I had started looking for a place of my own.'

'Had?'

'Yeah, I went to see Gordon Ferguson at the bank to suss out whether he would consider me for a mortgage and so I sent him all the accounts and stuff ahead of the meeting and once he read them, he asked me why I wasn't thinking about opening another restaurant.'

'Bloody hell, a banker trying to give money away, you must be doing well.'

'To be honest, I never really thought about it. This whole year has been such a whirlwind,' I admitted.

'Tell me about it,' he said.

'Yeah,' I said and we paused briefly, acknowledging that both of our lives had been hijacked from their expected path to something quite extraordinary.

'Go on,' said Jack.

'Oh, erm,' I hesitated, bringing myself back to the here and now, just before I lost my thread. 'So yeah, I was totally shocked. I mean, it hadn't even crossed my mind.'

'So, what did you say?' he said, eyes bright.

'To hell with a flat,' I joked, which made Jack laugh. 'And now he's put the notion in my head, I can't think about anything else. I even met a commercial property guy yesterday to get the lie of the land.'

'God, Maddy, you don't waste any time, do you? That really is exciting.'

'Yes, it is, isn't it?' I replied as the waiter arrived back to top up our drinks and deliver the menus. Sitting back, we waited until he left us alone again.

'Well, today is a big day for me, too,' he said.

'Thirty, it's a biggie,' I said.

'Not just that,' he went on. 'Today is the day I inherit the estate.'

I sat back. 'Really?'

'Yes. Tradition dictates Kelso Estate passes to the eldest child on their thirtieth birthday,' he explained.

'Gosh! What about your dad?'

'Well, the outgoing laird and spouse can live on the estate for the rest of their lives but is expected to contribute in some way. Of course, when my father inherited, he was still floundering around in London, so my grandfather stepped up to the plate and ran it virtually until he died. On reflection, that was a blessing as during the past thirteen years Barclay has systematically run the whole place into the ground. I am just glad my grandfather didn't live to see the worst of it. So, what I am inheriting is a great heaving pit of debt, less of a blessing and more a curse.'

'Don't worry, I keep a table in the Birdie for the down at heel, you can eat there anytime you like, but you will have to do the dishes,' I joked. I sat forward, dropping my voice to a whisper, 'But seriously, are things that bad?'

'In a word, yes. The venison business is good, so it managed to accumulate some cash to invest in the estate, but it's a drop in the ocean compared to everything that needs to be done. It is not going to be easy to drag any of it into the twenty-first century.'

We both looked at the tablecloth – this was not shaping up to be the jolly celebration I had imagined at all.

'OK, that's enough about that,' he said, sitting up, shoulders back. 'Let's talk about cheerier things. To you, the next Deborah Meaden.' He smiled, leaning forward as we clinked glasses again.

Raising the glass to my lips I looked at him in what I hoped was more seductive than stalker, when suddenly, out of the blue, the smell of the fizzing alcohol turned my stomach. Instead of swigging it I put it back on the table.

'Oh sorry, could I have some water please?' I said, suddenly feeling very green.

Jack's hand shot up immediately, concern across his face. 'A jug of water please,' he said to the passing waiter, who was back in a moment with a large glass of chilled water. I gulped it down at speed, hoping it would settle my stomach. Eyes a bit watery, I sat back.

'Sorry about that,' I said.

'You OK now?' he said, watching me carefully.

I nodded and insisted in a high voice, 'Yes.'

'Are you sure?' he asked.

'Yes, really,' I said, my voice warbling, 'If you will excuse me just for a moment,' I added, standing up and making my way over to the stairs that led down to the ladies' loo. Slipping my heels off in case I took a purler, I padded down the stairs, feeling distinctly wobbly. Once in the privacy of the loo, I locked the door, stood over the sink and looked at myself. I seemed to be having some sort of hot flush, I thought, as I splashed my wrists, neck and hands in cool water. I didn't touch my face and was relieved to see my makeup had stayed put, despite the rest of me going to hell in a handcart. I took some solace in that. It must be nerves,

I thought, as I gathered myself and headed back up to join Jack.

As I approached the table he stood up. 'Are you OK?'

'Yeah I'm fine,' I said. 'I don't know what that was about.'

'Maybe low blood sugar. Have you had much to eat today?' he asked.

'Erm . . .' I said, remembering the carrot cake and hot chocolate I had had with Mouse oh and the vast bowl of macaroni cheese Claude had whipped up. 'No, I don't think it's that.' God, maybe I had worms, I thought, but chose not to say that out loud. Hardly an aphrodisiac.

'Could be dehydration then, that can make you feel very odd,' said Jack.

'Yes, that's probably what it is. I can't remember the last time I had a glass of water.' And with that he poured another full glass of iced water for me, which I dutifully drank down in one.

'Aaah, that's better,' I said, immediately needing the loo again.

It had to be anxiety, there was no other explanation. I willed myself to get a grip and not ruin Jack's birthday and the evening I had been so looking forward to. The waiter tentatively approached, proffering menus which we both took.

Scanning the menu, the array of delicious food on offer was fabulous. The words were swimming in front of me. I really didn't feel well at all.

'Mmm, oysters!' said Jack. 'I love them. Fancy sharing a dozen to start?'

'Erm . . .' I said as my mind's eye visualised a plate of oyster shells open, the bivalve slick and salty, twitching, sliding down my throat in one slimy glob. Standing up I bolted across the room, this time clattering down the stairs in my heels, getting to the loo just before I was sick. Five minutes later, I was a mess. My face splashed with cool water, the mascara gone, lipstick but a dim and distant memory, and even my hair damply clinging to my sweaty face, I clomped back upstairs and this time when I emerged at the top of the stairs, Jack was waiting, holding my jacket and handbag.

'I'm sorry,' I said, quite worn out and teary by this point.

'It's not your fault,' he said. 'These things happen. Listen, let me take you home to bed.'

An hour ago, those words would have been music to my ears and now those very same words brought connotations of hot water bottles, woolly socks and a Lemsip.

'Thanks,' I said, wobbly as he helped me on with my jacket and led me out of the restaurant.

Clomping back along the Scores, in the direction of home, I leant into him, as he held a protective arm round me, supporting me. For once I was silent.

'Listen, Maddy, we can do this another time, when you're feeling up to it,' he said gently as if reading my mind.

'I'm so sorry, I've completely ruined your birthday,' I said.

'No,' he said. 'Seeing you has completely made my birthday.' He squeezed me as he said it.

'Thank you,' I said, and despite feeling bloody awful, I smiled.

We parted at the front of Noel's shop. There was no point in him coming in, the place looked like a bomb had hit it, and I just wanted to lie face down in my pit of misery.

'Do you want me to take Frank?' he offered. 'Save you walking him?'

'Would you?' I said. 'That would be great.'

And so, I wobbled in, clipped the dog on his lead and led him out to Jack, who got an ecstatic welcome. 'I think he prefers you to me anyway,' I said.

'You really are feeling sorry for yourself, aren't you?' he laughed.

Promising to text me in the morning, he kissed the top of my head and I watched as he waved a sweet goodbye, walking off with Frank marching along beside him without so much as a backward glance. Bloody dachshunds.

Back inside I boiled my mini kettle, made myself a lemon and ginger tea and began to perk up. Typical, I thought, reliving the past few hours and kicking myself. Hopefully I'd be feeling brand new in the morning. Lying in bed I was suddenly ravenous, having missed dinner, so two Pot Noodles later, I put on the radio and drifted off to sleep.

Chapter 20

I awoke surprisingly late the following morning to a WhatsApp from Jack.

'How are you feeling?'

'Better, I think,' I said.

'It's a gorgeous day. I'm heading out to Kelso lodge, fancy a walk? Frank's pining for you,' he said. 'I'll pick you up in thirty minutes.'

Just as he clicked off, I remembered I had my new car but decided to leave things as they were. I had enough to do, I thought, glancing at my mirror. Yikes! Damage limitation required and fast! I grabbed my dressing gown and headed into the shop for a shower.

Just as Jack's Land Rover pulled up outside Noel's shop, I practically fell out the door and onto the pavement with seconds to spare, smiling casually with my heart yammering in my chest, as his rangy body swung down from the driver's side to come around and open the door for me. The first time he had done this I nearly swooned but now I was quite used to it.

'Och, there's no need for that,' I said brightly, opening the passenger side door, only to be faced by a baby seat and a strapped-in and well-wrapped Scarlett. My heart sank. How could I forget?

'Oops,' I said, gazing at this tiny human. 'Hello, you wee scone.' I gave her wee chubby leg a squeeze.

'Sorry, you're in the back,' Jack said, opening the back door as Frank threw himself at me as if he hadn't seen me for years, which made me giggle as I clambered in and shuffled along the utilitarian back seat. Duke and Gaston nudged me as I hauled the little zeppelin-shaped dog up and hugged him tight, as he exhaled and fell into an immediate snooze.

'Morning,' Jack grinned, looking at me in the rear-view mirror. 'He's exhausted, trying to keep up with my two.'

I squeezed the sleeping dog, assessing Jack's very cheery chops. 'You look happy.'

'I am,' he said. 'Scarlett cut her first tooth. I was worried sick about her, she was off her food, grizzling, crying, drooling and then this morning her wee face broke into a huge grin and there it was! A tiny wee white dot in the front of her gum,' he finished, demonstrating with his finger in his own mouth.

'Aw, that's lovely,' I said, the usual feeling of dread dragging through my heart. It felt ridiculous being jealous of a baby, but he was so inveigled with Scarlett...

'So how are you?' he asked.

'Great,' I lied.

Sitting in the back, straining to hear Jack over the noise of the diesel engine, I sat forward. As the four-wheel drive lurched round a corner, I grabbed onto the headrest and swallowed. He eyed me in the mirror. 'You OK?'

I nodded, not trusting myself not to throw up if I opened my mouth. 'Still not quite hundred percent.'

'Yeah, I always feel sick when I sit in the back,' he said, smiling and winding down his window which brought a blast of fresh chilly air into the car. 'This should help, shouldn't it?' he added to Scarlett. Let's hope so, I thought, focussing on the horizon, a technique I knew worked for seasickness.

Three minutes later we pulled up outside Kelso Lodge.

The garden to the front looked idyllic, a sugaring of frost evident in the spots as yet untouched by the low winter sun. Jack hauled on the handbrake as the dogs all began clambering around and pushing to get past me. Opening the back door, the three of them tumbled out and began tearing around on the lawn, sniffing and chasing one another, Frank slap bang in the middle of it, with no clue he was any smaller than his two giant pals. Inhaling the fresh cold air, I watched as Jack opened the doors of the landy, heaved Scarlett out and popped her in a sling which he expertly fixed around his body. A natural. Heading out over the lawn following the dogs, on the route I always took towards the woods and hill beyond, Jack stopped me in my tracks.

'Where are you off to?' He smiled. 'Come on,' he said, nodding in the direction of the house. 'I've got something I want to show you.'

Intrigued, I followed him around to the back of the house, cringing as we passed the door which I had so recently skedaddled out of doing the walk of shame after the wedding debacle. Shaking my head as a flashback of Javier naked appeared in my mind's eye, I marched on, focusing on Jack as he trudged through overgrown weeds and grass, past the bin store, woodshed and on towards the huge stone perimeter wall where a rotting door stood propped up against it. Checking Scarlett was secure, Jack carefully picked it up and moved it to one side, revealing a doorway.

'This way,' he said, leading me through the small drystone arch into an overgrown knot of weeds.

'In here?' I exclaimed. 'I didn't even realise there was a door here. I thought this was the way out of the garden, not the way in ...' I said, tramping in behind him, from cut lawn to knee-deep foliage. Speechless, I tried to take in my surroundings, turning around and around, a jungly mass of overgrown weeds, tangles, nettles, sticky willies, grasses, thistles, and ivy. A lush, lumpy, bracken cushion mingling up and into gnarled, rumpled trees, spider's webs, and espaliered tress clinging on to the undulating, bulging three metre brick wall.

'The walled garden,' he said.

'Wow,' I said, gazing round. 'It's extraordinary. The atmosphere in here is … magical.'

'It's two degrees warmer in here,' he said. 'In the summer, the wall absorbs the heat of the sun and dampens the noise of the outside world …'

I listened. 'It's like the garden of Eden. I had no idea this was here. I thought I'd explored the whole place, but this is literally a secret garden.'

'Yeah this was where they grew the fruit and veg back in the day for the whole estate,' he said, trudging on.

'And what are all these?' I asked, waving my arm in the general direction of the trees.

'Well, this part was the orchard.'

'God, it must have been amazing.'

'Now, let me see,' he said, stomping over and scrutinising them. 'Apples, pears, cherries, they are all here, they have just been completely neglected over the years. Some of them are struggling with all the ivy in here.' He leaned over, wrenching a broad branch of ivy up and off a tree trunk. 'It literally strangles them. And over there.' He pointed to further clumps of weedy mass in one corner. 'That was full of raspberries, gooseberries, plums—' he turned, his eyes twinkling. 'They were all planted a long time ago. Mum was the gardener in our family. She just loved it, spent hours out here when she lived here – when *we* lived here – but the moment we left, Dad just let it go to rack and ruin.'

Sensing a deep sadness, I was relieved the moment was

broken by a sudden yelp. Looking in the direction it had come from, all we could see was Frank leaping up and down unable to keep up with Duke and Gaston, which made us both laugh heartily. I made my way back to where he stood, completely surrounded by broom and shrubbery, which I stamped down to reach him, picking him up and tucking him under my arm so he could look round without straining his back.

'It's so peaceful in here,' I said, with the slumped sausage dog in my arms, as we stood in the middle of the mass, the outside world somehow muted.

'Yeah, I loved this place as a kid,' he said. 'To be honest, I haven't thought about it for years. But I called Hamish when I got home last night, and he came round with some beers.'

'I'm so sorry about ruining your birthday.'

'Oh, don't worry, we can do it another time,' he said. 'So, a few beers down, Hamish started mithering on about wanting to expand his horizons in terms of his gardening and having nowhere to go. And it got me thinking about this place.'

'For Hamish?'

'Potentially yes. I wanted to have a proper think about things and come and remind myself of what it's like before I said anything to him – you know what's he's like.'

I smiled at him. 'Yes, he would be off like a whippet if he got a sniff of it.'

Stopping at one end we looked back and assessed the space.

'It would certainly take a lot of work,' I said.

Jack nodded. 'Yeah, but going forward this place is my responsibility and I need to be as creative as I can with ideas to generate some activity and hopefully money. I also need to have a more regular presence out here, so between Hamish and I, we could work on this together and keep an eye on the place. I need to keep the venison business going and I can't be in two places at the same time.'

'It is a mighty step up from the wee back gardens he's looking after just now ...'

'Yes, that's why I need to talk it over with him. You're right, it is huge, and may well be too big, but there is no harm in discussing it.'

'Absolutely,' I said, imagining my cousin being hysterical when he heard about it. I slipped my arm through his. 'Exciting stuff.'

He grinned at me, those eyes fixing on mine, eliciting an involuntary shiver of animal lust which he mistook for a chill.

'Come on, it's too cold out here. Let's go and have a coffee and I will send Hamish a WhatsApp to see what he thinks,' he said, snuggling Scarlett up closer to him and leading us back through the jungle towards the house.

As we pushed the door open, Jeannie appeared.

'Hello, Jack, and happy birthday!' she grinned. 'I heard you arrive a while ago, your tea will be cold.' And then addressing Scarlett, she exclaimed, 'And look at you! You've got wee pink cheeks like a sugar mouse.' She gently pinched the baby's face, eliciting a happy gurgle.

The warmth enveloped me as we entered the kitchen and Jack unclipped Scarlett's papoose, lifting her out and placing her on the battered couch beside the Aga, propping her up with a cushion so she stayed upright. He really had the knack for that, I thought, as he set himself at the table, took out his phone and texted Hamish.

'You make the coffee, Maddy,' said Jeannie as she popped a small tray of scones into the oven to warm up, before busying herself to get some butter and homemade raspberry jam on the table in preparation.

'God, they smell fantastic,' Jack enthused, Scarlett's wee fat legs straightening and kicking with joy in full agreement.

'She could charm the birds off the trees, that baby,' I giggled and poured the coffee as Jeannie slid the tray out of the oven and popped the scones on the table on front of us.

'I'd like to take credit for that,' she said, 'but it was Claude ...'

'What, the baby?' I joshed.

'No! The scones,' she said, snorting with laughter. 'Claude loves them, and I was teaching him how to make them yesterday.'

'Huh! Busman's holiday round here,' said Jack as Jeannie blushed.

I looked at her. She looked back at me for a nano second and looked away, flustered. Oh my God, I thought, are Claude and Jeannie ...? I recalled seeing them sitting next to each other at the boys' wedding and remembered remarking to Javier about the animated conversation the two of them were having, heads together, Claude slapping the table as he delivered one of his food obsessed monologues, Jeannie sitting quietly smiling, and listening intently. Well, well, well.

I eyeballed her. Jeannie must be at least ten years older than Claude ... but so what? Mmmm, I was going to keep a close eye on the pair of them, to see if I could spot any clues before saying anything. I just love it when people get together, I thought, and then exhaled rather long and loudly as I considered how the only person that wasn't sorted was me. And Javier. My stomach squirbled, giving away my consternation.

'Actually, do you mind if I make myself a hot chocolate?' I said, standing up. 'The smell of that coffee is making me feel a bit...'

Jeannie looked at me with concern. 'No problem, let

me get it,' she said, preparing the milk while chatting all the while, distracting me from any questions about Claude; questions that I filed away for another time.

With my legs tucked under me, snorkelling a gulp of creamy hot chocolate and scoffing my warm buttered scone, I felt worn out. The heat of the Aga having the desired effect, I curled up on the couch with Frank and listened as Jack gave Jeannie an update on his proposed plan for the walled garden, jiggling Scarlett on his knee.

'Ooh, that makes my heart sing,' Jeannie said. 'It's been neglected for years but it was your mum's pride and joy. Mind, it won't be cheap to clear it out, it will be some job...'

'Yeah,' said Jack. 'I wanted to talk to you about that...' He turned to face me as I eased another scone onto my plate greedily.

'Me?'

'Well, according to Hamish everything he grows you use in the restaurant.'

'Yeah,' I said, nodding, wiping the crumbs from my stuffed mouth and swallowing. 'Maybe a slight exaggeration but theoretically let's say yes.'

'OK, well, if he likes the idea of cultivating this place, we could put up a polycrub?'

'A what?'

'A polycrub. Like a weatherproof poly tunnel, made in Shetland to withstand all the weather that gets flung at us.'

'Oh, right, and...?'

'Well, he could grow stuff for you all year, and more of it, so he could supply you – or whoever. As you've seen for yourself, that walled garden is just wasted at the moment, but the bare bones of it are still there, and with a polycrub I reckon we might just have a chance at making it work.'

'You mean like a market garden sort of thing?'

'Exactly,' he said, his eyes sparkling, synapses firing.

'That sounds like a brilliant idea!'

'That's what I thought!' he grinned.

'What about your dad?' I said, nodding in the direction of the cottage he lived in with his harridan wife Tooty.

'He's got no real say in it now. He can like it or lump it.'

I laughed. 'I know which one it will be.'

'Yeah.' He grinned back at me.

Chapter 21

At this point Jeannie asked Jack to help her with some maintenance issue so off they went chattering along the corridor, leaving Scarlett and I sitting on the couch. She was propped up and staring at me in that direct, unblinking way that babies do, like she could read my mind and she was not very impressed. Brushing some of the crumbs from my recent feeding frenzy onto the floor, the dogs hoovered them up as I smiled back at the baby, who continued to stare at me with a screwed-up look on her face. It looked like she was holding her breath because her complexion changed from healthy pink to a considerably darker shade.

I looked at her. 'You OK, sweetie?'

Her gaze intensified as did her colour, verging on purple. Afraid her head was going to rotate, or she was going to combust, I stood up and was just about to call for help when Jeannie and Jack walked back in.

'Oh, thank God!' I said, jumping up and pointing at Scarlett, as Jeannie swiftly scooped her up, sniffing her well-wrapped bottom.

'Yup, she needs to be changed. I'll take care of that for you' she said, marching out.

'Thank God,' I said, hugely relieved, Scarlett happily gooing and giggling as Jeannie took her off to be changed, leaving a malodorous waft in her wake.

'Thanks, Jeannie!' shouted Jack, smiling and placing his

hands on the Aga to warm them up before chuckling conspiratorially. 'That was good timing.'

God, I really didn't have a clue what to do with babies, I thought, watching Jack and thinking how much I fancied even the back of him. Turning, he grinned at me, walked over and sat down next to me. We both started talking at the same time, then laughed, then stopped as he leant towards me and—

BANG! The door flew open, nearly ripping off its hinges.

'Jack, man!' shouted Hamish, marching straight over and taking his hand, shaking it vigorously. 'I fucking love you!'

Jack stood up, embracing my ecstatic cousin.

'So, you like the idea?' he joked, rolling his eyes at me over Hamish's shoulder.

'I swear it's the most exciting thing that's ever happened to me. Ever! I'm so happy.' He stopped in his tracks, dropping Jack, and stepping back. 'I know it's not a done deal, like you said, but Jack, man, I am so up for this ... and,' he stopped dead in his tracks, 'I told Mouse ... I hope you don't mind?'

Jack laughed. 'No, no, of course not, and?'

'She's more excited than I am! We need to go out and celebrate! We've got a lot to celebrate now: the garden, your birthday and Mouse's exhibition!'

'You're right,' said Jack. 'When?'

'Tonight...'

They both looked at me.

'Why not?' I said.

'Yes, why the hell not?' Jack grinned, then hesitated. 'I'll need to find a ...'

'I'll babysit,' I said.

'No! You come, too!' said Jack. 'I can try to find someone else to babysit.'

'You only get one night off a week, Maddy. Come on!' said Hamish, egging me on.

'Honest, guys, I am absolutely worn out after last night, I'm not firing on all cylinders. All I need is a sofa and the telly.'

They looked at me, looked at each other and then back at me.

'OK, well, if you're sure? Thanks, Maddy, that would great,' said Jack, looking at me, then back to Hamish. 'Right, where are we going?'

'Aw, Maddy, you are a doll,' said Hamish. 'Mouse and I will meet you in the Hoozier then?'

'Seven OK?' Jack asked me.

'Perfect,' I said as Jeannie came back in with a clean, smiling Scarlett.

'Can we go and have a look at the garden now?' said Hamish to Jack, eyes sparkling.

'Erm, I don't want to desert Maddy,' said Jack, taking Scarlett from Jeannie and strapping her back into the sling.

'Don't be daft,' I said. 'On you go. I have loads to do, and I'll see you later. What time do you want me?'

'Quarter to seven?'

'No problem,' I said as Hamish hopped from one foot to the other, desperate to see the garden.

'I can give you a lift into the town just now, Maddy. I'm meeting someone for coffee,' Jeannie said, blushing.

'Thanks,' I said.

'Oh, OK, if you're sure?' said Jack, looking at me.

'I'm positive,' I said and with that they were off out the door, chatting excitedly as they clomped along the corridor to inspect Hamish's potential new empire.

Chapter 22

As I suspected by her schoolgirl blush, it was Claude Jeannie was meeting for coffee. Between shifts, Claude stayed in the restaurant, preparing his menu for the evening, and seldom left the premises, but clearly, he was making an exception for Jeannie. When he did leave it was to his digs, at Kelso Lodge. So, it was all very cosy. Sitting in the passenger seat mulling this over as Jeannie drove, I cut to the chase.

'So, are you and Claude …?' I ventured.

'Oh no, no, no, no, no,' she said, grinding the gears.

'I wasn't sure about him when I first met him. I thought he was a bit bossy and formal but now I realise he is a bit of a softie underneath it all,' I said, just leaving it hanging.

'Yes,' she mooned.

I was right! There was something going on. Jeannie changed the subject deftly.

'So, you know the walled garden has quite a history,' she said.

'Yes, Jack said his mum loved it and spent a lot of her time working in it.'

'No, I mean well before her time. Going back … gosh, to the Second World War.'

'Really?'

'Yes, I can't remember the exact detail of it all. It's the sort of thing Jack might remember or if not him, his grand-mother.'

'Flora? Do you think she would remember?'

'Well, it might be worth a try, and if not, well, the one thing about this town is that the university has every piece of history of the area tied up and written down so I am sure you could find out more if you were so minded.'

It was at this point I spotted Claude standing outside the Birdie, eyes peeled, clearly looking for Jeannie's car. Clocking it, he waved and smiled and then, seeing me in the passenger seat, got flustered, jamming his hand in his pocket. Jeannie drove right past.

'Are you not stopping?'

'I will drop you off first,' she said, slowing down and stopping right outside Noel's shop. Before I got out, she turned to me, looking rather het up.

'Och, don't say anything to him, will you, Maddy? He's a really private man.'

'Don't worry, I won't say a word,' I said as she wheeched out a lipstick and applied it quickly, before saying a hasty goodbye to me and walking back to meet her beau.

Chapter 23

My inaugural journey in the custard beast was out to Jack's. It took rather longer than I thought because weirdly the gear stick stuck out directly from the engine, so it took a bit of getting used to. I smiled at the irony of me cringing at Jeannie's gear grinding earlier; compared to me she was Lewis Hamilton, I thought, as I wrenched on the handbrake and it coughed to a stop.

I was late and I knew Jack would be raring to go. The front door flew open as I approached.

'Sorry I'm late.'

'What is that?' he said, pointing at the custard beast.

'That's my new car.' He laughed. 'What?' I asked defensively.

'Nothing,' he said, tamping down his cheesy grin.

'Hamish got it for me.'

He smirked and, looking at my face of indignance, chose to leave well alone. Sensible move. 'Come in, come in. Listen, thanks so much for this; honestly I can't remember the last time I had two nights out in a row,' he enthused and then stopped. 'I wish you were coming, too. You know I would have tried to find someone else to look after the baby?'

'I know. I know. Honestly, I am more than happy to help out. I'm knackered, and God knows you deserve a night out after last night's carry on.'

We stared at each other for no more than a second when

that insistent visceral connection flared between us. Time stopped. Dry-mouthed. Fat-tongued.

'When you're feeling better, we can celebrate.'

'Yes.' I smiled. 'You better watch your time!' I said, dragging my eyes away from him and looking at the clock.

'Yeah, right,' he said, snapping out of it and launching into a list of dos and don'ts, the practicalities of looking after the baby. Gulp. The best news was she was already asleep. He'd put her down about twenty minutes beforehand and, 'that's usually her until about one in the morning,' he said. He then laid out instructions as to what I was to do if Scarlett woke up, where to find made-up bottles, and how to heat them. 'She shouldn't need her nappy changed because it's just been done,' he said. More excellent news – faced with a full nappy the way I was feeling it could frankly push me over the edge. Sensing my apprehension, he stopped and looked at me.

'Are you sure you are OK with this?'

'Yes, yes, I'm just concentrating,' I lied, thinking how surreal it was to be having such an exchange.

'OK, good. I think that's everything. My phone's on and don't hesitate for a second to call if you need any help,' he said, patting his jacket down, taking out a set of keys from the pocket and looking anxiously around.

'We'll be fine,' I said as he grabbed his mobile phone off the table and prepared to leave. We endured a typically awkward hug and peck on the cheek before he was off in a flurry.

'Oh,' he said, swinging his head back round the door. 'The dogs are in the kitchen. I let them through to lie by the fire in the evening, after Scarlett's in bed.'

'OK. Frank will love that,' I said.

'Right, I'm really off this time. I'm taking the car and will get a taxi back,' he said. 'No later than ten?'

'Ten!'

'Yes, she wakes up at one so I'll get a few hours before that.' He grinned.

'Och, anytime is fine with me,' I said, secretly relieved he'd be back sooner than one.

'Are you absolutely sure about this? It feels … weird,' he checked for a final time.

'Of course! Now bugger off,' I said, cheerily half-pushing him out the door and closing it behind him.

Watching out the window as his brake lights chuntered down the drive, I exhaled and looked around. First things first, I tiptoed upstairs to see Scarlett, her wee pudgy body tucked lightly under a cover, her shiny hair catching the lowest light, and the round of her chubby cheek visible. She was perfect. Satisfied that she was sound asleep, safe and warm I went back downstairs.

Spending an evening in Jack's cottage without him was weird. I had been here a few times but never on my own. The memory of the first time still made me heat up like a spitting skillet. The most romantic night of my life, the night Jack and I finally got together, after what felt like an endless build up. The sexual tension at breaking point, the night I drank my bodyweight in champagne and behaved like Phyllis Dixey the stripper, believing at long last everything had fallen into place. And boy, had I let my guard down, inhibitions out the window, and then, nausea rose at the memory, the awful humiliation of the following morning, when Jody had bowled in with Scarlett turning our lives upside down.

The mere thought of it had me raiding the fridge. Disappointingly empty, apart from SMA milk cartons, olives, butter, a banana and some Tennent's lager, Hamish's chosen poison. How things had slipped in Jack's world.

Our love of food was something we'd shared from day one; his speciality had been producing tasty morsels in the most unlikely places. His scope of delicious food ran the gamut from venison carpaccio to home-smoked salmon, Scotch eggs made with game wrapped around an organic duck egg and homemade chocolate and shortbread that melted in the mouth – and these were just snacks in between meals! These sad droopy fridge contents smacked of someone who was seriously struggling.

Every surface was covered in stuff.

Highchair, playmat, playpen, endless toys, wooden and plastic rattles, wipes, nappies, creams, potions, and lotions. It was completely overwhelming. Poor guy, I thought, wondering how I could help, really help, when my ears were assaulted with a screech.

'Shit, she's awake,' I said out loud to Frank who shut his eyes and continued snoozing between the deerhounds in front of the fire. I took a deep breath, grabbed my list of instructions and tramped upstairs to see the wee pudding.

If the baby wakes up soon, she could be cold or have wind.

Hoping it was the former as winding a baby was not in my skillset I tiptoed in and sneaked a look.

The blankets she had so recently been snuggled under were all ruggled up at the bottom of the cot, so pulling them up gently, I tucked her in, rubbing her back, placing her dummy in her mouth, which she began to suck on, and before she even opened her eyes, thank God, she was snoozing again. Phew, I thought, slipping out and down the stairs where I sat, quiet as a mouse on the couch, staring at the fire.

What the hell was Jody thinking? Was she just having a sabbatical from the responsibility of motherhood? Would she come back and reclaim the baby? How would Jack react if she did? And if Jack wasn't the baby's real father, then who the hell was?

There was no doubt in my mind, despite the fact I knew it would cause an argument, I had to encourage Jack to do a paternity test.

With this set in my mind, I flicked on the TV, kept the volume low in case it woke the baby and was joined on the couch by Frank, then Duke and finally Gaston. It was so cosy being folded into a pile of dogs I soon dozed off.

Chapter 24

I was awoken by Jack opening the front door to find me snuggled on the couch with the dogs, as they all stretched and sleepily made their way over to greet him. Turncoats.

'I must have just dropped off,' I said with no idea what on earth the time was.

'It's only just after ten.'

'Ten! You're early.'

'I drove,' he said.

'You drove?' I couldn't hide my surprise.

'Yeah, I had to keep it together in case Scarlett wakes up. It's a helluva responsibility,' he said, suddenly looking drained, which made me want to give him a hug.

'She usually wakes about now for a bottle and I ...' he hesitated.

'Thought I might drop her,' I joked.

He smiled. 'Well, I don't know how many times you've said you know nothing about babies and that you're better with dogs ... and restaurants apparently.'

I grinned at him. 'No one is more surprised than me about that.'

'Fancy a dram?' he said, taking his jacket off, picking up a bottle of Bells and a couple of glasses.

'I'm driving,' I reminded him.

'Och, of course,' he said. 'The death trap.'

'Oi!' I said.

'Just pulling your leg,' he grinned. 'Well, I need a large one after three hours of Hamish, he is on one. What a night!' He chuckled, taking a seat in the battered old leather winged armchair opposite the couch. I sat back down, which meant I was level with his chest, peering up at him, and on the back foot.

'So, tell me what happened?'

'Light blue touch paper and retire. Hamish, as predicted, is cock-a-hoop and didn't shut up all night. He has hundreds of ideas, some of which are brilliant and some of which are ridiculous.'

I grinned. 'It's so great he has found his thing... really, he's such a bright guy but up till now has never stuck at anything.'

'That's my only worry,' said Jack in a more serious tone. 'That he starts this whole thing and then loses focus and buggers off.'

'Well, for what it's worth I have never seen him like this. Day and night he's out in that garden at the back of the Birdie, he just loves it.'

'Yeah,' agreed Jack.

'And let's not forget about Mouse.'

'How could I?'

'Those two are just two halves of a whole ... They are mad about each other.'

We shared one of those stomach-flipping looks.

'You're right. By the time I left them they were talking about moving lock, stock, and barrel out to Kelso Lodge.'

'Both of them?'

'Yeah, well, it was me that suggested it, to be honest. Hamish was going on and on about working 24/7 on the new garden and asked if I minded if he pitched a tent in it so he could immerse himself in the whole thing...'

I laughed. That was such a Hamish thing to say.

'And what about Mouse?'

'Well, of course we were celebrating this exhibition of hers, too, and I could see there was something bugging her. She's been fretting – she needs space to paint, she has no room left in her place.'

'It's a bedsit for one, how Hamish can get in there at all is a mystery,' I laughed.

'Well, by then I was completely caught up in the moment,' he said, 'so I said there's plenty room for her, too.'

I released a hearty guffaw. 'Sounds like you were the over-excited one.'

'Yeah.' He took a sip of his whisky. 'They might wake up in the morning and think it was a bad idea ... but to be honest, having people living in Kelso Lodge is very appealing. Even if they can only afford a minimal rent, it's better than nothing. There's ten rooms in the place and with just Claude and Javier renting rooms it is costing a small fortune to run.' He raked his hair back again, that look of worry writ large.

'What is it?' I prompted.

'It looks like I am going to have to let Jeannie go.'

'Oh no,' I said.

'Yeah, I know,' he said. 'I just can't work out how to keep her on. It was Philip Stefan – the guy who leased the house from Dad to run it as a B&B – who kept her on, and now he's out of the picture. Javier and Claude look after themselves, and the truth is we don't really need her.'

'She will be gutted.'

'I know,' he said. 'I am dreading it.'

We sat in silence of a moment.

'Yeah and then there's my father and Tooty. They are still

in Gardener's Cottage which they are now entitled to stay in.'

I nodded and managed to remain silent. It really was none of my business and the last time I had waded in and given my honest opinion on his dad it had gone down very badly indeed. He looked at me expectantly so, clenching my buttocks, I launched in.

'Do they pay rent?'

'No. Dad had a deal with Stefan, free rent for him and Tooty if he did some odd jobs round the place and the idea is the retiring Laird contributes in any way they can.'

A snort emanated from my nose. 'Sorry,' I said.

'No, no, you're right. I'm not sure he has ever done an honest day's work in his life. So, they are an additional drain on the estate.'

'He must be good at something?' I said, trying to see the positive.

'Well, if he is it's eluded me so far,' said Jack, staring into the fire and looking rather deflated for a moment before changing tack.

'So, Madeline, your ears must have been burning tonight?'

'Me! Oh my God. Why?'

'Well, I wasn't going to say anything tonight but ...'

'What? Well, you have to now!' I said, scooting out of the slumped couch and perching on the edge so I could see him eye to eye.

'OK, now I don't want you to feel pressurised in any way, or think that I have been plotting this behind your back ...'

'Jack!' I said. 'Spit it out.'

'OK,' he said, putting his glass down. 'It was just with Hamish having his brainstorm and all these ideas flying around ... I hope you don't mind but it just slipped out that you were thinking about opening another restaurant.'

'Oh.' I sat back. 'No, I don't mind but thanks for warning me, as I know Hamish finds it impossible to keep his mouth shut so it will spur me on to speak to Claude and Javier tomorrow. I need to do that anyway.'

'Sorry,' he said.

'No, honestly, it's fine,' I said.

'Well, the pair of them were very excited about your news and then, it was Hamish to be honest, said why don't you open the Birdie Two, out at Kelso Lodge?'

'Kelso Lodge? How?'

'Well, it's hard to see through the stour in there at the moment but in that tangled mass of weeds, believe it or not, on the perimeter wall of the walled garden, there's an old bakehouse.'

'Really?'

'Yes, it has a real history, but along with everything else it's been lost in the mists of time. I have no doubt it is in a complete state but if it's something you think might be of interest, we could have a look and see if it was fixable ... if you were interested, I mean.' He looked at me, uncertainty in his eyes.

'Well, I ...' My heart clattered hard in my chest.

'Of course, it's totally up to you. I know we all got very over-excited tonight,' he said. 'I wish you'd been there but—'

'I love it!' I said, interrupting him. 'Oh my God,' I went on, my head whirling.

I looked at him. He looked at me.

I jumped to my feet. 'What a fecking fantastic idea! I mean, I love it!'

'You do?' said Jack.

'I do!' I beamed.

'Maddy!' He launched onto his feet, picking me up and whirling me round. 'That is fantastic!'

'Put me down,' I squealed, not meaning it.

Frank, the overprotective sausage, released a staccato yap, unused to sharing me with anyone and launched himself off the couch, jumping up and punching Jack's legs with his fat paws. Duke and Gaston, picking up on his cue, joined in with a series of deep bassy woofs.

We laughed heartily as Jack put me down and it felt like the most natural thing in the world. We leant into one another.

'Waaaaahhhhhhhhhhhhhhhhhhh!' The most blood-curdling scream ricocheted down the stairs and out of the baby monitor at the same time. Without missing a beat, Jack dropped me and was on his feet, galloping up the stairs. I watched him go.

'Fuck,' I said to no one, sitting back down, my shoulders slumped, as the baby continued to screech, inconsolable, despite Jack's soothing tones. Frank looked at me, as terrified as I was. It sounded very serious, I thought, out of my comfort zone. I put my jacket on and resumed pacing. A few minutes later Jack came padding down with the wee snuffling baby, all hot and fretful.

'I've got Calpol in there,' he said, gesturing to the kitchen.

'Calpol?'

'Small bottle, in the fridge, pink and white label. It's for babies when they're not well.'

'OK,' I said, rushing through and retrieving it for him.

'Spoon,' he said and I disappeared back into the kitchen and grabbed the first spoon I could find.

'There's a small plastic spoon,' he said, putting the wooden spoon down on the coffee table.

Dashing back in, feeling very foolish, I found the white plastic spoon, took it through and handed it to him. Opening the bottle, balancing the clinging baby to him, he deftly poured some onto the spoon.

'I think it's the teething thing. Sarah told me it can be agony for them, and of course they can't tell you. Her first tooth appeared last night, so maybe she's on a roll,' he said, propping Scarlett up and gently sliding the spoon into her mouth.

'Aw, the wee soul,' I said, smiling at her, as she turned her wet face away from me and stuffed it into Jack's chest. 'Listen, it' s late, I'm going to head off. I have a lot to think about.'

'OK,' he said, stroking the baby's back, glancing at me briefly.

'OK,' I said, scooping Frank up, who stuffed his head under my oxter, unsure about what was going on.

'Thanks for tonight, Maddy. I'm so happy you like our idea. Why don't you sleep on it and we can talk about it more tomorrow?'

'Yeah, good plan,' I said.

'Maddy,' he whispered over the head of the wee baby. 'Sorry.' He gave me an apologetic smile.

'It's OK. I hope the wee soul's OK. Night,' I whispered back and let myself out.

Chapter 25

Sleep on it? Well, that was a bloody joke.

I drove the Custard Beast back into town, with the radio blaring, singing my heart out.

The idea of the Birdie and Bramble in the walled garden kept me awake late into the night.

I just loved the whole idea.

All my misgivings about opening something too close or similar to the original restaurant were taken care of.

It was far enough away from the original restaurant not to rain on Claude's parade; his ego was something that was very easily bruised, and I knew I would have to handle that very carefully, especially now that Jack had let it slip to Hamish that expansion was on the cards. Hamish, the unofficial town crier.

But, in essence, a rural restaurant in a walled garden was a dream. At this stage it was hard to imagine exactly how it would look, but if the walled garden was anything to go by the potential was more than exciting.

As the hours passed, I gave up even trying to sleep, light on, sketch pad on my knees, writing lists of things I would need to do. By dawn I had decided a less formal business appeal. The whole garden thing would lend itself to being more of a daytime operation. I would make it dog-friendly and child-friendly, too, I thought, as Scarlett was top priority these days. I would need to think about numbers of covers, type of menu, hell, what sort of permission we would need to open, and a name! We would need a name. The branding. The social media. William! I would have to tell William what had happened. I dug out my phone and WhatsApped him.

'I have news.'

Eight in the morning as Northpoint opened, we were waiting to get in and within seconds, sitting opposite each other. When I told him, William's eyes bulged.

'Oh my God.'

'Good OMG or bad OMG?'

'Good OMG ... teetering on great.' He grinned.

'Brilliant!' I said. 'I knew you'd love it. The only thing is, this is happening a hell of a lot faster than we thought.'

'It certainly is,' he said, 'and I know I have to tell Noel, but I feel great and everything at the Birdie feels so ...' he searched for the right word, '... settled. We have a great team with Claude and Javier. Honestly, sometimes I feel like the spare wheel.'

'Me, too!' I said. 'And this is the opportunity of a life-time ...'

'Yes,' he enthused. 'So, tell me more.'

And I did, well, as much as I knew. There were so many unanswered questions, so I texted Jack to ask if William and I could meet him out at Kelso Lodge.

A text pinged back from Jack. I broke off mid-sentence and read it.

'He's good to meet us out there at three.' I grinned at Will. He looked at me.

'What?'

'When you talk about him your eyes change.'

'How?' I said.

'I dunno, they sort of go all ... big and watery.'

'You make me sound like a spaniel,' I laughed.

'So, I take it things are going well on that score?'

'Yes,' I said, not sounding too sure.

'That would be my only misgiving if I'm absolutely honest ... you and Jack mixing work and play and all that. What if you fall out?'

'Yeah, I know, I did think about that.'

'And?'

'Well, we seem to have been thwarted at every turn since Scarlett arrived,' I moaned. 'It's bloody hard work having a baby.'

He laughed. 'Yeah.'

'Timing is all, and there is always something, and if that something is a gorgeous wee pudding like Scarlett, then second fiddle is where I am likely to stay for the foreseeable future and that is not a good feeling,' I said.

'No, quite.'

'So, I have been thinking that it may be a sign that we are meant to be together as business partners and not as lovers.'

'Gosh,' said William, tilting his head slightly. 'Do you really think that or are you just saying it?'

I looked at him. 'Just saying it.'

'Thought so.'

'OK, I can see your point but really, the way things are at the moment we would have to fall in before we fell out ... there are lots of things to do before we get to that stage.'

'Yeah, like Noel,' said William, looking very serious for a second. 'I'm going to strike whilst the iron's hot, tell him now.'

'OK, and I will have a word with Claude today, too,' I added as William put his scarf on and prepared to leave, giving me a look of dread as he waved goodbye. 'Good luck!'

Chapter 26

Fifteen seconds after the door closed it opened again, and in came Mouse.

Sunglasses, a long black coat and a shuffle that suggested a hideous hangover. I grinned at her as she baulked when the chair she pulled out to sit on scraped along the ground.

'Don't smile, your teeth are too bright. I can't handle it,' she said, reaching out for my half-drunk coffee with her fingerless-gloved hands.

'Good night?'

'Yes, I think so.'

'How did you know I was here?'

'Hamish said he saw you and Will waiting outside to get in earlier.'

'Of course. The oracle. So, it sounded like you all went berserk last night; Jack filled me in when he got back. Hamish and you moving out to Kelso Lodge?'

She groaned. 'Yeah, I know ... we were on a roll, and all talking at the same time. It was mad.'

'So? Are you going to?'

'Well, I need studio space, that's for sure, but moving in with Hamish ... well, we talked about it vaguely. I just didn't think it would happen quite so fast.'

'And?'

'And ... well, what the hell?'

I laughed. 'Great. You two are like two peas in a pod. I, for one, am delighted.'

'I will be too if I survive,' she said, waving her arm at the waiter who came over and took her order for a hot chocolate and a cheese toastie.

'And did Jack talk to you about it?'

'If you mean the Birdie, then yes! And the good thing was he was sober.'

She groaned again. 'I know, it makes it worse.'

'What?'

'Our drunken rambling, and carrying on,' she said. 'I can't remember getting home.'

'Oh, it didn't bother him, he was on a complete high when he came back and told me about you and Hamish and then asked me what I thought about opening the Birdie out there.'

'Well?'

'Well, I love the idea.'

She slid her sunglasses down and looked at me over the top of them. 'Really?'

'Yes!'

'That's fabulous news,' she said, sliding them back up again. 'Sorry I can't hug you; I might be sick.'

I snorted. 'Yeah, in fact I just told William, who loves it too, and we are both going out to see it this afternoon to have a proper look around. And what about you? You were going to send me over the contract you signed with Adrian De Witt when he emailed it over to you.'

'Yes.' She looked anxious.

'I haven't got it, did you send it?'

'Erm no.' She reddened. 'You'll go mad.'

'Why?'

'He hasn't sent it to me yet.'

She took her phone out, scrolled, and passed it over to me.

Dear Dorcas

Enjoyed showing you around Edinburgh. Things are progressing, the date agreed upon regarding the launch is 12th of August. It is the mid-week of the Festival.

Venue: The Space, Albert Street, Edinburgh. Why not come down next week to see it, measure up and we can take it from there?

Don't have a scanner in the office so can't send copy of contract, send me your address and I will send it by post, or I can give you it next week?

Yours,

ADW.

'Oh well,' I said, handing her phone back, not wanting to make her feel any worse than she already did. 'Certainly sounds like he is making progress. So, are you going back down then?'

'Yes,' she said. 'I need to see the space and plan the exhibition, measure up, decide what I'm going to do.'

'Bloody hell, it's really happening! And that is great news about your potential new studio space at Jack's!'

'I know.' She visibly perked up. 'I am going out to see that later today, too.'

'Do you want a lift?'

'Yeah, that would be great. Hamish was up at the crack on his way out there this morning, doing his dad's deliveries then going straight back out to the walled garden. He is a man possessed.'

'Never thought I'd see the day. Will's meeting me at the

bothy at quarter to three. If that suits, come along then and we can all go out together.'

'Great,' she grinned. I looked at her. I heard a rattle and, looking closer, I noticed two small lip rings were back in place. Duly noted.

Chapter 27

Arriving at the Birdie, Javier had the place looking sharp, set and ready with an hour to spare.

'Claude in?' I asked.

'Yes,' he said as I thanked him and marched into the kitchen.

'Hi Claude, you got a sec?'

'Morning, yes, of course,' he said. Following me through to the restaurant, he asked Javier to go into the kitchen and keep an eye on his stock, which left us alone. Perfect.

Claude placed a bowl in front of me, and one in front of himself before placing a soup spoon neatly to the side. 'Soup du jour,' he announced, 'cream of celeriac and star anise.' Thanking him I took up my spoon, and reverentially began sipping the delicious soup. Claude was the slowest eater I had ever met so I was finished and collecting my thoughts as he spooned his soup, intent in the way it looked and tasted with every sip, ever the perfectionist.

'Delicious,' I said.

He nodded.

'So, I said I was hoping to talk to you about something.'

His eyebrows rose but he kept hold of his spoon, raisin-black eyes focused on mine.

'As you know things are going incredibly well at the Birdie.'

He nodded.

'And you and Javier are running a tight ship, the part-timers are doing well, with William being back and, well, me being here, too ... I have been thinking now might be a good time to grow the business.'

Give him his due, he didn't flinch, just watched me carefully.

'I see,' he said, placing his soup spoon down, and lifting his napkin to dab the side of his mouth.

'So, an opportunity has arisen to explore that possibility.'

His eyes gave the game away, as they darted from his soup to meet mine.

'Oh?'

'Yes. At Kelso Lodge, not in the house itself but in the walled garden behind the house. Apparently there used to be a bakehouse there which Wiliam and I are going to go have a look at.'

'Ah yes, the bakehouse.'

'Oh, you know about it?' I said, surprised to say the least.

He reddened. 'Oui, Jeannie mentioned it.'

Jeannie! Of course, I had forgotten, she must have told him about Hamish's plans.

'So did she tell you about the market garden?'

'No, but Hamish did. He was delivering early this morning, such excitement,' he smiled.

'So, I just wanted to keep you in the loop. Nothing is set yet, but the plan would mean the Birdie as it is would be run by you and Javier, the A-team as it were,' I said, which I could tell went down well. He seemed to grow a little taller, and a smile played round his lips. 'With you two officially running things here there is no need for William and me to be here all the time as well. Too many cooks and all that.'

He nodded. 'We can run this place standing on our feet,' he said.

'Head,' I corrected.

He shook his head. 'Of course. Head,' he said.

'So, you are supportive?'

'Why yes, of course. To expand is to live, to stand still is to die,' he said, rather dramatically.

Well, he could say it any way he liked, the main thing was he was on our side, which was going to make my life a whole lot easier.

'Thanks, Claude,' I said and held out my hand to him, which he took and shook gravely.

'Keep posting me.'

'Keep me posted?' I clarified.

'Yes,' he said.

'Good.' I smiled as he stood and made his way back into the kitchen to attend to his stock.

I asked Claude to get Javier up to speed, too, saying I didn't have time as I had to go meet Will. It was true but to be frank I still felt desperately uncomfortable being alone with Javier, despite him being so mature about the après wedding fiasco. I knew my mortification would die down in time, just not yet.

Chapter 28

'Dear God, I am not getting into that,' said William when I unlocked the passenger door of the Custard Beast.

'Why?'

'It's a death trap, that's why.'

'It's not. It just needs a lick of paint and—'

'A hoover,' said Mouse, peering in the back window.

'Och, well, please yourselves,' I said, rather put out, opening the driver's door. As neither of them had a driving license they both relented, William taking off his jacket and putting it on the passenger seat before reluctantly climbing in as Mouse clambered into the back with Frank. Thankfully it started first time and apart from taking a corner at slightly over fifteen miles per hour, which caused everyone in the car to slide over to one side with the distinct feeling that the wheels on one side left the road, we arrived, safe and sound, at Kelso Lodge. William's hand stayed on the door handle the whole way, and the second we ground to a halt he released his seatbelt and was out.

'See? It wasn't that bad, was it?' I said, grinning at him.

'If you say so,' he said, sliding his jacket off the seat, shaking it vigorously and slipping it back on.

'I think it's cool,' said Mouse as she helped Frank down.

'Thank you,' I said, smiling at her.

Jack's Landy was already there, as was Uncle Fraser's van, which meant Hamish, too.

'Come on this way,' I said to William and Mouse, leading them round to the rear of the house. Someone had already cut back the foliage and branches that previously concealed the door into the walled garden.

'In here,' I said as the three of us filed through. 'Hellooo!' I shouted into the undergrowth.

'Maddy! Hey, we're over here,' my cousin's happy voice hollered.

'Nope, can't see you,' I said. 'William's here, too.'

'Hi Will,' shouted Hamish.

'And me!' said Mouse.

'Mouse!' he said gleefully.

'Is Jack here?' I asked.

'Yes,' said a voice right behind us. Turning, we saw him clomping into the garden with Scarlett secure round his chest in a papoose. She grinned at me, last night's upset and bawling long forgotten. Seeing her like that, her legs dangling down, I could see she was growing like a bean, charming everyone who met her, with her extraordinary eyelashes and alabaster skin. It was no wonder no one questioned her parentage, she looked so like Jack, but, as Sarah pointed out more than once, her mother was a dark-haired elfin beauty, so it was fifty-fifty in my book whether she was a MacPherson or not.

It was over three months since Jack had been left literally holding the baby, which the burning hole in my heart reminded me every time I saw them together. If Jack ever looked at me like that, I would die happy.

William was pulling silly faces and tickling her toes. Another fan.

I poked him in the ribs, reminding him there were other people present, too.

'Oh Jack, hi. Sorry, I didn't mean to ignore you,' he said, 'but she is so sweet…'

'Yes, she is,' Jack grinned, looking down at her shiny hair. 'William, it's good to see you.'

As the two men shook hands, Hamish emerged like Stig of the Dump from deep within the undergrowth.

'Maddy,' he said, stepping forward and giving me a very leafy hug.

'Hamish!' I said. 'I've just come from work, get off!'

Laughing, he released me as I brushed leaves and spots of mud off me, waving at Will and wrapping his gangly arm round Mouse.

'Well, cuz, what do you think?' His eyes ablaze, he surveyed the jungle beyond.

'I think it's brilliant!' I grinned back at him.

'Yeah!' he said. 'Me, too. And what about you, William?'

'I think it sounds like a wonderful opportunity and I'm looking forward to hearing more about it,' he said, in a far more restrained manner.

'OK,' said Jack. 'Let's have a tour.'

'Come on then,' said Hamish, loping back.

It was clear Hamish had already made good headway. He had clipped and cutback a ton of foliage, revealing in places an old stone path through the undergrowth which allowed us to wend our way carefully through the garden.

'This is the west wall,' Jack said, pointing. 'As you can see, this door,' he said, whapping the old wooden door with his hand, 'is directly opposite to the one we came in through and in theory this would be the proposed way in.' He grabbed the handle, pulling it hard. It didn't budge.

'Let's have a look,' said Hamish, moving Jack to the side and grabbing the handle with both hands. But as he strained and grunted, the door remained stuck fast.

'Och, don't worry, Hamish, we can sort it out later,' said Jack, just as the handle pinged off, launching Hamish backwards onto his backside as the rest of us roared with laughter.

'Right, see what you mean,' he said, standing up and brushing off his trousers. 'Bit stiff, that.'

'Anyway,' said Jack. 'I can show you it from the other side, but I think that's a possible parking area that keeps the house private – we want to try to keep it separate if we can. Now if we head this way,' he continued, turning off down the path to the left, 'this leads to the south-facing wall.' He pulled a great knot of sticky twisty ivy and yanked it with his hand to clear our path. 'You can't see properly yet, but if you look over there you might be able to make out a bit of the old tiled roof.' Poking our heads into the eye-high grass and squinting, just visible was the peaked tip of something that looked like mossy tiles.

'Oooh, I think I can see it,' I said.

'Let me through,' said Hamish, pushing past with his great big clippers to hand, and scant regard for his own safety, his progress accompanied by swearing and yowls as he snagged various parts of his body on vicious branches that he cut down.

'OK, coast's clear, come on through.' Forging on, the four of us bent almost double, Jack with his arm protectively round Scarlett, we moved together until, a few feet further on, the tangled mass cleared, and we could stand straight again.

'Oh my God, it's like a Hobbit house!' I exclaimed as an ancient looking stone house revealed itself.

'My God, it's beautiful,' marvelled William.

We saw a quaint, nearly round structure made of thick stones, a window on each side of the round doorway, and almost all of it covered in shells. William could not hide his surprise.

'What an extraordinary structure,' he said.

'Yes, my mother was mad about the garden and this was where she spent most of her time. When it rained, we would shelter in there, but it is very basic inside.'

'Running water?' asked William.

'Not that I can remember,' said Jack. 'But then it was years ago.'

'It would be great to get in, how big is it?' I said, peering in through one of the windows.

'God knows, have a look,' he said as he turned the handle and pulled but the door was stuck fast.

'Stand aside,' said Hamish, going through the same unsuccessful routine as last time.

Mouse stepped forward. 'Allow me,' she said, Hamish smiling at her in a condescending way.

Reaching forward she took the handle and pushed. The door opened slightly.

A gale of laughter. 'See?' she smiled.

'Ha!' shouted Hamish as he put his shoulder up against it and pushed hard, managing to force it open nearly wide enough for us to squeeze through. One last shove caused it to fall off its hinges and hit the floor with a WHUMP, releasing a puff of dust and spores. Pissed off pigeons eyed us suspiciously, and there was an obvious hole in the roof, just big enough to let in daylight, birds and rain. Tentatively, we filed in. The windows and walls were covered in ivy, which tangled in and out of the building. Hamish, clippers at the ready, began to snip. Leaving him to it, mindful of the baby, Jack emerged back into the garden followed by Will. Hamish and Mouse followed on, eyes wide as they got accustomed to the light again.

'What a place,' said Hamish.

'Yeah,' agreed Mouse.

'What do you think, Will?' I asked.

'Well, it's an extraordinary place, but rather small.'

'Ah well, that's why you really need to see the plans, but what we have here is just the ante room, aka Hobbit house. The main structure is actually on the other side of the garden wall. There is a small door in here that leads through to the bakehouse. This part was really just a private access for the family.'

'Oh, that makes sense,' I said, craning my head back inside and clocking the other door. 'So how big is it?'

'Well, this part I estimate is around two metres across, but the main bakehouse, looking at the plans, I'd say ten metres by five.'

'Gosh,' I said, my fantasy of a small bijou brasserie dispersing as the scale of the project hit home.

'Unfortunately, it is so overgrown on the other side that we can't get to it yet, and this door is jammed shut so we can't get through that way either... but I can show you the plans and as soon as Hamish and I cut everything back, we can regroup and have a proper look.'

William and I must have looked unsure.

'OK, well, you two need to have a good think about it but remember there's no pressure. It's just an idea at this stage,' said Jack. 'But whilst you're out here, Will, I might as well show you around the garden so you can get a real feel for the whole set up.'

Will was rapt at the myriad of trees and plants, many still clinging to the wall helped by ancient small metal clips. Fruit lay unpicked and rotting on the ground, while some remnants were shrivelled and hanging from branches as the green shoots pushed through.

'Some of these still look remarkably healthy,' said William, as Hamish followed on, examining them closely.

'White fly on this one,' he said, squishing a bug between his fingers. 'Black bug.'

I looked at him. 'Will the trees die?'

'Not these two, these are treatable,' he said, 'but trees, like humans, have a life span, and some of these are in their dotage. I will need some help with this though, I'm no expert.'

'Hmm,' said Will, off on a flight of fancy. 'Just imagine using all of this produce in the kitchen.' I could tell he was very taken with the place.

'Yeah, cider,' said Hamish, licking his lips.

'Apple pies, plum pudding, apricot crumbles,' Mouse added.

'Chutneys, compotes and jams,' added William.

Smiling at Jack I watched as they continued pinging ideas around, my tummy rumbling at the mere thought of it.

'Listen, guys, this one's getting tired,' he said, stroking Scarlett's hair. 'I'm going to take her back to the house and give her a bottle, then how about I show you your potential studio space?' he added to Mouse.

'I can do that if you like,' said Hamish, giving Mouse a soppy grin.

'Great,' she said, returning his look.

'OK,' said Jack. 'I'll leave that to you because I am gagging for a cup of tea.' He turned to me and William. 'Coming?'

Giving him the thumbs up, we made our way back to the house. Jeannie was on hand to take a very tired Scarlett off Jack's hands so we could make a pot of tea, and scoff some more of her delicious homemade scones. We arranged to meet back at Kelso in twenty-four hours by which time Jack was confident that they could get access to the bakehouse and William and I could have a chat about things, too. Time was marching on and as Jack announced he had to get Scarlett home for tea, I realised I had to get back to St Andrews for the evening shift, so we said our farewells. As Will and I wandered back to the car we saw Hamish emerging from the stables, grabbing a wheelbarrow and marching purposefully back towards the garden. Clearly, he had no intention of leaving, possibly ever, I thought, as a familiar figure walked towards us coming from the same direction.

'Mouse!'

'Hi, I was coming to find you.' She grinned. 'Come and have a look, I think I've found the perfect studio space.'

William and I followed her past the house to the long stone stable block.

'Tooty used to keep her horses in there,' she explained. 'There's still one wee pony, but it's mostly empty and the bit I've got my eye on is up there.' She pointed to the first floor above. Clomping up the chunky wooden steps, we found ourselves in a long thin room with a low ceiling, the unmistakable smell of hay and horses everywhere.

'What do you think?' she said, an expectant smile on her chops.

'Rustic,' I said, removing some fronds of hay from her hair, the remnant of some rough and tumble, I thought.

'I just love it,' she said. 'I can make as much mess as I like up here and there's no one to tell me off. Loads of storage for canvases and supplies, walls are just tall enough for me to hang the finished art.' Her eyes glistened. 'Honestly, it's perfect!'

'Fantastic. So, are you moving out lock, stock, and barrel or just your stuff?' I asked.

'Just my stuff for now but yeah … I think I might.' She beamed.

'If you don't then God knows when you will see Hamish,' said William.

'Yeah, I know,' she giggled. 'Thanks for the offer of help, Maddy, I might take you up on that depending on how Mellors is getting on.'

'Mellors?' I repeated, puzzled,

'The gardener in *Lady Chatterley's Lover*,' William answered.

I laughed. 'Ha. Ha. OK, too much information. Just let me know.'

As Will and I drove back into town, I noted he wasn't hanging onto the door handle.

He had more important matters on his mind. 'I have to say, Maddy, if this goes ahead, which I really hope it does, this old jalopy is going to be worth its weight in gold.'

'You've changed your tune. You should sit your test, you know.'

'Oh no! Honestly, I am the worst driver on the planet. Seriously, the last time Noel took me out he asked me to indicate, and I wound down the window. My brain just doesn't compute this sort of thing.'

I laughed. 'OK then, I will be the official driver for the Birdie.'

He smiled. 'Deal.'

We travelled on in silence, both lost in our own thoughts.

'There's a lot to think about, isn't there?' I stated.

'Yes, there certainly is. I'm off tonight so I'm going to talk it all through with Noel. What are you doing?'

'Saturday night? Usual social whirl,' I joked. 'Working. I'm out front tonight so I better get going.'

'OK. Have fun,' said Will. 'Speak tomorrow.'

Chapter 29

Twenty minutes later, I arrived at the Birdie. The bookings slate was full: two sittings, the first one kicking off in under an hour, which was pretty much the norm these days. Pouring myself a glass of water I allowed myself the luxury of sitting back and observing. The tables were set, linen starched and flawless, cutlery gleaming, napkins folded beautifully, candles ready to be lit, a small bone china vase on each with a sprig of heather, and the wine and water glasses sparkling.

'The place looks wonderful.' I beamed at Javier and Claude who were going over last minute details about the night's menu. They were ready to roll once Jimmy the Fish's second delivery of the day arrived. The phone rang and we got the news that Jimmy had fallen and broken his arm so the fish, lobsters, crab and langoustines were still in the sea and he was in hospital.

There was a moment of stunned silence. Claude's reputation as a superb seafood chef meant a lot of our customers booked specifically for his crab, lobster and langoustine platter, seafood bisque and dressed crab salad. I felt panic rise as Claude silently retrieved a clipboard and a notebook and the two of them sat calmly talking, rearranging things, rewriting the menu and introducing some lip-smacking delicious-sounding vegetarian options and alternatives. I was full of admiration. I knew myself well enough to acknowledge had that been up to me, I would have been like a headless chicken flapping about, achieving nothing. They were more than a safe pair of hands and with potential expansion imminent after this incident my confidence in my team was at an all-time high. There was no doubt now, I could confidently take my eye off the Birdie and concentrate on the potential bakehouse project.

Jack and I were in touch constantly, first thing in the morning and last thing at night, but only between Scarlett and everything we were about to put in motion. We were all running flat out, so recently our flirting had been curtailed dramatically. The idea of spending more time with Jack was very appealing, and I was so excited to go and see our potential new site again, I was up with the lark.

I texted Will. Keen as mustard, we arrived at Kelso Lodge, wellies on, and thirty minutes early for our meeting with Jack, so we took Frank for a daunder in the woods whilst we waited.

As we tramped through the damp mossy wood, William confirmed Noel was theoretically supportive but, 'with a few conditions, none of which were deal breakers,' said Will without going into detail. 'What are you thinking?' he asked.

I updated him on the previous evening's fish debacle, and he was just as impressed as I had been.

'It makes me realise those guys are at the top of their game,' I said.

'Yeah,' he said, trudging on. I could see he was pensive.

'What's up?'

'Well, we really need to think what we are going to open out here, if we are going to open anything,' he said. 'A restaurant will be a lot more work than, say, a cafe. With a restaurant, we will need a serious kitchen, a head chef, a sous chef and, well, basically a replica of what we've got in town.

So, we need to think carefully about that … imagine in a few months' time if what happened last night happened, and we had two fully booked restaurants to deal with.'

'God, yes,' I said, with a bolt of anxiety.

'And that's presuming we can find another Claude and Javier,' he went on.

'Sounds like you've gone off the idea …'

'No, far from it. But I do think it's important we talk these things through now and give it proper thought, before we get the ball rolling … I know what you're like, Maddy.'

'OK, how about we have a look at this place today and then if we think it might work, then we can decide?'

'Deal,' he said as the noise of a vehicle crunching up the drive interrupted us.

'Jack,' I said as we saw his Landy drive past us and park up. Leaping up, he strode around to the passenger door, opened it, and within seconds produced the baby, who he deftly strapped into her papoose.

'God, he's certainly got the hang of that,' said William as we emerged from the trees towards him.

'Morning, guys,' he shouted. 'I'm not late, am I?'

'No, we were just over-excited, so we arrived early.'

He grinned and smiled, this time guiding us around the exterior perimeter wall of the garden, rather than through it. A few minutes later we arrived in a big muddy patch, in the middle of which stood a digger, surrounded by massive mounds of earth, and my great galoot of a cousin in the driver's seat with a cheesy grin.

'Morning!' we said in unison to Hamish.

'Giant mole hills,' I said to him as he swung down, giving my hair a scuffle with his hand.

'Morning all,' he said.

'What time did you start?' I asked, impressed at his work ethic.

'Worked till dark last night and was up and at it by seven this morning.'

'My, you have been hard at work,' said Will, following Jack and marching along the perimeter wall. He stopped and turned to me. 'Look!'

Behind a vast pile of branches, weeds, and twigs there it was, a rather unremarkable looking structure. Long, brick built, traditional steading, four windows running horizontally along the front and a door at each end. Honestly? It was rather underwhelming.

'The Bakehouse,' Jack announced.

William and I glanced at each other and followed on, walking through the door which was wedged open. The moment we stepped inside it was immediately apparent it was a lot bigger than it looked.

'Whoa,' said William into the cavernous darkness.

'It's like the Tardis.' I gawped.

'Yes, it's a lot bigger than you think,' said Jack. 'I haven't been in here since I was a kid; things always seem bigger when you're a kid, but this still is!'

'I'll say,' said Will, clomping over the undulating floor, which seemed to be made up entirely of mud.

'It's hard to see properly but it looks pretty sound to me.' Jack stomped round peering at the space and stroking the walls.

'It looks like it would withstand a nuclear holocaust,' I added.

'Jack! Look!' Hamish exclaimed.

'What?' he said into the gloom where Hamish was ferreting about.

'These look like the original ovens!'

'Oh my God!' said Jack, joining him. 'So they are.'

'Do you think they still work?' asked Will.

'Well, they're wood-fired so it would depend on the chimneys, but I don't see why not,' said Jack, patting the chimney breasts and assessing them.

'We could reinstate the whole thing!' I said.

'Get money from Historic Scotland,' William chipped in.

'Make it a tourist destination,' said Jack.

My initial disappointment evaporated. This was perfect: an authentic bakehouse, original stone ovens, a secret door into a walled garden through the Hobbit house – it was the stuff of dreams.

All four of us were by now stroking the vast stone ovens.

'Gosh, these are substantial; they are built into the actual structure. God, it would be great if we could get them working,' enthused Will.

'Mmmmm, the smells would be amazing,' I said, my tummy rumbling as usual at the thought of food.

We were all buzzing with the possibilities, but agreed that without decent light there really wasn't that much else to see, so after Hamish and William measured the floor space, we made our way into the big house. Jeannie, as ever psychic and prepared, had coffee on the stove and ginger biscuits hot from the oven which we duly demolished. Jack unclipped Scarlett, and Jeannie spirited her away leaving us to talk.

'Right,' said Jack, taking out and unfolding a map. 'It's the original plan of the walled garden and bakehouse ... circa 1824.'

'Bloody hell, I thought it was built in the Second World War,' I said.

'No, that was when it became a community hub but up until then the garden and bakehouse was private, for the family, staff and workers on the estate.'

'So, it's Georgian,' marvelled William. 'Even better.'

'Gosh, those were the days,' I said, scrutinising the intricate map in front of us, pen and ink drawn, intricately marked and labelled, in such good condition it was as if it had been done yesterday.

'Where did you get this?' I asked.

'Well, after all the chatter the other day, Jeannie had a dig about. We have a cabinet in the house which is packed to the gunnels with documents and pictures, and she vaguely remembered seeing it before. She persevered on the search and came up trumps.'

'It's terrific,' said Will.

The overview clearly showed the large rectangular walled garden, and where it sat within the estate. What we called the Hobbit house was labelled the Summer House and it sat right in the centre of the south wall, directly opposite the gate. In the interior of this wee house was the doorway into the bakehouse on the other side of the wall. The map included the old access to the bakehouse, a road or path that led from the main drive in, away from the house, and up around the back.

'This is the perfect spot to put the car park,' said Jack, pointing to it. 'It keeps everything away from the house, so it remains completely private.'

'It's like it's just waiting for us to come and bring it all back to life,' marvelled William, eyes glued to the magical map.

'And look here,' said Jack, digging into a large buff envelope, producing various photocopies and clippings all held together with a bulldog clip. 'We have Jeannie to thank for this, too. Most of this lot came from the library. These pictures show how important the bakehouse was back in the day.'

Silently we loomed over the table, reading the cuttings.

'Local landowner opens the doors to community to feed the hungry.'

Grainy black and white pictures illustrated queues of people at the bakehouse, smiling, holding armfuls of loaves, paper bags bulging with goodies, large sacks of flour leaning up against the old stone walls, flat caps, ruddy cheeks, a couple of scruffy looking dogs, and in the middle of it... Jack!

'Oh my God, is that your grandpa?'

'Yes,' he smiled.

'You are his doppelgänger, that's incredible,' I said, picking up the cutting and looking more closely. 'And oooooo, there's Flora!' I exclaimed. Jack's delightful grandmother was in her early nineties now, but she was instantly recognisable by her sweet smile and extraordinary cheekbones. Dressed like everyone else, she was so very obviously part of the community, as they all gathered together to smile for the camera.

'These really are extraordinary,' said William. 'A living history.'

The door opened and in came Jeannie.

'Jeannie, thanks for doing this, it's fantastic!' I grinned at her.

'Och, you're welcome,' she said. 'It was well before my time, but as you can see back in the 1940s the estate was the heart of the community. The corn was grown here, the grain milled, and the flour sold to all comers. The head cook would produce bread for the big house and apparently, he started giving surplus to the locals and then it grew from there. When war broke out the laird, your grandfather stopped selling grain and began to make it into bread for anyone in need. It was a mainstay of the community back in the day.'

'I had no idea,' said Jack.

'Well, it's not the sort of thing your father would be interested in and when your grandpa passed, and Flora left...'

Jack nodded. 'How sad.'

The comment was left hanging.

Once the excitement of the cuttings died down and Jack confirmed he was more than happy for us to use the history and photographs for our PR and marketing, we settled down to do the more mundane elements.

I'd spent most of last night online and found out the Bakehouse was a listed building, as we suspected. This meant we were very restricted as to what we could do with it. As long as we don't change the basic structure and anything we want to do is in keeping with the original design, then we shouldn't have any problems with repairing it, painting it in heritage colours, and replacing the broken glass and wood in the windows. But it did not mean the idea of creating something that was state of the art and modern would be a big fat no.

'Do you think we can work around it?' I asked.

'Yes, with clever design, creative thinking and... come on, Maddy, you've done it before,' said Will.

'Well, Mouse has done it before.'

'OK, well, Mouse and you then,' he said. 'But I think it sounds very exciting.'

'Yes, I suppose,' I said, reaching for my third ginger biscuit and taking a major bite out of it.

'OK, you two,' interjected Jack. 'The good news is that if we are theoretically bringing it back to its original purpose, we can apply for a grant from Historic Scotland. If we are successful, that would potentially take a lot of the financial pain out of our plan.'

'That is good news,' I said, mindful of the fact that he was the one who was going to be footing that particular bill.

Next came what I would call the boring bit.

Rules, regulations and permissions any food operation anywhere had to adhere to. That was a long, long list, but it was William's speciality – he just loved this sort of thing, thank God. So, the well-known t-crosser and i-dotter offered to take on the red tape and bureaucracy of the project with the intent of getting necessary planners and officials out ASAP to see the project in person.

By the time the meeting had come to an end we each had a long list of things to do. There was one thing I needed to ask Jack and there was no polite way of doing so, so I just came out with it.

'Can we – or should I say you – afford to do this?'

'Well, I will be able to answer that once I have talked to George the contractor, who's coming out this afternoon to have a look around. I've known him for years and he will give me a ballpark figure as a starting point. But a lot of it will be how we fit it out inside.'

'And I imagine that's how long is a bit of string,' William said.

Jack nodded. 'Yeah, but with Mouse and Maddy's magic touch, I hope it won't be totally out of the question.'

I grinned. 'Great!'

'OK, so it is over to you two,' said Jack. 'You need to go and discuss if one, you want to do it and two, what sort of business it's going to be. Once that's been decided, we can proceed accordingly. The sooner the better.'

There was a fizzing excitement as we all made to leave, Will subtly saying his goodbye, leaving Jack and I to say our own farewell, which consisted of a delicious kiss punctuated by Scarlett grizzling for her lunch.

He opened his eyes and crossed them at me. The little cherub had done it again.

Best contraceptive in town.

'I'd better be off,' I smiled at him, knees like jelly.

'I'll call you,' he said as I reluctantly released him to take care of his fatherly duties.

Chapter 30

And so, a new rhythm of life began.

Every morning I checked in at the Birdie, which was more of a habit than necessity. Claude flourished even further with this newfound vote of confidence that he was going to be running the restaurant.

Of course, Jack and I saw each other most days but it was hardly quality time, as everyone was up to their eyes in work.

Hamish had wasted no time moving into Kelso Lodge and though Mouse had kept on her bedsit for the time being, she was spending most nights with Hamish out there. The two of them were still thick as thieves.

Mouse had moved all her supplies into the studio and was working hard, appearing in overalls occasionally to get some fresh air and snap some photographs of the garden project, documenting the transformation as it took place. She was so wrapped up in producing work for the exhibition that she was holed up in the stables most of the time, but she did take an afternoon off to spend time with me in the bakehouse to talk through how we both imagined it, and sketch out some plans. During this process I noticed her piercings reappearing; at the time I put it down to her spending so much time on her own in her studio, which was bound to make her appear more withdrawn.

From dawn to dusk, people came and went. Suppliers of

plants, shrubs, dung, builders, officials, planners, councillors, and two very serious people from Historic Scotland.

Amongst all this activity one day Barclay, Jack's father, appeared in the garden, curiosity having got the better of him, in his usual bull in a china shop sort of way.

'So, what's going on here?' he barked, causing us all to stop dead in our tracks.

Jack dropped what he was doing and, teeth gritted, steered him back out the way he'd come in, talking to him in a low voice. He reappeared a few minutes later, a little red in the face, assuring us he had secured Barclay's support.

'How did you do that?' I asked him later when the two of us were enjoying a well-earned cup of coffee.

'I merely pointed out it might be in his best interests to give us a hand if he was so minded, as if this place goes under, he will be going under with it and out on his ear, homeless.'

I looked at him.

Quite.

Hamish had adopted the role of foreman directing operations, keeping everyone busy and on their toes. Jack had employed a guy they had both known for years, Gordy, who lived locally and had a seemingly endless supply of plant machinery. One day he'd pitch up with a tractor, the next a digger, and the next a cherry picker. He was a man mountain who could pick up and move things that would have defeated Desperate Dan without batting an eyelid, a very obliging character, willing to help in any way he could.

Skips were hauled in and out as they were filled with earth, foliage, huge stones, dead and dying trees of all shapes and sizes. The biggest culprit of destruction in both the garden and the bakehouse was the ivy, the strong strangling snakes of it worked into every nook of the garden, sticking to walls and stones, creating webs of knotted weeds in the interior of the Bakehouse too.

The Bakehouse roof was going to be the biggest expenditure, the majority of tiles well past their best, but between Gordy and Hamish they managed to source vintage tiles to match the ones that were salvageable. So once the tiles were taken care of, Jack mentioned the next thing they needed was a roofer and no one was surprised when Gordy piped up.

'Aye, aye, I know a brilliant roofer. Sheep Shepherd.'

'Sheep? The same Sheep from school?' asked Jack.

'Aye, one and the same.'

'Why's he called Sheep?' I couldn't resist asking.

'His surname is Shepherd, and they look after sheep; we came up with that in Primary and it stuck from that day to this,' snorted Hamish.

'Did you have a nickname?' I asked Gordy.

'Aye. Gordy.'

'Oh. So, what's your real name?'

'Stuart Gordon.'

'Another P4 creative genius at work,' said Hamish.

'What about you?' I asked Jack.

Hamish sniggered.

'C'mon then, what was it?' I pressed him.

Jack shook his head, grinning.

Hamish chuckled. 'Maddy, do you not remember mine was Chops cos my dad's—'

'The butcher,' we all finished in unison.

'And Jack?' I asked Hamish, because Jack wasn't going to spill the beans.

'Popeye,' he answered.

'Because you were big and strong and ate a lot of spinach?' I said, turning to Jack admiringly.

Hamish wheezed with laughter.

'Erm, no,' he said, looking rather embarrassed.

'Why then?'

'Well, you see this,' said Jack, pointing to the mole that sat tantalisingly below his left eye, perched on his deliciously defined cheekbone.

'Yes.'

'Age six we thought it looked like a guinea pig poop, so one day I called him Poopeye,' said Hamish, before losing the plot. 'Poopeye became Popeye.' Gordy and he wheezed away like a couple of emphysemic mongrels as Jack scuffed the pair of them on the top of the head. 'Ah, the joy of lifelong friends', he said as the three of them thumped each other on the arm. So, the boys were having the time of their lives, pulling each other's legs, doing the heavy lifting, clearing and hefting the soil and materials from one place to the other, which was a blessing as at this stage I found some days it was hard to put one foot in front of the other. I felt absolutely exhausted.

Things inevitably came to a head. One afternoon William and I convened in his cottage to continue our debate as to what kind of business we wanted to open. With the news of the building being listed and the good possibility of getting a grant from Historic Scotland for Jack, it seemed things were pointing to more of a daytime operation such as a bakery/cafe.

We did a long list of pros and cons to help us make the final decision.

The cafe option won out by a country mile. Fife Council had agreed in principle to us running the bakehouse, so we would not need change of use, saving us a lot of time and money.

A cafe meant we wouldn't need a Class Three Restaurant

licence, which would mean a simpler business model serving hearty soups, sandwiches, salads, home bakes, cakes, soft drinks, coffees and teas – no restaurant menu required.

This would also mean we wouldn't need an all-singing, dancing kitchen, nor all the appliances that come with it, such as, commercial dishwashers, to stoves, mixers, fridges. Will worked out that would be a saving of over a hundred thousand pounds. Eyewatering.

The staffing was easier, too, no head chef, commis chef and cover when they were off.

A daytime operation would mean that work and life balance was far more manageable, which Noel would certainly approve of, and we would all appreciate. This had to be fun.

And the clincher for me, the fabulous home cook and exceptional baker we would need to really make the bakehouse fly was right under our noses, of course. Jeannie. And I just loved the idea of her being involved. Whether she would be interested was another matter. What with her kids all grown up and away from home, as well as her recently acknowledged budding romance with Claude, she had a lot going on. I tried not to get too ahead of myself as she might feel she didn't want to be tied into anything, as she had long talked about what she would do when she retired. But I would do my damnedest to at least make her consider it. I've adored her since we met, and she had seamlessly slipped into a surrogate mother position in my life, a steady, calm influence in addition to her culinary talents. It was a win-win whichever way we looked at it.

So, the decision was made, and the Birdie Bakehouse was born.

As tradition dictated, the agreement was sealed with a handshake and a hug just as William's phone rang.

'It's Noel,' he said. 'Mind if I take this? I want to give him the news.'

'Of course not,' I said as he stepped outside to take his call, leaving me alone. The heat of the kitchen combined with tiredness rolled over me, so I momentarily gave in to the urge to lay my head flat on the table. What could have been seconds or hours later I woke with a start as William nudged me gently.

'Maddy,' he whispered. I sat up, momentarily confused as to where I was.

'Oh Will, gosh, I'm sorry. I—'

'You don't need to apologise. Noel was hugely relieved and supportive that we're going down the cafe route, he feared the whole restaurant thing would have been too much for me.' He looked at me. 'Actually, for us both.' He pulled a chair up right beside me, keeping his hand resting on my arm. 'You look exhausted, Maddy. Absolutely worn out. And I am speaking as someone who knows only too well how that feels,' he said. 'Don't forget we are just at the beginning of a long road with the bakehouse and you really need to take care of yourself better.'

I nodded, annoyed as tears sprang up in my eyes.

'If you run yourself into the ground the way I did then where will we be?' I opened my mouth to speak but he interjected. 'Let me finish. Please.'

'OK.'

'You've said yourself Claude and Javier have the Birdie under control. Hamish, Jack and big Gordy are doing all the heavy lifting out at the walled garden. I can crack on with the paperwork and license permission because now we know what sort of business we are going to open. So, from now it's just a waiting game until the fun part starts and you want to be up and running for that, don't you?'

I nodded.

'Good,' he went on. 'So, this makes it the perfect time to have some time off.'

He detected that I was about to object and held his hand up again, this time more forcefully.

'Remember how I was when you came back from your travels?'

'Yes, of course.'

'You said yourself I was a shadow of my former self. With the benefit of hindsight, I can see now that I had lost perspective and I can see the signs, Maddy, I feel it is my responsibility as your friend and business partner not to sit back and let you end up in the same position. Maddy, I need you. We all do,' he said.

He had hit a nerve big time. I had not one iota of energy left to answer; what he said was true, it all made perfect sense. I did not feel like me at the moment, and if the truth be told, I hadn't for quite some time. I was wrung out, strung out, and bless Will for noticing.

'I know you're right,' I said. 'Everything just seems so overwhelming and I don't know why. I mean the Birdie is great, and the Bakehouse is so exciting. I suppose I just thought by now Jack and I would be ... would have ...' I sighed. 'And then there's Scarlett ...' I added as my chin wobbled, and tears spilled over.

'Come here,' he said, opening his arms up, and inviting me in for a major hug. 'This is what I was talking about, perspective. You *have* run yourself into the ground. You need time out, to rest, recharge. Maybe even a few days away ...'

By the time he released me, I had ruined his shirt shoulder with mascara and tears and agreed to take a day off. He suggested a whole week which terrified me, so we compromised on a few days but, and I was adamant about this,

I wanted to speak to Jeannie ASAP. The sooner we knew whether she was onboard the better, and if I timed things the right way, she would never have to go through the stress of even hearing the word 'redundancy'. William agreed.

I voiced my only other concern.

'What will I say to the others?'

'Don't worry about them. They are so wrapped up in their own stuff, just say you're working from home.'

Unbelievably the floodgates opened again. 'Aaaaaah, and that's another thing, I want a home,' I snottered. What the hell was going on? I was an emotional wreck, who even was this mercurial bubbling fool?

'Right, Maddy, that's enough,' he said, calling a halt to my self-indulgent wailing long enough to instruct me. 'Go and blow your nose and splash your face with water. I am sending you home to bed.'

Thankfully his words snapped me out of it, though I was in no fit state to argue. So off I went, trudging around to the bothy, boiled the kettle, ate two Pot Noodles, climbed into bed and called Jack.

Chapter 31

'Maddy, hi!' He picked up immediately.

'Jack, hi,' I said, putting on a cheery upbeat voice which took what little energy I had left. 'Just a quick call. I wanted to let you know Will and I have just decided, the Birdie Bakehouse and Cafe it is.'

'Love it!' came the instant reply. 'I think that is the path of least resistance. Great news. So, we can crack on now, it's a much easier ask and I reckon it won't take long to sort everything out. Proposed opening date?'

'Gosh, well, we haven't quite decided on that yet.'

'Yeah, fair enough, I'm just getting ahead of myself.'

'Brilliant,' I said, grinning stupidly into the phone. 'Oh, and the other thing I wanted to run by you ...'

'Yes?'

'Well, as you know now, we don't need a chef, thank goodness, but we do need a bloody good baker and home cook, so Will and I were thinking, if you're OK with it, we might ask Jeannie?'

'My Jeannie?' He sounded surprised.

'Yes, your Jeannie,' I said.

'Yes! That is a fabulous idea. I have been so worried about her job and you're right, she would be perfect ... if she goes for it. Oh my God, it couldn't have worked out better. I am so relieved.' He laughed in an exhausted sort of way. 'When are you going to ask her?'

'Soon as I can. I wanted to let you know first, see what you thought... I will text her now and arrange to meet her on Sunday at the big house.'

'OK, so will you come and find me after you've seen her? I can ask her to take Scarlett, and the two of us can walk the dogs and you can get me up to speed. I feel like I haven't seen you properly for ages...'

'I know,' I croaked.

'I look forward to seeing you then, Madeline,' he said gently. 'And good luck with Jeannie.'

'Thanks,' I whispered, just as the phone clicked off.

It didn't seem to matter how many times I spoke to him, the effect he had on me was extraordinary, I thought, picking up my phone and dialling Jeannie's number, losing myself in a little fantasy.

'Hello?'

'Oh Jeannie, hello,' I said, sounding surprised.

'You phoned me,' she giggled.

'Yes, sorry, just having one of those days,' I said. 'I was hoping to catch up with you. You around on Sunday morning?'

'Yes, I am. I will be out at Kelso, by the back, at nine, so anytime you like, dear.'

'Super, I'll aim to be out about mid-morning.'

'OK, dear, cheerio,' said the bright wee spark.

So, we were all set.

Chapter 32

When I awoke the next day, I felt much improved, and I was starving. All the mini Budweiser fridge held was a big chunk of Arran cheddar, which I bit into and as I clambered back into bed my mobile pinged.

WhatsApp from Sarah. 'What are you doing later?'

I replied, 'Nothing.'

Sarah was gloriously unaware of my recent meltdown.

'Want to come around for an early supper? I have not had a conversation with anyone over the age of four for two days and need some adult company ... pleeeeease?'

I smiled and looked at the clock, it was nearly two! I hadn't slept that long for years. Glancing down at my rumpled dressing gown, trackie bottoms, and old t-shirt, I wondered if I was up to going anywhere, but one look at Frank who was standing by the door, looking disgusted at my slovenly behaviour, and my tummy which gurgled and grumbled as it needed stoked, so I texted her back.

'Yes please! What time?'

'Five. Is that too early?'

'No, perfect, see you then.'

I felt much better after doing my hair and putting on minimal slap. I dug through my rag bag of clothes, which were strewn around the place. I was delighted to find my favourite skinny jeans that had been missing in action for some time under a clump of discarded clothes on the arm of the only chair in the place, which doubled up as a holding pen, wardrobe and general dumping ground. Grabbing them, I sat down on the bed and snaked them on, one leg at a time, realising, as I stood up and wiggled from foot to foot trying to inch them up, that they were tight. Tumble drier has done for them, I thought, as I continued to wiggle and squirm my way into them. After a real wrestling match, I managed to get them up over my bum, and lay on the bed trying to get the top button done up but the zip was gaping and straining and refusing to come up even a centimetre. Sitting up breathless and frustrated, I looked at the cheddar cheese packet and Pot Noodle containers sitting on the chair ready for recycling and admitted to myself that my diet recently had left a lot to be desired. I was eating two meals a day at the Birdie, the second of which was usually late at night, after which I would go home to bed. Without a kitchen in the bothy, breakfast consisted of whatever I could grab. Chocolate, crisps, Pot Noodles, hunks of cheese, Tunnocks Caramel Logs. Hmmmm, I thought, I'd really better get a grip as I noticed the linen drowse I had bought for my hot date a few days ago was still lying on the floor. Size fourteen.

Giving the jean zip one more yank, I conceded defeat and wiggled out of them which took almost as much time. I pinged them off my leg into the corner of the room, plumping for my baggy denim jumpsuit, a far more forgiving cut, and was horrified to feel the usually baggy bottom now skimming my own enhanced bahookey. A bum like Kim Kardashian, minus the muscle tone. Oh dear.

Makeup on and swearing off food and drink for the rest of time, starting tomorrow, I clipped Frank to the lead and popped in to get some handmade chocolates for Sarah and a giant bag of Doritos on my way round to her place. She answered the door like a desperado.

'Maddy, a human, thank God. Come in, how are you?'

'Fat,' I said, traipsing in behind her and into the lounge, a rare treat as this was where the kids usually hung out.

'Where are the little cherubs?' I asked, opening my bag and plopping the chocolates and Doritos on the table.

'Cherubs?' she guffawed. 'They are driving me mad. I love them but Charlie is going through a rumbustious phase where he won't listen to anyone, but Phil, his hero, and Tilda has to be attached to me 24/7 or she screams the house down so ...'

'You've sold them on Gumtree?'

'Haha, no, Phil has taken them to his mum's for the night.'

'Oh hallelujah,' I said, slipping off my shoes and lunging at the bag of Doritos I had just plopped on the table whilst getting settled on the couch.

'So, I thought we'd order in?' said Sarah.

'Great idea,' I said. 'I'm starving.'

'Me, too,' she said, picking up the menu for the local delivery. 'Pizza from Papa John's?'

'Oh, God, yes,' I said. 'My diet can start tomorrow.'

Large and fattening pizzas ordered, we sat back with two glasses of iced water.

'Exciting times, Maddy, such a lot going on. How are you feeling?'

'Fine,' I lied. 'Why?'

'You just look a bit pale,' she said, scrutinising me.

'Well, I am feeling a bit tired,' I conceded.

She nodded. 'I'm not surprised.'

'Look at us!' I laughed. 'Saturday night. Drinking water. Changed days.'

'There is a bottle of wine in the fridge, help yourself,' she said, 'but obviously–' she prodded her tum, '–no booze for me until this wee one is fully cooked.'

I smiled. 'No thanks, I'm fine … I'm not in the mood for drinking.'

She looked at me. 'Are you ill?'

'Not exactly,' I said.

'So, spill the beans,' she said.

And I did. About me ruining Jack's birthday celebration, my tummy bug, the overwhelming tiredness, my meltdown earlier, the fact I had eaten about a pound of cheese before coming around and …

'I could eat a bloody horse again!' I unzipped my jump-suit. 'And look at this! I'm turning into a Teletubby.'

She continued looking at me before standing up and leaving the room.

Shrugging, I re-examined the pizza takeaway menu hoping I had ordered enough extras on my margherita – pepperoni, tuna, capers, anchovies, and chilli oil – as Sarah came back into the room and put something down on the couch next to me.

'What's that?'

'A pregnancy test.'

I laughed heartily. 'Fuck off.'

She wasn't laughing.

I sat up. 'Really?'

'Yeah, really.'

'Why? What? Why?'

'Nausea, hunger, exhaustion, crying a lot …' She patted her tum. 'Your recent expansion … all signs your hormones are raging, woman. Did it not cross your mind?'

'No!' I said, shocked to the core.

'When did you have your last period?' She looked at me.

'God, I don't know … I'm pretty sure I would have noticed if I hadn't had my period,' I said, racking my brain for any memory of the monthly tampon purchase. 'It's been so busy, and when I was travelling my period was all over the place, never very regular, it's just one of those things that happens if I'm not leading a normal life.'

'Well, you're certainly not leading a normal life right now, you're right,' she said, sitting back. 'But it won't do any harm to eliminate this from your enquiries.' Clocking my dazed expression, she went on.

'I'm sure you're not, but I got a multipack off Amazon when we were trying and there's a couple left ... you might as well.'

Panic rose in my chest.

'Jesus, it never crossed my mind that I might be ...' I couldn't bring myself to say it. Taking one and opening the packet, my hands were shaking. Reading the leaflet, I went on, 'It says do it first thing in the morning and not to drink water for two hours beforehand.'

She looked at me. 'Maddy.'

'It says here!' I objected, pointing at the leaflet, but she wasn't budging.

'Well, ignoring the instructions isn't the best bloody start. But OK if it shuts you up,' I said, standing up.

She grinned and got to her feet.

'Right. Easiest way to do it is pee in here,' she said, handing me a paper cup. I looked at her.

'Thank you, Ali Bongo, resident magician. Where do you get that?'

'Experience has taught me this is the best method to avoid peeing all over the place.'

I held up my hand. 'OK, Ok,' I said, slightly irritated that I was being railroaded into this.

'I'm just trying to help,' she said, following me through to the loo.

'OK, that's far enough,' I said, nudging her back out of

the loo door and closing it behind me. 'I think I can manage this part on my own.' A couple of minutes later I reappeared with the paper cup and handed it to her.

'Thank you,' she said, marching back to the lounge and putting it on the table.

She unwrapped the test and dunked it into the cup and sat down on the couch, where I joined her. Suddenly at a loss for words, we both stared at the aperture on the stick which held my future in its hands, as the longest three minutes in history began to tick down. After about a minute, a very clearly defined pink line appeared.

'Not pregnant,' I shouted grabbing Sarah's arm.

'Hang on,' she said, holding her hand up, still staring at it. Releasing her arm, I watched as a second very clear pink line developed right next to it.

Sarah's face drained of colour as she looked at me.

'Pregnant,' she whispered.

I stared at it. 'What?' I grabbed it and shoogled it about, hoping it might change its mind.

I looked at it again. Nope, same result.

'I can't be,' I said, absolutely sideswiped. 'It's a false positive. There is no way I can be pregnant.' My heart was yammering in my chest, legs like water.

'OK,' she said, marching off and coming back with another test. 'You're right, try another one.'

This time I tore through the bathroom and ran the tap for a few seconds before the urge was upon me to pee again. Once I did, I opened the door, and like the relay at school I passed Sarah the baton, this time a paper cup with a life-altering result teetering on the brink of it as she marched through, ripped open the second test and dunked the stick. This time two pink lines came up within a minute.

I sat back, jaw hanging open, speechless, shocked, unable to think.

Sarah put her arm round me. 'OK. Take a deep breath.'

I looked at her. Inhaled.

'And out.'

Exhaled.

'Right, Maddy, everything is going to be OK. It's the most natural thing in the world.' She paused. 'I mean, if you think about it, it's really exciting. This means we can go through the whole thing together!' Still dumbstruck, I stared at her. 'I will be with you every step of the way, and our babies will be lifelong friends, like us!' she said, which was my cue to burst into tears. Then, as fast as they started, they stopped. I stood up and began pacing.

'I need a drink,' I said.

'Well, you're not having one.'

'Oh shit, I can't drink,' I said, the magnitude of the situation hitting home. 'OK, give me some crisps,' I demanded instead, as Sarah handed me the half-empty packet of Doritos. Jamming my hand into the depths of the bag, I took out a handful and stuffed them into my mouth. And then spat them out, jumping back. 'Oh my God,' I said, doing a mental rewind of all the booze and rubbish I had been snorkelling over the past few ... weeks? Days? Months? I was terrified. Plus, there was one small matter to clear up. I sat down with a slump on the sofa and looked at Sarah.

'Whose is it?' I exclaimed.

'Oh my,' said Sarah. 'I never thought about that.'

'How pregnant am I?' I asked.

'Well, when did you—'

'Last have a period? I don't know.'

'No, when did you last have sex?'

Oh, God. 'With Javier, it was the night of the wedding.'

'Well, that's fairly definite and what about—'

'Jack? Erm, we've only slept together once, that time at his cottage.'

'Once!' she said.

'I know!' I said.

'OK, when was that?'

'Three or four weeks before that …?' I stuttered to a stop, the magnitude of what we were talking about beginning to sink in. 'Have you got a paper bag?' I asked.

'Why, are you going to be sick?' she said, jumping up.

'No, I am going to have a panic attack,' I said as she ran back into the room with a Tesco carrier bag,

I couldn't help but laugh.

'Are you trying to kill me? Asphyxiate me …'

The sense of relief on her face caused us both to start laughing uncontrollably which quickly transmogrified from guffaws to gulps, as we then started crying.

Sarah squished up next to me on the couch and put her arm round me as I slumped my head on her shoulder and sobbed.

'Hormones,' she said. 'Brace yourself, they are in control. You are now in a hostage situation.'

'What a bloody mess,' I said.

'Don't worry, Mads, we can handle this. Really.'

And so, as we scoffed our vast pizzas, she talked me through what to expect and what I needed to do. With her support I realised it was a surprise, yes, but hell, I was an independent woman, I was nearly thirty, it wasn't ideal timing, but I could do this. I wouldn't be on my own, I would have Sarah, William, Noel, Hamish, Mouse and …

'You need to establish the most likely father and then decide how you want to handle that.'

I agreed to make an appointment with my GP who

would tell me how pregnant I was, which would give me the answer as to who was most likely the father.

'Until then mum's the word,' I said and gulped, never a truer word.

From then the evening took on a rhythm, of crying, eating, crying, hysterical laughing, eating and some more crying until I was absolutely puggled. But before leaving, despite the huge pizza, I managed to horse down a cup of tea and some chocolate digestives.

'Eating for two?' I ventured.

'Bullshit, you're just a greedy pig. Always were, always will be.'

By ten we were both lying on the floor, cushions under our heads, half-asleep watching *Love Actually*. The idea of having to move anywhere seemed awful, especially back to the cold, dark bothy, so when Sarah asked me if I wanted to stay, I jumped at it. Borrowing some jammies, I was soon tucked up in Charlie's room, reading a copy of *Pregnancy and Birth* magazine that Sarah gave me, Frank watching me very carefully, wondering what on earth was going on.

Once in bed my mind was like a toyshop. I put the radio on and chatted to Frank, trying to block out the screaming in my head. I lasted thirty-five seconds in bed, before I was up again pacing. A baby. I was having a baby. I was with child, pregnant, oh my God. Mindful not to disturb Sarah, I forced myself back to bed and spent a fitful night, punching pillows. I woke up, sweat crawling over me, Frank's beady eyes watching.

Throwing the covers off, I got up as a roll of nausea swept over me. Grabbing my dressing gown, I just made it to the loo and was rifling through the herbal teas in Sarah's kitchen when she turned up in her dressing gown looking equally green.

'I hope this sicky feeling passes soon,' I said as she took the kettle, filled it up and flicked it on.

'It should do,' she said. 'Ginger tea is good for nausea.'

Suddenly the front door opened and in came Phil, Charlie and Tilda, a whirlwind of activity.

'Good morning,' said Phil. 'Oh, hi Maddy, what a nice surprise. Did you stay over?'

'No, I always dress like this,' I said, indicating the floral jammies and matching dressing gown I was currently modelling.

'Fair enough,' he grinned.

'You're up early,' I said, looking at the clock, which said half past eight.

Phil and Sarah looked at each other.

'Pre-children, this used to be early, but now this one is up at six playing with Lego, and I am almost ready for lunch and a beer,' said Phil.

Phil looked at Sarah, and she gave an almost imperceptible nod before turning to me.

'I hope you don't mind, Maddy, but Phil phoned after we went to bed last night and we were talking and, well, your news just sort of slipped out,' she said.

'Of course, I don't mind,' I said. 'You are both my oldest pals in the world.'

Phil's face broke into a cheesy grin. 'Congratulations. It's just the best news ever. Welcome to the club,' he said.

'Thanks,' I said, feeling my face heat up.

'How are you feeling?' asked Phil.

'Bit sick, bit tired, oh, and I can't stop farting,' I said.

Sarah laughed. 'I have to say that isn't something that's been an issue for me.'

Phil burst out laughing. 'It may not be an issue for you, but it has certainly been an issue for me.'

This set us all off, and then amidst the gales of laughter I let a monster rip and we were uncontrollable for at least five minutes, during which Sarah announced her pelvic floor was shot and ran to the loo at speed. An hour later I was showered and ready to go. I thanked them, swore them to secrecy and left them and their lively household to it.

Chapter 33

Once outside, I realised I needed to do something to distract myself. I couldn't go back to the bothy and listen to the voices in my head, so I headed off in the direction of the beach but, nausea gone, suddenly the allure of a coffee and a huge bowl of porridge lured me along to the Birdie. Closing the door behind me, I was impressed. The place was immaculate, and already set for lunch. Claude ran a tight ship, I thought, flicking on the coffee machine. Normally the smell of coffee beans had me in raptures but this morning, they seemed utterly repellent. My head spinning, legs shaky, I ran to the loo and splashed my face with water until the nausea passed again. When I recovered sufficiently, I emerged, and came face to face with Javier, his wee face looking very concerned when he saw me hunched up coming out of the loo.

'You OK?' he said.

'Yes,' I lied in a voice so high only a dog could hear it.

'Maddy, what is it?" he asked so sweetly, placing his hand on my arm and looking deep into my eyes and damn my hormones, I just burst into tears.

One swift step and he was by my side, helping me into a chair, before pulling up one for himself right next to me. He sat down, putting his arm round me.

'Come. Tell me?'

Racking sobs now, as my nose and eyes began leaking at the same time.

Wheeching a folded napkin from the adjacent table, he handed it to me.

'Come on, blow,' he said.

And I did, loudly, which made me laugh and broke the moment.

'What is so wrong?'

I swallowed, cleared my throat. I didn't know where to start so I just blurted it out.

'I'm having a baby,' I said, nose filled with snot again.

'That's wonderful!' he exclaimed.

I stopped short. 'But I don't know whose it is,' I wailed.

'Well, it's yours, of course,' he said.

'The father,' I said.

'Oh.' He sat back, his face serious. 'I see ... So, who do you think? I mean how ... well, you know.'

I looked at him, then at the table, and I had to say the words I had been dreading.

'Well, it's Jack or you,' I said, humiliated that I had got myself into such a ridiculous position.

He sat back and laughed.

'What's so funny?'

'Is not mine.'

I looked at him with watery eyes. 'How can you be so sure?'

'We have never done eeet,' he said.

'What?'

'We have not done sex,' he said.

'But the wedding.'

'You sleep in my bed, yes, but I am not the man who takes advantage of drunken girls,' he said, clearly offended.

'No, but ...'

He looked at me, as a flashback to his naked body caused my face to heat up.

'You were naked,' I said accusingly.

'I am Spanish,' he said. 'I always sleep naked, and I was drunk, too, but nothing happened. You talked about Jack for hours, over and over, how much you love him, until I fell asleep. Maddy, you know me, I would never...'

I looked at him and nodded. My honourable friend. What on earth was I thinking?

'I'm so, so sorry,' I said. 'I just thought that—'

'No, no, no. Maddy, you are like a sister to me. And anyway, I prefer blondes,' he joked.

'What a relief!' I said.

'Thanks,' he said, laughing.

'No, I mean... I was so mixed up.'

'So, you need to talk to Jack, no?'

'Yes,' I said. 'But until then will you please keep it between us?'

'Of course,' he said. 'You have my words.'

'Thank you,' I said, giving him a hug, as there was a bang on the window.

'Break it up, break it up, and open that door, will you?' said Hamish. 'I've got some pheasants for Claude.' He shoved the feathery mass at us through the glass door.

And so, another day began.

Leaving them to it, I needed some fresh air to clear my head and think.

Stomping the beach even when it was wet and windy had a cathartic effect. The rain cleared my head as I marched along the dunes with Frank. I addressed the elephant in my head: when and how to tell Jack. I had to do it soon. Sarah and Javier already knew about the baby, and Jack would be so upset if he found out from someone else, so I began to formulate a plan.

Jack was currently living with Scarlett, allegedly his child from another woman, the result of a one-night stand. I cringed remembering my cynicism that he could possibly have fathered Scarlett after a one-night stand, and yet here I was in exactly the same position. Up the duff and feeling guilty about judging poor Jody, I stomped on.

I would tell him tomorrow, I needed one more day to really get my head round what was happening. He had a right to know and, I shivered, God knew how he would react. From no children to two in under a year from two one-night stands. You couldn't make it up.

But before I told him, I would make a plan, a plan for me and the baby. From here on, whoever was growing inside me and I were a team, and no one was going to change that. I would decide on my course of action accordingly.

As I walked and walked, my right hand gravitating to my belly, I realised the idea was growing on me. 'Hell, I am the perfect age to have a child. I have a successful business and I am about to open a second,' I shouted into the wind. Of course, that might have to change depending on Jack's reaction but whatever happened, the baby and I were not going to starve. If I had to be less involved on a day-to-day basis with the Bakehouse then so be it, William and the rest of the team were more than capable, I would just reorganise things to be back at the Birdie. I would separate my business and personal life. That's when it dawned on me, the sudden overwhelming desire to have my own home must be my nesting instinct and I felt very strongly about that indeed. There was no way I would bring my child into the world to live in a damp outhouse behind an antique shop. So, once I had spoken to Jeannie, I would leave her and Jack to talk things through, come back into town and hit the St Andrews property centre. I was now determined to find a place to buy or rent ASAP. As long as we were warm and with a roof over our heads, the baby and I would be fine.

Chapter 34

I spent a good twenty minutes repairing the damage the day had already wrought on me; my hair was like a burst mattress, and my face pink from the windy walk and intermittent tears. By the time I arrived at Kelso Lodge, externally I looked like me as I strode into the kitchen.

'Hi,' I said brightly, instantly clocking a magnificent carrot cake, the aroma curling up my nostrils. Dropping my bag, I headed straight over to the table and gazed at it.

'What a beezer,' I said, my tummy giving out a loud rumble.

'Still warm,' said Jeannie. 'I can't ice it until it's cold. Do you want to wait?'

'No,' I said, without hesitation.

Smiling, she cut a generous slice for me and went about making the icing as I helped myself to a cup of tea from the pot and sank my teeth into the lightest, moistest, most delicious sponge. 'Mmmm,' was all I could muster.

'Jack gave me the news this morning that you're going to call it the Birdie Bakehouse and make it more a daytime thing,' she said.

'Yesh,' I said through my cake-laden chops. 'Do you approve?'

'Oh yes,' she said. 'It will bring much needed life and energy to the old place, without spoiling it.'

'Quite,' I said. 'We decided against putting a full kitchen

in, and all the other things needed to run a restaurant, well, it would cost a fortune and—'

'It's a lot of work,' she said.

'So,' I said, pushing a few crumbs round my plate.

'Spit it out,' she said.

'Have you always been psychic?' I laughed.

'Pretty much,' she said, smiling at me over the mixing bowl.

'Well, William, Jack and I agree you are just the best baker in town.'

She blushed. 'Och, away you go.'

'No, seriously, we do.'

'Uh huh,' she said. 'Go on.'

'Anyway, we wondered if you might consider, and you don't have to if you don't want to, but if you do then that would be just brilliant—'

'Maddy,' she said, calling a halt to my unintelligible waffle.

'Sorry. Right. OK. Would you like to be our head baker?'

She laughed.

'I mean it.'

'Oh lassie, no, surely not. I'm over sixty and anyway, I've got a job,' she said, flapping her arm round.

'Of course,' I said, 'but theoretically is it the sort of thing that you might consider if things were different?'

'Well, 'tis very flattering,' she said.

'That may be but it's also true,' I added.

'Well, if I can be candid, I have been thinking about handing in my notice here.'

'Why?'

'It's no secret money's more than tight, Jack's been very open about that. It's no longer a B&B so no guests are coming and going, Claude and Javier are both chefs so they don't need me, and Hamish—'

'Lives like a giant hamster,' I interjected.

'Quite.' She smiled. 'So, my role is more or less redundant, but I've known Jack since he was a baby and he would keep me on out of loyalty, even though he can ill afford it.'

I remained silent.

'Don't get me wrong, I'm not flush,' she said, 'but I've put money aside over the years so I could get by, but what you're talking about is something completely different. It would be a paid job, a proper job, a new start.' Her cheeks pinked up.

'Exactly,' I said.

'The only reason I've not resigned before now is I just didn't know what I would do with myself. This place is in my blood, it's been my life,' she said.

'So, is that a yes then?' I said, trying to jolly her along a bit.

She laughed. 'I think it is, yes!' And then on a more serious note, she added, 'But if you don't mind, let me talk to Jack about it first.'

I nodded. 'Of course.'

This was my get out of jail card. God knows I loved the bones off Jack MacPherson, but I was not in a fit state to see him this morning. I'd just found out I was carrying his child, my head was like a toyshop, and another twenty-four hours wouldn't make much difference.

'Well, I was going to catch up with him for a walk this morning but why don't you go and have a word with him instead? I can see him tomorrow,' I said, getting ready to go before he came looking for me.

'You don't mind?'

'No,' I said. 'The sooner it's all sorted the better.' Relieved that I was off the hook, I asked Jeannie to pass on my best and tell Jack I would call him later. Jeannie cut three huge slices of the now iced carrot cake, put her coat on and headed off in the direction of the walled garden.

Dashing outside, I quickly called him. He picked up straight away.

'Shhhhhh,' I said.

'Oh, OK,' he sniggered. 'What?'

I loved that he got it. He didn't ask me what on earth I was playing at, he instinctively understood my sense of urgency and that skulduggery was afoot and he needed to pay attention. With that in mind I very quickly blurted it out.

'I just asked Jeannie about the job. She's keen, but worried about you. She's not daft and knows you've only been keeping her on out of loyalty so she's on her way around to speak to you, to resign, but don't worry, I didn't tell her you were going to make her—'

'Jeannie,' he said loudly, 'is that your famous carrot cake? Come here, you wonderful woman.' And then back into the receiver, 'Thank you for phoning, much appreciated. Goodbye.'

Phew. I leaned up against the wall, and grinned. I was living in a Brian Rix farce.

Chapter 35

I didn't hang about; I drove straight back into town to the property centre where I sat poring over potential flats and drinking hot chocolate.

Thirty minutes later Jeannie called me to officially accept her new position at the Bakehouse. She reported that Jack had been lovely about everything and had made it completely painless for to hand in her resignation. She was over the moon. Great news.

Five minutes later Jack's number flashed up, and with a dry mouth, and fluttering heart, I picked up and tried to sound as normal as I could. His version of events was more or less the same.

'That's brilliant,' I said.

'Yes, it is,' he said, 'but why did you run off? I thought we were going to walk the dogs?'

'Oh, I know, I'm sorry, something came up,' I said, my heart rate increasing to attack zone. 'I was going to ask, if you're going to be working out there tomorrow, why don't I grab a picnic? We could have lunch together?'

'Aw, that's a lovely idea.' The smile in his voice said it all.

'And maybe Jeannie could look after Scarlett, give us some ... privacy.'

God, that sounded like I was going to seduce him. If only, I thought, putting my spare hand back on my belly and patting it.

'I'll ask her, I'm sure she'll be up for that. And Maddy?'

'Yes.'

'No Pot Noodles.'

I laughed as we said goodbye, my hands trembling.

That night I began a Pinterest board for the Bakehouse but I couldn't concentrate, so I read *Pregnancy and Birth* magazine from cover to cover instead. Then I spent a good hour Googling lots of things about babies and pregnancies. I wish I hadn't. I scared myself half to death with horror stories. So, snapping shut my laptop I turned my attention to the telly, only to be faced with a seventeen-year-old girl, knees round her ears, screaming like a banshee as she pushed a baby out. *One Born Every Minute*. I clicked that off sharpish, texted Sarah, and arranged to go around to see her for a cup of tea tomorrow and listened to a meditation audiobook instead.

Mouse phoned me and we had a long chat. She admitted to feeling very stressed about it. Adrian De Witt was in touch daily, and she was feeling the pressure.

'What is it that's bothering you?'

'I think it's the size of the canvases he wants, they are just massive. Much bigger than anything I've worked with before,' she said.

'Oh, right. How big are we talking?'

'The smallest is two metres by one metre.'

'Gosh, and the biggest?'

'Four by four.'

'Metres?'

'Yes!'

'Bloody hell. You'll need to buy a few tins of Dulux paint to cover that lot.'

She giggled.

'I'd love to see what you're doing,' I said.

'You will,' she said. 'Just not yet.'

Choosing not to press her, we moved on to speaking about the Bakehouse; what Will and I had discussed, how it might look, what sort of things would be on the menu, the marketing, in other words, as Will had called it, 'the fun stuff.' Before we said bye, Mouse agreed she would dash off some preliminary sketches over the next few days so we could start pulling it together.

Phew. There was a lot to think about, but this was the perfect time to do it; on my own, feet up, Pinterest, sketch pad, sausage dog and Diet Coke. I would have to stop drinking the latter, because, according to Sarah, it was nutritionally bereft of any vitamins and everything that went into me now went into the baby, too. A sobering thought, as I lay awake for hours worrying about what I had eaten and drunk since the night of conception. Remembering the amount of champagne I threw down my throat at Will and Noel's wedding, I flipped open my laptop and Googled drinking and pregnancy and burst into tears. That was a mistake. Foetal alcohol syndrome was a real thing, so with sweaty palms I went online and made an appointment with my GP. I needed to confess and tell him I was having a baby, which would make it official once and for all.

First thing the following day I texted Will to see if I could pop around. I decided it was only fair to let him in on my secret, too. Bless him, he was seriously worried there was something really wrong with me, so I couldn't help but smile when I thought about his likely reaction. I was on the doorstep by nine.

'You look better,' he said, opening the door.

'Thanks,' I said.

'So, what was so urgent?' he asked as I followed him

through and sat in my usual chair by the Aga, accepting a cup of tea.

'I have news,' I said coyly.

'What now?' he said, intrigued, sitting down and eyeballing me.

'Good news. I am not having a breakdown, I am not losing the plot, but I am, according to Sarah, currently a hostage to my hormones.'

He looked at me. 'Sorry, you've lost me there?'

'OK. Let me put it another way,' I said.

He waited.

'It seems, rather unexpectedly, I am having a baby.'

His eyes bulged, and jaw dropped.

'You're not!'

'I bloody am.'

'Maddy! Oh my God!' he said, jumping up. 'Thank God, I've been so worried about you.'

'I know.' I grinned at him. 'Everything I am feeling are normal symptoms of pregnancy apparently.'

'Oh, I don't know what to say ... I'm speechless,' he said, sitting down again with a thump.

'Tell me about it,' I said.

'I take it it's Jack's?'

'Yes.'

'Awwwwww,' he said, his head tilting to the side.

'I haven't told him yet ... in fact today's the day.'

'How long have you known?'

'Just a couple of days.'

'Well, well, well, Maddy Campbell. Who'd have thought it, you're going to be a mummy,' he said and took my hand across the table, smiling at me with such a soppy face, I felt my chin wobble.

'Stop it,' I said as I felt my eyes fill with tears. 'You know I am not normally a blubber but these hormones! The slightest thing sets me off. There was an advert on TV for Dogs Trust last night and I was inconsolable.'

'Don't worry, I know the one, it gets me every time,' he warbled.

As I scoffed some toast and jam, I updated him on my plan to take Jack for a picnic and break the news gently.

'OK, well, I can help you with that,' he said, standing up and opening a drawer. 'First things first. Linen napkins.'

'Classy,' I said.

'And a proper tartan rug,' he added, striding off along the hall and then, shrieking, ran back and looked at me, clapping his hands, 'I'm going to be an uncle!'

After much excitement, hugging and chatting I escaped Uncle Wills' house.

Ten minutes later I was in the St Andrews deli following his instructions. Olives stuffed with garlic, roasted red peppers and feta, smoked salmon, scotch eggs, bresaola, parmesan, sourdough rolls, posh crisps, a bottle of elderflower cordial, fresh figs, local honey, and a quick pit stop into the Birdie for some cutlery, side plates and a bottle of Jack's favourite wine. Nerves building in my tummy, as I packed the picnic into the basket William had lent me and hauled it into the boot of the Custard Beast, I inhaled a deep breath, and I was off.

Chapter 36

One on the dot I pulled up outside the big house, and my heart was in my mouth. All the bravado was gone, leaving me a watery-legged wreck. Taking a deep breath, I got out of the car, went around the back and retrieved the picnic basket, tucking the rug under my arm as Frank leapt out.

I gave a brief wave to a beaming Jeannie through the kitchen window as I stomped around to the back of the house and into the walled garden.

It was really coming together now, the stour and piles of detritus long gone, replaced by military drills of plump, moist-looking soil, seeds being planted, and green shoots coming up everywhere which was where I found Hamish straddling a raised bed, pushing cuttings down into the soil.

'Looking good,' I remarked.

He grinned back. 'It's really coming together, isn't it?'

'It certainly is, you've performed a bloody miracle,' I said.

'Yeah ...' he said, smiling over his garden.

'Seen Jack?'

'Oh yeah, sorry, I was meant to tell you, he had to go.'

'What?'

'Yeah, he said to say sorry, but he had to go back to the cottage.'

Gutted, I asked, 'Any idea why?'

He shook his head. 'No, sorry, he got a phone call and then just ran off, that's all I know.'

'Oh dear,' I said. 'That sounds serious.'

'Yeah,' he said.

Clearly I wasn't going to get any more information from Hamish, I thought.

'OK, I'll pop in to see Jeannie on my way, see if she knows anything.'

'OK,' he said, bending back down and continuing with the job in hand. He was oblivious to the devastation I was now feeling, having psyched myself up for this moment, brandishing my posh picnic and very near tears. Again.

Heading into the house to use the loo, I popped my head round the door to see Jeannie.

'Maddy, hi!'

'Hey, you don't know what's happening, do you? Jack and I were supposed to be having a picnic, but I gather he's disappeared.'

'Yes, I saw him run off, said he had to go home, something urgent.'

'Did he take the baby with him?'

'Yes, and we'd arranged that I was going to take her,' she said, 'so it beats me.'

Slightly relieved that at least it wasn't anything wrong with the baby, I was at a bit of a loss.

'Come in for a moment,' she said. 'He might be on his way back in a minute.'

So, I did.

'Thanks for phoning me to accept the job,' I said. 'Will and I are both over the moon.'

'Me, too,' she smiled. 'Actually, I've started making a few notes on the sort of thing you might like,' she said, going over to the oven and opening it up, taking out a tray of big cheesy scones.

'Oh,' I said, eyes wide.

'Fancy one?'

'Well, as I don't know when I'm going to get my picnic, yes please!' I said as my stomach burbled, and I put my hand on it.

A moment or two later, I settled down with a mug of soup and a vast warm buttery scone. Jeannie looked at me strangely.

'So, when are you going to tell him?'

'What about?' I said, my voice shrill.

'About the baby.'

'What do you mean?'

'Maddy. I'm not as green as I am cabbage looking. I may be as old as the hills, but I have four grown-up kids of my own.'

I tried to look as if I had no idea what she was talking about as she went on, 'You have stopped drinking, you go to the loo every five minutes, you've taken a sudden liking to baggy sweatshirts, gone off coffee and you are sitting there stroking your stomach.'

I looked down. So I was. I stopped.

'All classic signs,' she concluded.

She tilted her head and smiled at me, her genuine warmth and kindness causing my eyes to fill with tears. Sitting down beside me, she put her arm round my shoulder and pulled me in for a motherly squeeze.

'And your hormones ... How far gone are you?'

'About fourteen weeks,' I warbled.

'I take it Jack's the father.'

I nodded.

'Right,' she said. 'So why haven't you told him yet?'

'He's so wrapped up with Scarlett.'

'Yes, he is,' she said, 'and you can see what a wonderful father he is. What are you scared of?'

'He might not want it.' She looked at me, almost shaking her head as I waffled on. 'I had so many plans, things I wanted to do and now I'm–' I hesitated, '–pregnant.'

'For God's sake, lassie, you are having a baby, it's not the end of anything … it's just the beginning,' she said gently, 'How long have you known?'

'Day before yesterday,' I said, emptying my hooter into the kitchen roll she handed me.

'And who else knows?'

'Sarah, she guessed, Javier, Will, and now you.'

'Aw, Maddy, come here,' she said, holding me close as all my bluff and bluster ebbed away, leaving me feeling like a rather small, insecure child.

'I just don't know where to start,' I said in a small voice.

'Don't underestimate Jack,' she said.

I nodded. 'He's going to have a conniption,' I gulped, my hands in the pockets of my sweatshirt rested on my tummy.

She was right. I had to tell him about the baby today. I felt sick. Jeannie cut to the chase.

'Have you tried phoning him?'

'No,' I said.

'Well, just pick up the phone. If he doesn't want to answer he won't,' she said.

Logic always won the day, I thought, my throat closing up as my shaky hand picked up my phone and I dialled his number.

He picked up straight away.

'Maddy, did you get my message? I'm so sorry, I had to come back to the cottage.'

'Is everything OK?'

'Erm … well … I just got a call and …' His sentence petered out, sounding so unlike him.

'Do you want me to come over?' I asked.

'Erm … yes,' he said and hung up very abruptly.

'Maybe it's something to do with one of the dogs,' said Jeannie, when I reported what he'd said.

'Yeah,' I said.

'Well, he didn't tell you not to go round, did he?'

'No.'

'Well, what are you waiting for, woman? Go, go, go!'

Chapter 37

Pulling up outside the cottage, Jack was watching out the window. Seeing me, he made his way out.

'What's going on?' I asked, turning round, wondering what he was looking for.

'Come in, come in,' he said, ushering me inside and just as he opened his mouth to speak, we heard another car pulling up on the gravel outside. He looked at me, his face white and then before he got a chance to utter a word, the front door flew open and in came Jody. Ignoring Jack and me, she rushed forward, scooping Scarlett up, crying, hugging her and apologising, overwhelming emotion writ large on her face. I thought the baby would freak out but bless her, her wee fat fingers locked onto Jody's jumper and her face lit up like a Christmas tree.

Jack and I sat speechless, watching this unexpected re-union.

God, this woman does nothing by halves, I thought.

Once the tearful stroking, kissing and cuddling abated slightly, she sat back on her heels, holding Scarlett close. Jody turned to her audience.

'Hello,' she said.

'Hi,' I said as Jack stood up, went over to the cupboard, took out a bottle of whisky and poured himself a dram.

'Maddy?'

'No, thanks,' I said.

'Jody?'

She shook her head. 'I'm fine.'

Walking over, he sat down again.

I stood up. 'I think I should go, leave you to it,' I said.

'No, Maddy, stay,' said Jack.

I looked at him, nodded and sat down again as Jody slipped off her jacket and sat on the couch, reattaching herself to a beaming Scarlett.

'How's she been?'

'Great. She's been great. She's got a lovely temperament,' said Jack, looking at the wee girl, smiling gently. He returned his eyes to Jody. 'I'm looking forward to hearing this.'

Sitting forward, clamping her knees together, her hands between them, Jody looked diminished, smaller than I remembered, and so young. This was a different Jody to the one that had left just fourteen weeks ago.

'First, I want to say sorry,' she said. 'I'm so, so sorry.'

Jack inhaled, not saying a word, waiting.

She went on. 'I don't know what the hell I was thinking. Well, I wasn't. I was struggling and I didn't know what else to do. I needed to get my head together. I tried to tell you how I was feeling but I couldn't really put it into words. The whole motherhood thing was so overwhelming. I was scared. I didn't know how to look after a baby!' She stopped and smiled at the rapt wee pudding before continuing, tears in her eyes. 'I know being a mum should be as natural as waking up and breathing in the morning, but for me it was ... different. I was terrified that what I was doing was wrong. I was on my own, I had no one to ask. My lifestyle over the past few years has been nomadic so I thought she would be better without me, that it wouldn't be fair to bring her up like that. I thought she needed stability and that wasn't me. That was you. You seemed so together, so ...'

she hesitated, 'stable. You've lived here since you were born, you know your place in this world. Everyone knows you and that sense of belonging is something I had never seen before. Suddenly it came to me, this is what Scarlett needs: a real home, a real father and a normal life and so I ran.'

'So where did you go?' asked Jack, sitting back, having sunk his dram.

'Well, I just jumped on the first bus I saw, and it took me to Perth where I found a hostel. I was in a terrible state, a blubbering wreck. Believe me, leaving Scarlett was the hardest thing I have ever done, and the people there were lovely. Obviously, I didn't tell them what I'd done but they could see I was in distress so one of the girls took me under her wing. In fact, that's not quite true … I would say she saved me.'

'How?' I asked.

'Well, Helen had been traveling for over three years, and finally she was on her way home, so she just asked me to go, too. And I did.'

'Where's home?'

'Findhorn.'

'The Findhorn Foundation?' I asked.

Jack looked lost.

'Yes,' she said. 'It's the most amazing place, it was set up in the 60s by a woman called Eileen Caddy. At the time it became a Mecca for hippies all over the world and some of their ideas were seen as a bit wacky so people in the area were initially suspicious of these incomers, but over time they integrated and were an accepted community. Now, their ethics and way of life is used as an example of how sustainable living can work. They were way ahead of their time. In fact, NATO now send people to Findhorn from all over the world to learn from this community. It's an amazing place.

'Anyway, this was where Helen was brought up. Her folks are still there, and she was heading back to settle, so I went with her.'

Jody smiled, a confident smile, as she looked at her baby.

'For me, it felt like coming home. It was what I had been searching for. A community of people helping and working together for the common good. It's an amazing place and the perfect place to bring up a child,' she said.

'So, you're staying.'

'In Scotland, yes,' she said. 'I have never felt more sure of anything in my life.'

'Well,' said Jack.

Jody went on. 'I will never be able to apologise enough for what I did to you. Or to thank you enough for what you have done for Scarlett.'

'She was easy to have around,' said Jack, choosing to brush over the stress and anxiety the past weeks had caused him. The elephant in the room was still there. I wondered who would address it first.

'So, there is another thing,' said Jody, with an expression that suggested the elephant was about to be tackled.

'The matter of parentage,' said Jack, kicking that elephant right into the centre of the room. I gulped.

'Yes,' she nodded.

'Well, I can help you there,' he said. 'The first thing I did after you left was do a DNA test.'

I stared at him with my mouth open.

'So, you know?' she said.

'Yes. Do you?'

She nodded.

His demeanour changed as he sat upright. 'So if you knew I wasn't Scarlett's father, what the hell were you doing leaving her with me? A virtual stranger?' he asked.

My head was reeling taking this all in. So, he had done a DNA test. He knew Scarlett wasn't his and yet he hadn't uttered a word about it to anyone.

Jody teared up again. 'I'm sorry, really, but what I told you about my ex-husband was all true, he is not a good person. Even during our marriage, he was sleeping around and when I told him I was pregnant he told me he didn't want me or the baby, which is when he told me to get an abortion.'

'Back up,' said Jack. 'So, you're telling me when we slept together, you knew you were already pregnant.'

She went beetroot.

'Yes.'

'Jesus,' he said, sitting back, the magnitude of what she had just admitted sinking in.

FFS, I thought, this was like *EastEnders* on acid, you couldn't make it up.

'I can't believe this!' said Jack, who got up and began angrily pacing. 'Jody, what the hell were you thinking?'

'Well, I wasn't. I was so upset. There I was at my sister's wedding, she was so happy, and I was so miserable. Adam was there with some bimbo and knowing everything he knew, he completely ignored me. I just felt so alone and then I met you and–' she glanced at me, '–and ... well ... you know.'

I'm sure I went beetroot at this stage. Boy, did I know, I thought, but I kept schtum.

'You really played me,' he said, shaking his head.

'No!' she said. 'It wasn't like that. I just left it as it was, a one-night stand, end of. And then after I had Scarlett, I was a mess. Desperate, alone, unable to sleep, and I had no idea what to do, so I got to thinking you seemed so nice, and normal, and I just thought ... what a great Dad you would make.'

'Jesus, and you had the audacity to turn up out of the blue

on my doorstep, telling me I was the father of your child. That is unforgivable,' he said.

'I know, I know, but I was totally on my own. I haven't seen my parents for years, my brother in Japan is useless, and if I hung about in Darwin, word would have soon got out that I was having the baby, and my ex-husband would have made my life hell. That's why I came over here and had the baby.'

'You had her here?' Jack was sideswiped again.

Shit, this was getting worse, I thought.

'Yes. I had to get as far away from my ex as possible. If he found out that I had had the baby, I was terrified he would change his mind, want to see her or even worse, try to take her from me. After all, on the surface he is the successful one, a businessman with plenty of cash in the bank, on paper he looks the better bet ... and I couldn't bear that. I couldn't stand the thought of him having anything to do with her or me.'

'So how on earth did you find me and why?'

'It wasn't hard,' she said. 'On Gordon's Facebook. You're quite memorable.' She had the audacity to flutter her eye-lashes at him. His face was positively thunderous.

'So, what are your plans now?' he growled.

She looked at the door and then the floor and had the good grace to appear embarrassed.

She looked desperate. 'Well, erm ... Helena's outside, she drove me down.'

Jack stared at her, watching as Scarlett clung to her mother's finger in a familiar comforting way.

'So, I wanted to tell you the truth, explain what happened and then ...' she petered out.

'Crash out of my life just like you crashed in. Jesus, Jody.' He was exasperated. 'I could have been anyone, any kind of man. How could you leave your own flesh and blood with a stranger? If I let Scarlett go with you, how can I be sure you won't hand her over to the next poor sod you have sex with or meet on a bus?' he barked.

She looked terrified, like he was going to assert some sort of ownership over her child, which was when my instinct to interfere kicked in.

Jumping up, I said, 'Listen, why don't I put the kettle on? We can all have a cup of tea and calm down a bit.' Jody looked at me gratefully, Jack sitting back and seeming done in. 'And it's bloody freezing out there. Why don't you ask Helena to come in and join us?' I added.

'Thank you,' said Jody, nervously looking at Jack before quietly opening the door and waving to Helena, walking out to meet her friend.

I turned to Jack. 'I know this is a bloody nightmare, but surely this is for the best?'

He looked at me with an expression I had never seen before.

'The best for who?' he snarled. Ouch. I stepped back, not quite sure who that barbed comment was directed at.

A whip of cold air arrived in the room with the two women and as they closed the door and took their jackets off, I made my way through to the kitchen, put the kettle on and stayed there as long as possible before reappearing with teapot, mugs, milk and sugar. Jody was sitting on the lumpy sofa with Scarlett still clinging joyfully to her. Next to her sat an older woman with a smiley fresh face scrubbed of makeup. She wore a brightly coloured dress, black boots and was talking directly to Jack in an English accent.

'Yes. I have a twenty-three-year-old daughter, Tallulah,' she went on. 'Had her when I was fifteen. We had a difficult start, Tallulah and I.' She smiled at me as I put the tray down and continued, 'I was young, I couldn't settle, but in time it all came good. We are great now. She's at Exeter Uni, studying anthropology. When she finally left home, I did the travelling I always wanted to do when I was younger. Got it out of my system once and for all, and on my way home, well, that's when I met Jody.' She smiled.

Jack was clearly interviewing her.

'Tea?' I asked.

'Yes please,' she said, taking the mug from my outstretched hand and smiling. 'Thanks.'

'Jody?'

She nodded, still nervous as a cat about what Jack was going to say or do next.

'Jack?' I asked.

He shook his head and continued the inquisition. 'So, what are you going to do now?' he asked both women.

'Well, I am going to help Jody get all her paperwork in order and we are going to try to get her UK citizenship.'

'So, you really are staying?' He addressed this question to Jody.

'Yes,' she said, slipping her hand into Helena's. 'Like I said, I have finally found where I want to be and ...'

Helena returned her gaze. 'With whom.'

I smiled. It was rather sweet. They were clearly in love. Helena looked like a woman who knew her stuff and Jody, underneath her understandable nerves, looked well, and, when she gazed at Helena, clearly happy.

'What about Scarlett?' asked Jack.

'Well, she will be with us, of course,' said Jody.

'I have had an empty nest for three years,' said Helena, 'and meeting Jody wasn't in my life plan, but you never know, what's around the corner, do you?' She smiled. 'We want to spend our lives together, that much we know, and

Scarlett–' she looked at the rapt wee pudding, '–is the icing on the cake.' She picked up the pink-cheeked baba for the first time and addressed her directly. 'I was told you were the cutest little person on the planet, and I can see that was not one word of a lie, you are a gorgeous wee thing.' She grinned at the baby who fluttered her eyelashes, and rewarded Helena with a face-splitting gummy smile.

'She's got teeth!' gasped Jody.

'Two,' said Jack.

'Oh, look,' said Helena, putting her hand into Scarlett's mouth. 'Aren't they wee beauties?'

Scarlett held her mouth open proudly as the two women cooed and cuddled her.

Jack and I sat silently watching as this new little family joyfully met and re-met each other. I looked at Jack. His expression of loss confirmed he knew what he had to do.

'Well,' said Helena, standing up.

'Yes,' said Jody, taking the cue. 'There is no point in prolonging this. I think we had better be making a move. It's a long drive back...'

Jack stood up. 'I'll get Scarlett's bits and pieces together,' he said, striding across the room and loping up the stairs two at a time.

'He's going to miss her,' I said.

'I know but I promise we'll keep in touch,' said Jody. 'Let him know how she's doing. I can never thank him enough for what he's done for her, for me...' she finished, tears in evidence.

'Right, well, I better have a check around here,' I said, standing up and picking up some of Scarlett's bits and pieces, which were everywhere. A few minutes later Jack was back downstairs with a large rucksack overspilling with clothes and toys.

'Gosh,' said Jody. 'She's got some new stuff.'

'Hmmm,' was all Jack managed to say, not trusting himself to speak. He took the bag I had filled, unplugged the baby monitor that sat on the table next to the TV, wrapped the flex round it and popped it on top. 'The other half is in the rucksack,' he said to no one in particular.

'Oh, and you will need this,' he added, digging around in the pile of coats that hung on the back of the door, retrieving her padded, pink snowsuit with rabbit ears, and handing it to Jody.

'Thanks,' said Jody, smiling gently.

'OK,' he said. 'I think that's about it. If I find anything else I will send it on ...'

His voice broke, giving away that he was finding this a lot harder than he was letting on.

'OK,' said Helena, realising this was agony for him and as with all farewells, brevity would be the best course of action.

'Here's our address,' she said, handing over a handwritten note. 'Come and stay anytime.' Jack took the note and put it on the table.

'I'll take this lot,' she said, heaving up the rucksack and bag. 'And wait for you outside,' she said to Jody tactfully, nodding at me and Jack and taking her leave.

'You'll need her car seat,' said Jack. 'Land Rover's open.'

Suddenly feeling superfluous, this was my cue to make myself scarce.

'I'm just on my way, too, so I can give you a hand with that,' I said, giving Scarlett a peck on the cheek. 'Bye, darling.' I dashed out after Helena.

Once I had wrangled the car seat from the jeep into the back of Helena's stalwart old Volvo, I stood back.

'There was no easy way to do this,' she said.

'No,' I said, 'but it's for the best. She needs her mum.'

'Yes. And Jody is so much better. She's settled, she's ... well, maybe in time you can both come up and see her,' she ventured.

'Oh, Jack and me? We're not ...'

'Oh,' she said. 'I thought ...'

'No,' I said.

'Oh. OK. Well then, please tell Jack he is welcome anytime. Time is a great healer.'

'I will,' I said, warming to this woman I had only just met, kindness emanating from her in waves.

Then the front door opened and out came Jody, tears running down her face, Scarlett glassy-eyed in her arms, looking a little confused. The front door closed behind her. I helped her put Scarlett in the car seat before saying goodbye.

'Is he OK?' I asked, indicating to the cottage and the broken-hearted man within.

To which she just burst into tears.

As they drove off, I stood watching their brake lights disappear down the drive. I was unsure whether to go back to see Jack, or just head home. The closed door made it clear he wanted to be alone, plus I had no idea what to say. It was a heart-breaking scene. Taking a deep breath, I hesitated before knocking on the door and waited. Nothing. I tried once again, this time speaking to the closed door, imagining the anguished man within.

'Jack, it's Maddy. I understand you want to be alone, please know I am here for you when you're ready,' I said before adding, 'OK, I'll leave you in peace then.' I trudged back to the car.

The hurdle that had kept us apart gone, the insecurity of Scarlett's parentage no longer an issue, but instead of relief my heart was heavy as I climbed into the Custard Beast and chugged away. What a shocking turn of events.

Bloody Jody. I couldn't believe how much she had screwed things up again.

And I was shocked that Jack had done a DNA test months ago and known all along he wasn't Scarlett's biological father, and that he had chosen not to utter a word to anyone. Not even me. The most impressive thing was, even with that knowledge, he had invested so much of his time and emotional energy in that gorgeous wee baby. I had watched him closely over these past weeks, his genuine care, love, and concern obvious, which was why I had been sure he was convinced she was his biological child. But she wasn't, which was why Jody had just effectively ripped the child from his arms, disregarding his feelings completely once again. No wonder he was utterly distraught.

Chapter 38

In times of trauma my coping mechanism was to walk St Andrews beach. Miles and miles of golden sand, a churning sea, salty air, and the refreshing blast of wind never failed to bring me back to some sort of equilibrium.

It was not up to me to tell the others what had happened, so I would steer clear of everyone for a day or so, let the dust settle, and let him tell them in his own time. But right now, I was absolutely starving, so when I pulled up at the beach, with Frank straining to get out for a walk, I remembered the delicious picnic in the back. It was foolish to waste it so, opening the boot, I took the basket and rug and tramped down onto the beach. The tide was out, there were only a handful of people walking, so I walked about a hundred metres, unfolded the rug and flopped down on it. It was a warm enough day, so with my jacket on, I sat hunched up with Frank sitting under my knees, munching my way through the delicious hamper and was suddenly overtaken by an overwhelming feeling of melancholy. 'Alone again,' I said, as my sausage-shaped friend looked at me from under his unruly eyebrows, as if to say, 'No, you're not! I'm here, too.'

After eating far too much, I lay back on the rug, closed my eyes and concentrated on just breathing in and out, trying to make sense of what had just happened.

Anger boiled up as I recalled the moment Jody had marched in, ignoring Jack, and going straight over to the baby to reclaim her without any thought as to how it might impact the man she had trusted enough to leave her baby with. In one fell swoop she had completely upended Jack's life, for the second time. And mine.

I had no idea how this was going to play out. The idea of me adding to the confusion he must be feeling by telling him I was carrying his child might very well push him over the edge if he wasn't already over it. He needed space and time to come to terms with what had just happened. I would have to be patient. Whatever happened over the next few days would dictate how I was going to handle things. But now I felt absolutely done in. I had been up to high doh ready to tell Jack everything and here we all were, yet again, no further on.

Panic rose briefly but I managed to tamp it down as I realised whatever happened with Jack, I was wrong; I was not alone nor would I ever be alone again, and that gave me strength, I thought, instinctively touching my protruding tum.

'I'm sorry,' I said out loud to whoever was in there, listening to every word I said. I lay on the sand and began telling my innermost thought and secrets.

Firstly, I said sorry.

'Sorry for not realising you were there,' I warbled, both hands stroking my tum. 'You rather took me by surprise, but the most important thing you need to know is now I know you are there, I want you; I really, really do. And now I am getting used to the idea, I am so excited and so grateful that this has happened, and I know we will be just fine. So, little bean, know that you are loved, and though I have no idea how to be a mum, I promise I will do my best to look after you and care for you.' I hesitated as all the picnic items I had scoffed caused my belly to squirble and then I held my breath. 'That's not indigestion,' I said in wonder. My heart swelled, as I felt it again... a tiny fluttering silverfish of movement in my tummy and I knew then, without any doubts, everything was going to be alright.

Chapter 39

For the next two days I lay low.

I was mindful of giving Jack space but equally I was worried. I could see on WhatsApp he had been online, but he hadn't read or responded to my messages. I'd restrained myself to two messages. The first an hour or so after Jody had gone, and the second the following morning asking if he needed anything. As far as I knew he hadn't told anyone about what had happened, so in order to respect his privacy I concocted a story to explain his absence to the others.

Hamish was a pushover and would have believed anything. All he cared about was his precious garden. Hamish was working in the garden every hour that God sent. Living out at Kelso Lodge meant he could roll out of bed and work in it until dusk, and often longer, before rolling back into bed. His progress was impressive – once the donkey work of clearing dead and dying trees, plants, and ivy was done, the form and design of the garden began to emerge, marked by a series of reclaimed stone paths separating off individual areas. The stone itself had been indistinguishable from the earth until Hamish, bit by bit, revealed it from under the thick mossy floor that had accumulated over years. With all the ivy and weeds gone, the fruit trees stood, gnarled and ancient, breathing again in the space cleared for the first time in years. One lunchtime as we sat munching sandwiches and drinking elderflower cordial, admiring his handiwork, we were rather surprised when Barclay shuffled into the garden, in a far less blustering way.

'Afternoon,' he said. 'Mind if I sit?'

'No,' said Hamish with great trepidation.

'Would you like a cold drink?' I asked.

'Yes please,' he said, accepting a plastic cup of juice. His eyes scanned the garden. 'It looks like things are coming on.'

Of course, Hamish on his pet subject was off, delivering a full update and ended by confessing he was a bit stuck. Now he had freed up the trees, they desperately needed to be fed and pruned and he was terrified of doing the wrong thing.

Barclay listened and then suggested Hamish contact St Andrews University, saying there was bound to be a professor specialising in botany, so why not find out who he was and invite him out to see the project.

Hamish was very grateful and contacted St Andrews University immediately, who put him in touch with a Professor Leopold Harrison. The good professor was so thrilled to be consulted and he came out to visit the garden the very next day, and most days after that, too. His wee face was a picture when he entered the walled garden for the first time, reminding us all what a very special place we all had the privilege to be working in. Leo, as he insisted we call him, was rapt as he walked up and down examining the trees, shrubs and plants. We were fairly sure he would manage to identify the majority of things growing in the garden without any difficulty. He asked if we could help taking notes and labelling, but Hamish and Big Gordy were still doing a lot of heavy lifting work and helping with the Bakehouse. Will and I were up to our eyes in the marketing, menu and launch plan, so it was Barclay who offered to assist him. The first day Barclay was around for any length of time we were all a little nervous, but he and Leo seemed to hit it off, so we soon got used to the pair of them ambling about chatting, mapping and photographing everything. A few of the older rickety trees were even designated great examples of rare and specific species, so they had to be protected.

Hamish set about following Leo's instructions to the letter. And so, soil, minerals and great piles of manure began to arrive by the truck load. I swear it was just days till the trees began to perk up and very quickly after that one or two started to sprout green shoots.

Hamish was obsessed. His fingernails were constantly encrusted in mud, as was his face, but underneath the filth he exuded a healthy glow, a weather-beaten, sunburnt goodness which made his light blue eyes shine. He had never been happier.

Mouse wasn't much better. She had been holed up in her studio since she'd moved her stuff in. Periodically emerging covered in paint and a clarted smock, she would wander around the garden, sit quietly, smile, and occasionally chat but her mind was elsewhere. Despite this she had, as promised, sent over some rough sketches of the proposed interior for the Bakehouse which I loved. What a talented woman she was. She completely understood what William and I were trying to do, and that expenditure was limited. Her design celebrated the historic nature of the building, highlighting the natural assets of the stone with clever lighting. The colours and furnishings were carefully thought out to blend in, give it a sense of having been there for a long, long time. Everything was pared down, from the reclaimed oak for the floor to the plain walls, the only statement pieces being a couple of vintage lights which she put me on red alert to source on eBay. A substantial island would run parallel and in front of the huge stone ovens nearly the full width of the Bakehouse, the top made of thick reclaimed oak, the front covered in battered copper, a nod to the little oval bar in the Birdie which was dimpled copper and screamed 1970s which I loved. Open chunky wooden shelves would run along the entirety of the back wall for stacking plates, cups, mugs, jugs, and tea pots; all of which she wanted to source from Oranmore Pottery, a local potter who created colourful, hand-painted crockery to add real warmth. She had marked out four large pots in each of the corners of the room, suggesting that Hamish would be the one to decide on the right statement plant not so make sure it would survive in that environment.

Rather than lots of small tables, she had drawn three long refectory tables, each of which would sit up to twelve people, with a mixtures of benches and mismatched wooden chairs. More sociable, she said, which I also loved.

There was a shelf built along the outside wall, for dog bowls, and large brass rings for people to tie up their dogs.

The loos were in a separate bespoke building outside. Jack's idea. Rather than sacrifice valuable seating space, the planners had been amenable, as in every other aspect we were following their stringent rules, in renovating this historic site. Made entirely of ash, she proposed a standalone wooden box which held four loos and a large central sink. The idea is that the ash would weather nicely into the surroundings and look like it belonged.

She had listened to William and I jabbering on about how we imagined it and had amazingly captured the very essence of it. Yes, it was a lot to do, but I had a fire in my belly, as well as a baby, and I felt more than up to the job.

Neither Hamish nor Mouse baulked when I told them that Jack had gone off to spend a couple of days in Perthshire with his mum, who had sprained her ankle and couldn't get around very well.

Of course, Jeannie was another matter. The last time she had seen me I was all gung-ho, heading off to tell Jack I was pregnant. I told her the same story as the others, but she wasn't having any of it.

'Maddy,' she said, looking at me. 'I am not as green as I am cabbage looking.'

Denial was futile, plus I needed to tell someone, so I did.

'Oh, that poor baby,' she said.

'Scarlett?'

'No, I mean Jack,' she said.

'Oh, right. Yes. So, what do you think I should do?'

'I think you're doing the right thing by giving him time to come to terms with what's happened. And you say Jack knew she wasn't his flesh and blood all this time?' she asked again.

I nodded, 'Yeah.'

'Well, well, the mark of the man indeed,' she said. 'He will know in his heart of hearts that it's for the best in the long run, but that doesn't make it any easier to bear.'

I sighed, my hands resting on my belly as she went on, 'But when he does come out from under his buckie, and he finds out you're having his baby, he will be the happiest man in the world.'

'I really hope you're right,' I said, not quite as confident of the rapturous response she predicted.

'He's a good man, Maddy.'

'He is,' I agreed. Jeannie confirmed that she was more than happy to go along with my story about him being in Perthshire for a few days, but I would keep her up to speed with any changes.

Since the morning after Scarlett left, I had been messaging Jack first thing in the morning and early evening, attaching photos of our progress at the Bakehouse and garden, in the hope that might engage him. But no. Increasingly concerned he wouldn't be looking after himself, wouldn't be eating, just drinking, I had asked Claude to make me a pot of venison casserole which I left on Jack's doorstep with a note. I knocked and waited. Duke and Gaston barked in response, but Jack didn't answer. I really thought that this might work but no dice. The following day I returned to the cottage again and was relieved to see the pot and the note had gone but frustratingly still not one word from him. Working on the assumption that he had eaten the casserole, I began to drop off hot food out to him daily. It was easy to do. Claude assumed it was for me as he knew my cooking skills stopped at Pot Noodle, which appalled him, so he asked no questions.

Chapter 40

Gurgling, nausea and extraordinary farting seemed to be the three main side effects of pregnancy.

I mean, I can't imagine Kim Kardashian rushing to open a window and light candles in case she asphyxiates, before Kanye West gets in from work. But as I don't live with Kanye or anyone for that matter, it's not that important.

As I sip fresh ginger in boiling water in an attempt to quell said nausea, I cringed that I had seriously doubted the probability of getting pregnant after a one-night stand when Jody pitched up in St Andrews with Scarlett.

Almost one year to the day later Jack and I had our one-night stand and history had repeated itself so here I am up the duff, with a bun in the oven, pregnant.

Can I just say, and this is important, it so didn't feel like a one-night stand? It felt like the resolution to so many questions, feelings, doubts, relationships, wishes and yet in the cold light of day, the fact is, it was a one-night stand. So much as it irks me to admit it, Jody and I are on level pegging.

Chapter 41

I was in my second trimester now and I was experiencing a sudden surge of energy and drive to get things done. Top of my list, other than Jack, was somewhere to live.

Mouse was essentially living with Hamish out at the big house, albeit unofficially, which meant her bedsit was sitting empty. So I did a deal with her: I would move in until I found a more permanent solution, and whilst I was there, I would pay her rent. Still unaware of my pregnancy, she understood my need for a centrally heated place to stay with an inside loo, Wi-Fi, and no fungi growing on the walls. William and Noel were relieved that I was leaving the bothy behind and helped me put all my stuff into bin liners and lugged all my worldly goods, such as they were, to the bedsit the day after I did the deal with Mouse. The relief of being somewhere warm and safe was wonderful. On my first night, I soaked in the bath for over an hour which was blissful, so I bought Mouse's favourite biscuits and went out to thank her personally the following day.

Mindful of the fact that her studio was sacrosanct, I texted her when I was outside and was pleased to be invited in. The last time I had been in, half of the space was taken up with all fifteen blank canvases of differing sizes stacked up against one wall. The smallest ones were a mighty two metres by one metre and the mightiest one was a vast four by four metres, which wouldn't even fit into the studio, so it was propped up downstairs in the main stable area. The proposed sizes had been driven by De Witt who had gone to great lengths to reiterate the importance of creating real impact in the substantial exhibition space. The scale of these pictures was far bigger than anything she had tackled before and as a result Mouse had taken some time to put the first daub of paint on as she researched, walked, read, dreamt and drank, waiting for inspiration for the collection to hit and then thank God, suddenly, BANG! One day she was off. Like a demon.

Clomping up the stairs to her eyrie, rustling the bag of cookies, I hollered, 'Get the kettle on.' As I stepped into the studio, my jaw hit the floor.

'Oh my God, Mouse,' I said, walking up and down trying to take in what I was looking at. Bold splashes of every colour of green, glossy, delicate details contrasted with almost print block leaves, all insinuating nature, abundant, growing, lush, beautiful confident smears of oil. Up close it was impossible to understand what you were looking at but after taking a step back, they were jaw-dropping.

'You really like them?' said Mouse, blinking rapidly, flattening her fringe down repeatedly with the palm of her hand whilst biting her top lip.

'I love them. They are extraordinary,' I warbled, walking up to her, and giving her a massive bear hug. She giggled.

'You're the first person that's seen them,' she confessed.

'What about Hamish?'

'Nope,' she said. 'I wanted him to wait.'

'Wow. He's going to be blown away,' I said. 'I am so excited for you. These will cause a sensation.' She released her fringe, and full on grinned.

'Has Adrian seen them yet?'

'Only in photos – he just said he would leave me to get

on. I'm going down to Edinburgh to see him tomorrow, for the last time, before we send them down to be hung.'

'So exciting! So have you come up with a title for the exhibition yet?'

'Hamish's Garden,' she said.

'Perfect. These pictures feel like a living, breathing garden, they really do,' I enthused.

She visibly relaxed, flumping down on the burst sofa that had been dragged over from the old house, as I continued walking up and down, appreciating her extraordinary talent. She was on schedule for the stuff to be sent off in just six days, but the stress she had been under I was disturbed to see it manifesting in different ways. The confidence she had found in the past year was diminished, the thick makeup she once wore reappearing. Her long gone old habit of stroking her fringe flat repeatedly when talking had also made a return, along with the reappearance of half a dozen piercings. I suspected that underneath her painting smock, the propensity to drape herself in black clothing would be in evidence, too.

Wishing her well, I left her in peace, and I decided to speak to Hamish, see what he thought about it, so I made my way around to the garden.

'You looking for me?' he squawked from the branches of a substantial fruit tree, as he watched me tramp around the garden.

'Yes,' I said, walking over to the tree. 'You got a minute?'

'For you? Of course.'

'Just wondering how you think Mouse is doing. I haven't had a chance to have a proper chat with her for ages.'

'Me neither,' he said brightly. 'She's locked in that studio all day.'

'Yeah, but you see her at night presumably?'

'Well, to be honest I'm working out here till it's dark and she's in there until about midnight, so by the time she does come to bed I'm usually out cold. I've never slept so well.'

'Right, it's just that I noticed she's put some of her piercings back in.'

'Has she?'

'Has she? For God's sake, Hamish, there are holes in her actual nose, eyebrow, ear and lip.'

'Oh. Well, maybe she takes them out at night,' he said.

I rolled my eyes at him. 'You are a useless crater. I can see why you're so at home up there, hanging about in a tree, you're much further down the food chain than the rest of us,' I said.

'Cheeky besom,' he chuckled, from on high, plucking a plum and throwing it at me as I retreated, screeching. Bloody men. Observational skills of a donut, I thought, stomping off.

'Oh, Maddy, before you go, when's Jack back?'

'I don't know. Why?'

'Well, I think he's pissed off with me for some reason, he hasn't been responding to any of my jokes.'

'He's just busy, I'm sure, don't get paranoid,' I said, panning him off.

'Yeah, fair enough,' he mumbled.

'You keep an eye on Mouse,' I ordered.

'Aye, OK, will do,' he said, looking slightly embarrassed.

The fact that Hamish noticed Jack's lack of communication meant things were definitely coming to a head, so I swept off to have a word with Jeannie.

By the time I had updated her on Hamish's uncharacteristic observation that Jack hadn't even been in touch with him, she was frantic. She was set on driving straight over to his place, until I reminded her that he was eating the food I was delivering so we knew he was in there and not starving.

Nonetheless, we concurred that this couldn't go on much longer, so we made a pact; we would wait two more days, giving him a full week of space, before going around to see him.

Chapter 42

As I left Jeannie, I noticed Hamish heading up to Mouse's studio. He gave me one of his gangly waves and a thumbs up. I smiled back, pleased that he had heard me earlier, and took the opportunity to wander back through the garden to check progress. I'd not been into the bakehouse for a couple of days, because things had been so hectic.

Opening the door of the Hobbit House I walked into the ante room. It was now cleared completely and had a robust solid wood floor, while the walls were skimmed and waiting to be painted. Five arts and crafts wall lights glowed when I flicked the switch on. Even whilst it was completely empty, it had an almost magical atmosphere. There was still a good amount of work to be done, the walls less than halfway through being skimmed. The working island, which lay parallel to the massive stone ovens, had been marked out on the floor. Standing behind the chalk rectangle, looking over the length of the room, gave me a real sense of how it would feel when it was finished. Exciting stuff, I thought, investigating the other end of the room from where ladders, pots of paint, dust sheets and the like lay in a heap. Stomping over to what would soon be the main entrance, and unlocking the surface bolts, it opened smoothly, leading me to the generous parking area.

The exterior was looking sharp, the repointing finished, and the door itself daubed in various greens, blues and even a bright red as William and I debated what colour we thought it should be. Snapping a photo of the latest test pot colours I decided I would send that to Jack later to ask which one he liked best. You can't blame a girl for trying. The parking area was much more spacious, now that it was flattened and cleaned, the boundaries marked using logs. I reckoned there was easily enough parking for about twenty-five cars. Very ambitious, I thought, looking back at the Bakehouse and realising the roofers had taken down the scaffolding. It looked wonderful; the dull grey characterless building we had uncovered just weeks before had perked up considerably, the long chunky stone house set off by the newly repaired, fixed and cleaned red pantile roof. The tiles were now cleaned, so they were no longer covered in moss. I took pictures to show Will, and Jack, who I knew would be thrilled with the progress, as would the guy from Historic Scotland. Despite the day I had, I could not help but feel a sense of pride and excitement. We were nearly there.

Chapter 43

Wandering back to the car, deep in thought, I nearly crashed right into Claude and Jeannie.

'Where are you two off to?' I asked.

Jeannie looked coyly at Claude who appeared a little flustered.

'Dinner,' she said demurely.

'Nice,' I said. 'Enjoy yourselves.' I upped my pace to get into the car.

I was pleased their liaison was ongoing, Jeannie deserved to find happiness. She had been widowed some eleven years and the two of them looked good together, I mused, heading to the Birdie for my tea. I was starving again and if Javier was cooking, he would whip me up a poached egg on toast without making a production out of it whilst I sent these latest pics to Jack and Will and checked my to-do list for the next day. As I sat eating and reading, there was a sudden knock on the window which made me jump out of my skin. It was Sarah. Beckoning her in, she joined me.

'I've only got a few minutes, nipped out to get some milk and spotted you. How the hell are you doing? I haven't seen you for days.'

'Yeah, I'm feeling so much better,' I said, feeling guilty as I said it.

'You look it!' she said, scrutinising me. 'You're blooming.'

I looked back at her, specifically her lush shiny mane of

straight dark hair. 'If I'm blooming, you're blooming gorgeous,' I said.

She laughed. 'Ha! I presume you haven't told him yet?'

'No,' I said and then avoiding her eye said, 'Actually, he's been away for a day or two.'

'Ah, I wondered. I was due to look after Scarlett yesterday morning, but I didn't hear anything so assumed he must have had a change of plan.'

Oh God, how could I be so thoughtless? Poor Sarah, of course she was going to be upset at the sudden disappearance of Scarlett. After all, Sarah had had a lot more to do with the wee pudding than me. Yes, she looked after her occasionally, but more importantly, Jack had had Sarah on speed dial during those first few days and weeks, as she led him through the ABCs of how to look after a baby. I just couldn't lie to her, and it was only fair to tell her what had happened. So, I did.

As the story unfolded, she held her hands over her mouth, shocked to the core.

'I'm sure Scarlett will be fine,' I said. 'Jody was so much more together, and Helena was one of those capable sort of characters, you know the type. It's Jack I'm worried about.'

'Poor guy,' she said, shaking her head. 'I'm not surprised he's gone to ground. What a bolt from the blue.'

'Jeannie and I are going to flush him out if he doesn't make a move within the next forty-eight hours,' I said.

'Well, if you need my help, just say,' she said and then her hands went back up to her face again. 'God, Mads, I just can't believe it.'

Glancing at her phone, she said she had to go. Sworn to secrecy, she hugged me before she left, still trying to take on board the news.

★

After she left, I sent Jack the pictures from today to get his opinion, along with a hilarious shot of Hamish in the fruit tree.

Then I sent virtually the same message to William who came straight back to me.

Thanks, Mads. Looking good and re door defo not red. Yuk!
Love W XXX

I smiled and lingered another few minutes willing Jack to respond, too, but no, nothing. So, I said my thanks and goodbye to Javier and the guys and headed home.

Chapter 44

The combination of having a nice place to stay and this surge of energy, which was coursing through me courtesy of my hormones, had me up with the lark. My to-do list, which this time last week would have sent me into a spiral, didn't faze me at all.

The Birdie and Bramble continued to be busy. The boys had it all under control but nonetheless I liked to pop in every day just to give them a bit of moral support and let them know that they were very much a part of what was going on. Plus, my appetite was back with a vengeance, so I would have my breakfast there and work from there for a while, before heading to the Bakehouse to see what was happening.

On this morning, when I arrived, there was not a soul to be seen. Jeannie and I were meeting later in the afternoon with William to discuss the proposed Bakehouse menu, but I expected to see her as she was always up and at it early. I checked my watch. It was after ten, and there was no sign of her car.

I knew Mouse was in Edinburgh, but there was no Hamish or Gordy either, so I headed straight for the Bakehouse for a gander. The island was due to be built today, which I was very excited about and I wanted to check there was someone there getting on with things. Entering through the Hobbit house door, I was relieved to see there was already a hive of activity. Two painters, both with beanies on, stood on top of their ladders with rollers, covering the walls and ceiling in a neutral, chalky white in time to a tinny battery-operated radio that was blaring out dance music at one hundred and twenty beats per minute. If they kept in time, it wouldn't take them long. Lee the joiner had already begun construction of the frame and base of the island, the smell of freshly cut sawdust everywhere.

'Morning boss,' he said. Cheery chap.

'All good?' I asked.

'Aye, I'll have this lot done by the end of the day. The copper panel is coming later this morning and the worktop this afternoon. The shelves for the back wall here have been made off site so they're coming with the rest of the stuff. They won't take long to fit.'

'Brilliant,' I beamed.

'Aye, and once these two clowns have finished—' he waved at the young painters, 'we can start getting your floor down.'

'Great. Thanks. I will leave you to it,' I said, going back out the way I came in.

The signage for the Walled Garden, the Birdie Bakehouse, and the directions guiding customers where to park were all stacked up in the Hobbit house, so on my way back I unboxed and unwrapped them to check everything was the way it should be. They looked great.

I was keen to get online and keep an eye on the two light fittings Mouse had earmarked for us on eBay. The last time I looked I was the highest bidder, but there was only about an hour to go, so I didn't want to take any chances. With this in mind, I made my way over to the big house and settled in the kitchen. Jeannie was still AWOL, so I made myself a cup of tea, dug out my laptop and logged on. Satisfied I was still top bidder, I WhatsApped Jack the photos of the signs and the painters in their beanies and set about toasting my bum on the Aga, when Jeannie breezed in, looking very flushed.

'Sorry!' she said, sweeping in with a basket brimming over with stuff.

'What have you been up to?' I teased.

She looked at me, eyebrows aloft, and said nothing. I gave her a direct look, watching her pinking up further.

'Oh my God,' I said.

She smiled coyly again, and tittered like a schoolgirl.

'OH MY GOD,' I repeated. 'Really?'

Without a word, unless I was very much mistaken, this exchange of looks and giggles insinuated Jeannie and Claude had just spent the night together. Her head bobbled from side to side, her face was red, and her eyes sparkled. Most important of all, there was no denial.

'Now what time is William due to sort out this menu?' she asked, changing the subject and confirming my suspicions at the same time.

'Not till later,' I said, 'but why don't we make a start and have a look at what we've got?'

Reading through her ideas, she had been very thorough indeed. Included were the ingredients list, the costings, and the recipe for each item, too. I was impressed. Jeannie had done a sterling job; she was more than on point with everything William and I had discussed.

'You've absolutely nailed this,' I said.

'Thanks, but I can't take all the credit,' she said.

'Oh. I wonder who might have helped you with it?' I said knowingly.

She burst out laughing. 'Well, Hercule Poirot, as you've said yourself, Claude certainly knows his onions.'

'Oo-oer, madam,' I retorted and we both dissolved into laughter. After a moment or two, we calmed down again and were about to continue when Hamish's van pulled into view and came to an abrupt halt outside the kitchen window, scattering chuckies as he went. Very unlike him – he never rushed, never ran, always took his time.

'He's in a hurry,' said Jeannie as we both stood up to see what was going on. Hamish loped out of the van, ran around to the other side and, much to our surprise, helped Mouse out.

'I thought Mouse was in Edinburgh today,' said Jeannie.

'She is … well, was.' It became apparent by the way Hamish held his arm protectively around her that all was not well.

'I wonder what's going on?' I said as the pair of them walked over to the stable block studio, heads together.

'I don't know, but it doesn't look good,' said Jeannie. 'I'll put the kettle on.'

I kept an eye on the stable block. Not three minutes later, Hamish came tearing out, heading our way, so I ran along the corridor and out the front door to head him off at the pass.

'What's going on? Is Mouse OK?' I asked.

I could see by his face and the way he was holding himself that he was incandescent with rage.

'What is it?' I asked as he stomped past me, indicating with his thumb to get into the kitchen as he wasn't going to discuss it out here, so I trotted in behind him, where Jeannie stood, dishtowel in hand. He closed the door behind us.

'That bastard De Witt has bumped Mouse,' he spat.

'What?'

'She was on the train halfway to Edinburgh to meet him, to do the final measure of which picture was to be hung in which place, and he texted her and said it was all off.'

'Texted her! What did it say?'

'Said it was all off. Some big feckin' wig artist he knows

has come back to Scotland and requested to do a festival exhibition, a huge coup apparently, so he dropped Mouse just like that.'

I stared at him. 'Who the hell is it?' I asked.

'Oh, I don't know but apparently his stuff is worth hundreds of thousands. Chris Akaboome, he uses hippo dung.'

'Oh yeah, I have heard of him, but that doesn't mean he can just drop Mouse.'

'Exactly. Which is why I am going to Edinburgh right now to teach that snivelling little shit a lesson he won't forget,' he said and then softened for a moment. 'Look after Mouse, will you? She's in a terrible state. I have to go.'

And with that, he stormed out, got into his van and sped away.

Jeannie and I looked at each other. Holy shit.

'We've got to stop him,' I said.

'How?'

'I don't know but I'm scared what he will do to the guy if he gets his hands on him.'

'Or what the guy will do to him if he's the sort of man that behaves like that,' said Jeannie.

I felt sick.

'Mouse. I'll go over and see her now,' I said.

'OK,' said Jeannie as I marched off.

Climbing up the steps to the studio, the door was closed. A 'Do Not Disturb, Artist at Work' sign was on the door.

'Mouse,' I said gently.

Nothing.

'Mouse,' I said again, slightly louder this time.

Still nothing.

'It's Maddy. Mouse, please let me in!' I said in a more urgent tone. I listened and waited, but nothing. I tried, using the base of my hand, to thump the door this time, making it clear I was not going away. 'Come on, Mouse, it's me, please. We can work this out … just let me in.'

Still no reaction. I tried the handle, but it was bolted on the inside. I rattled the door.

'Mouse, open the door, please,' I begged, pulling and pushing the door with all my might. Out of breath I stopped and listened. You could have heard a pin drop, total silence. Panic was rising in my chest. Mouse was fragile at the best of times, her confidence never high. I knew no matter how many times she was told her work was brilliant, she never really believed it. She had imposter syndrome and never believed she was good enough. The piercings, the goth makeup, and hiding behind her long black fringe were all signs that her confidence had been eroded. Why hadn't I said anything to her?

'MOUSE!' I shouted, thumping the door.

That bastard De Witt, I thought, realising she was not going to respond. I ran back to Jeannie.

'I don't know what to do,' I said. 'Should I phone Hamish?'

'No, he's driving, and the state he was in when he left … it will only make things worse,' said Jeannie, pacing. 'And Maddy, you need to take care here. Come on and sit down, this isn't good for you or the baby.' Taking my arm, she led me to the couch where I sat down.

'There is one thing we can do,' I said.

Jeannie looked at me. 'What?'

'Jack,' I said. 'He would do anything for Hamish, anything for Mouse.'

'A friend in need,' said Jeannie. 'You're right. Phone him now.'

And so, hands shaking, I did. It connected straightaway and then rang and rang, finally clicking onto answerphone. I left a message.

'Jack. It's Maddy. Listen, we need your help. Hamish is on his way to Edinburgh to kill Adrian De Witt, who pulled out of the exhibition this morning. Mouse has locked herself in the stable and I'm scared she's going to hurt herself. I've tried battering down the door, but she won't answer. She'll listen to you; I know she will. Please help.'

I sent a text, too. *Urgent message on phone.*

'Well, if that doesn't sort him out, I don't know what will.'

'What can we do now?' I asked.

'Wait.'

Chapter 45

Feeling absolutely helpless we paced back and forth, the slightest noise or movement outside drawing us both to the window. I tried once again to get a reaction from Mouse, but I was met by a wall of silence. I looked at my watch.

'Hamish will be in Edinburgh soon,' I said.

'I feel sick,' said Jeannie.

'Me, too,' I said as Jeannie sprang up again and boiled the kettle just so she'd something to do.

A sudden movement caused a frisson of excitement, but it was just the joiner getting his packed lunch from his van. Seeing us both nosing out the window, he waved cheerily and disappeared again. Standing hip to hip, staring out the kitchen window, I thought I heard something in the distance, and Jeannie and I looked at each other. Jack's Land Rover came lurching around the corner, heading up the drive like Speedy Gonzales.

'Jack!' I shouted.

'Thank God,' said Jeannie as we both rushed outside, watching as he pulled on the handbrake whilst simultaneously getting out of the vehicle.

'Where is she?' he asked.

I pointed to the stable. 'Still in there, still won't respond,' I said, following hot on his heels, as he strode purposefully over to her studio, taking the stairs two at a time. I stopped in my tracks. This was as far as I would go. I'd done my bit, and now it was over to him, I thought, retreating to the courtyard where Jeannie stood pale, with her arms crossed tightly across her chest. Jack's hammering and shouting travelled to the courtyard, filling us with optimism. He was not one for giving up; it went on for over a minute and then suddenly, silence.

'Sounds like he's in,' said Jeannie.

'God, I hope so.'

'OK, let's leave them be,' she said, turning on her heels.

Following her back into the kitchen, she boiled the kettle again and we drank another cup of tea.

'Jack looked awful,' I said.

'Aye but the important thing is he's here,' she said.

'You're right,' I said, my hands slipping down to rest on my tummy, calming myself down. 'Everything's going to be OK,' I whispered to the bean and myself. After five minutes we settled down, taking it in turns to be on look out. It was over an hour before Jeannie announced, 'They're out of the stable and coming this way.' I jumped up and saw them, as Jeannie quickly busied herself with filling the kettle. I rushed over to the sofa, arranging myself in such a way so, I hoped, it looked like I'd been there idly chit-chatting for hours. Jeannie and I looked at each other as the front door clonked shut and the sound of steps got closer. The door opened and in they came, Mouse, then Jack.

'Hi,' I said, putting my magazine down and smiling casually, my nerves frayed.

'Hello, you two,' said Jeannie, wiping the kitchen table with a cloth. 'Cup of tea?'

'Yes please,' whispered Mouse in a tiny voice, as Jack led her over to the table and sat her down. So, we did what we always did in these circumstances, concentrated on getting the biscuit tin, pouring the tea, and making sure everyone was fed and comfortable before addressing the issue.

'Any word from Hamish?' asked Jack.

'No,' Jeannie and I said in unison, which elicited a sob from Mouse. Sitting up beside her on the bench, I handed her a napkin to blow her nose.

'When did he leave?' asked Jack.

'About half ten,' I said. It was near enough two o'clock.

'Have you tried phoning him?' he asked.

I shook my head. 'No,' said Jeannie.

'OK,' said Jack, picking up his phone and dialling.

'Jack, man, hi.' We heard the familiar voice booming down the line. 'How's it going?'

'I'm fine, it's you we're concerned about. Where are you?'

'Just coming into St Andrews.'

A collective exhale went round the table.

'I'll see you a minute then.'

'You at the big house?'

'Aye. OK, see you then,' Jack said and clicked off.

'He sounded OK,' I said.

'Thank God,' said Mouse.

'I'm looking forward to hearing this,' said Jack, getting up and taking his jacket off, settling in.

I was relieved to see a wee bit of colour had returned to Mouse's cheeks as I patted her hand and reassured her that everything was going to be fine. Silently, we awaited his arrival, munching our way through another batch of Jeannie's test cookies. Jack looked as if he hadn't slept for days; dark shadows under his eyes, his bedhead hair unruly, and he hadn't shaved either. His shirt looked like he'd slept in it, but then so did mine – neither of us were blessed with the domesticity gene. It was hard to see but I thought his jumper seemed looser round the shoulders, too. As I scrutinised him,

246

he looked up, caught me staring at him, his face spreading into a slow smile. My throat closed, my heart twisting.

'How are you doing?' he asked.

'OK now,' I said, holding his gaze, smiling back, my whole being flaring with hormones, lust, relief.

Chapter 46

A moment later, the butcher's van rolled up the drive, and we were all up on our feet again, this time to see Hamish, who waved and came striding straight in.

'Hi guys,' he said, as if nothing had happened.

We all looked at him.

'I could murder a beer, it's been a hell of a day,' he said.

Another tsunami of relief rolled over us as he was clearly unhurt. He poured a cold beer into a dimpled mug and sat down next to Mouse to tell us about his day.

'You're up to speed with that bastard De Witt?' he asked Jack.

'Yes.'

'Well, when I left, I was bloody furious but luckily I had time to calm down during the drive to Edinburgh. Dundas Street is easy to find, but I couldn't get parked, so I ended up parking the van on the pavement right outside his gallery. You should have seen his face—' he snorted '—he came stomping out with a face like a bulldog chewing a wasp and was about to give me hell when I took a step towards him. De Witt is a tall man, but I've seen more meat on a pencil, so he backed off and scuttled off inside but of course I followed him.'

Jack, Mouse, Jeannie, and I were absorbed as he continued.

'So, there he was, standing behind his desk waving his phone around.' Hamish did an impersonation of De Witt's posh, Edinburgh drawl. '"I'll call the police," he said, "if you don't tell me who you are and what you want!" Sorry, I said, how rude of me not to introduce myself. I'm Hamish Campbell, which of course meant nothing to him at all. So, then I said, "My friends call me, The Butcher of St Andrews".'

We all roared with laughter.

'Aye,' he went on. 'He damn near shat himself.'

'Oh Hamish!' said Jeannie, dabbing her cheeks as tears of mirth rolled down them.

'At that stage, I thought he might die of a heart attack as he didn't seem to have any blood left in his face, and I didn't want to end up in jail for murder, so I told him I was there to talk about the Dorcas Pratt exhibition.

'Then the penny dropped. I kept my eyes on his, and every step I took toward him he took one back. I asked him for the contract he had with Mouse, but she already told me he hadn't signed it, and he confessed that right away, too, so I knew it wasn't worth the paper it's written on. I told him that he made a mistake by crossing the wrong family. To scare him, I said I knew a hitman in Dundee, which worked because he was shaking so much that his glasses fell off and he locked himself in the toilet.'

By now he had us all in absolute stitches.

'I was enjoying myself a lot at this point, but I noticed a traffic warden making his way to the van. So, to avoid getting a ticket, I made my way back. But before I left, I shouted at De Witt, through the toilet door, that he would be met with pain if he ever darkened our door again. Even though I didn't do what I set out to do to De Witt, I managed to get this!' He whipped out some papers from his jacket and set them in front of Mouse, kissing her tenderly on the cheek.

'Oh Hamish,' said Mouse, her wee cheeks pink and her eyes sparkling as she scanned the pages.

'What is that?' I asked, gagging to know.

'It's his guest list,' said Hamish.

'Ooooooh,' I said, craning over Mouse's shoulder. 'For the exhibition?'

'For any and every exhibition he has ever organised,' Hamish answered proudly. 'There are literally hundreds of names on there.'

'Oh Hamish, he told me about fifty times that this list has taken him thirty years to build,' said Mouse.

'Holy shit, and look at some of the names on it!' I said, reading out a few. It was the who's who of Edinburgh's New Town.

'Hamish, this is priceless,' I said, patting him on the shoulder.

'You're a bloody genius,' said Jack.

'Aye, well, enough about me. So where have you been hiding yourself?' he turned to Jack.

Seeing a worried look pass over his face, I jumped in.

'Sorry to interrupt but Jack and I have a couple of things that we need to discuss. The joiner's only here for another half hour or so, if you don't mind?' I said to Jack.

As ever he got it straight away. I was giving him an out, which he took.

'Absolutely,' he said, heaving himself up, finding his jacket.

The moment had passed, and Hamish was reliving his trip again, and poring over the list with Mouse, who looked infinitely better. Jeannie winked at me as we walked out.

Chapter 47

Crunching over the gravel, we walked towards the garden.

'Thanks, Madeline,' said Jack.

'You're welcome,' I said.

'I'm sorry.'

'Sorry? You just saved the day.'

'You know what I mean, about the past week.'

'Oh, that,' I said, stopping and looking at him.

His dear sweet face was drawn, and his pallor was grey as his eyes searched mine. There was so much to say, but where and how to start?

'Come on. Let's keep walking,' I said, eager to get him into the privacy of the garden.

Silently we moved on, taking refuge on a bench in the orchard.

'Thanks for the photos,' he said.

'Just wanted to keep you in the loop,' I said breezily.

'And for the food,' he said, gently taking my hand.

'My pleasure,' I said, daring to look at him.

'And thanks for not cooking it yourself.'

I guffawed.

Silence once again, that comfortable, easy feeling, where there was no need to fill the gaps...

'I've thought long and hard about what happened,' he said. 'I honestly hadn't realised how much I loved that baby. I know she wasn't mine but honestly that didn't matter, all

I saw was a helpless child, a victim of circumstance, none of it was her fault and, well…'

'She was adorable.'

'Yeah, she was,' he said, slowly coming to a halt.

'You were great with her,' I said.

He smiled sadly. 'Spending every day and night with her, getting to know her. Her first tooth, her smile, watching her awakening to the world around her… it was amazing.

'It made me realise for the first time that, well, that's what it's all about, isn't it? It's not about us, it's about the next generation.'

'Jack,' I said.

'I couldn't help it, Maddy… I got ahead of myself and made plans with her, with you, for all of us… I hoped that you and I – and this place…' he couldn't bring himself to finish.

I stood up and faced him. 'Jack,' I said, and our eyes met, that visceral jolt as I took his hands in mine came over me, and I boldly placed them on my belly.

Chapter 48

Jack got it right away. His face as he realised that I was carrying our child melted my heart. Slowly, he stood up, opening his arms and locking them round me, holding me close and whispering, 'Madeline Campbell, you have made me the happiest man in the world.'

What happened that day will live with me forever. The hopes and dreams I had held securely in my heart were finally realised. At this point it would be handy to tell you the lens goes all smudgy and we walk off into the sunset together. But it was Jack and I, so you know that was never going to happen, we had too much to do. We talked over each other, excitedly making plans, kissing, holding each other, saying all the things we wanted to say, all in a rush and then we ran out of steam, the significance of what was happening to us settling in. Silently we sat there, a deep sense of calm descending on us. Everything was going to be OK.

It had been such a disastrous day already, and we decided not to add to it with our news. It was only fair to let Jack digest the news of his impending fatherhood, so with that agreed, we went back to the house to see how the others were doing.

As we re-joined the party, Jeannie looked at me and smiled. She knew.

William had arrived by now, too, greeting us with a wave.

He had joined Mouse and Hamish who were squished together on the bench, the table covered in paper and pens.

'What are you lot up to?' I asked.

'We've had an idea,' beamed Mouse.

'OK, you two, sit down and listen, see what you think.' Hamish jumped up and dragged us over to the sofa.

'Right,' he said, marching up and down the length of the kitchen, making sure to avoid the dogs. 'The Bakehouse is due to open in just under two weeks and if there is one thing we know how to do, it's to throw a damn good party,' he stated, 'so we were thinking, why not launch Mouse's exhibition at the same time?'

I looked at Jack who grinned back at me.

'We have the people,' enthused Hamish, picking up and flapping De Witt's guest list about.

'Have you seen who is on that list?' said William, his eyes boggling.

'Yes,' I said. 'Now I don't want to rain on anyone's parade, it is a great idea, but what about the canvases – they are far too big to hang in the bakehouse. I mean, you can't even fit one of them into the studio.'

'You're right, they won't fit on the walls, but they will fit in the garden,' said Hamish, grinning and sitting down next to Mouse again, kissing her on the cheek.

'The garden. Are you mad?' I said, sounding like a killjoy again.

'Just imagine,' Hamish said, leaping up again, arms flapping. 'Twelve stunning paintings, big, bold and beautiful, hanging on the ancient wall of the garden, surrounded by real trees, vegetables, plants and fruit.'

'It would be wonderful,' said William.

'Yes, it would, I agree, but this is Scotland, not St. Tropez.

What if it rains?' said my new sensible self, refusing to pipe down.

'Ah, we've thought of that, too,' said Hamish. 'Gordy's pal Clink is the marquee guy. I've texted him to come and have a look, and see what he can suggest, you know, tarpaulins or something like that, just in case the weather goes against us.'

Hamish stopped and looked at us like a kid about to be told if he was going to Disneyland or not.

Jack, who hadn't said a word up to this point, released his arm from round my expanding waist, stood up and turned to the rapt audience.

'Well, I think it's a fabulous idea,' he said. 'Let's do it!'

'Yeah!' said Mouse, jumping up, then clamping her hand over her mouth. 'Oh, sorry,' she said as I went over and hugged her. 'Welcome back,' I said, as she hugged me back.

Chapter 49

From that day to this, Jack and I haven't spent one night apart. That day when we left Kelso Lodge, I drove the Custard Beast around to his and just sort of stayed. We stayed in bed for a glorious two days, leaving the house only to walk the dogs, and then when we finally ran out of food, we rejoined the world, to help prepare for the big day. I am happy to report that it was at this stage that my recurring nightmare of Jody, Scarlett, Jack, me, and the bean living together in some polygamous cult stopped.

Speaking of big days, when Jack found out that I hadn't seen a real doctor yet, he insisted that we make an appointment which we attended together. The doctor said I was healthy as a horse and my due date was estimated at first of November, which is coincidentally the same date as Jack's grandmother, Flora. Coming up to sixteen weeks, the doctor offered to do a scan then and there to check that all was well. He said, if we're lucky, we might be able to see the gender of the baby, and he said we might be able to see if it's a boy or a girl. I wanted to know, but Jack didn't. Once the doctor had asked me everything, we were taken into a side room, the gel was put on my tummy and a nurse came in. As she ran the wand over my tum, we could see movement. 'There we are,' she said, 'a very lively baby.' We gazed at it for a moment or two, speechless.

'Now,' she said. 'Do you want to know what sex it is?'

'No,' said Jack, standing up.

'I do,' I said.

'OK, I will see you outside,' he said. 'And don't spoil the surprise, Maddy,' he added, grabbing his jacket and kissing me lightly on the cheek.

The nurse smiled. 'OK, now let's have a good look, see what we can see,' she said.

I could have stared at that wee screen for hours. It did take a little longer than I thought, and at one point, the nurse went off to get the doctor so he could give a second opinion. I realised that it wasn't going to be an easy secret to keep, that was for sure, but I would do my best to keep it for as long as I could.

Now Jack and I had an opportunity to talk and talk and talk, we decided it was only fair to wait until after the exhibition to tell everyone about the baby. The opening of the Bakehouse and the launch of Mouse's exhibition was more than enough for everyone to focus on. There was a lot to do.

Mouse was still reeling from the way De Witt had discarded her and her work, as if it were nothing. She's had a few wobbles already, and no matter what we said, she still didn't believe that she was good enough to have her own exhibition. To prove her wrong, we were determined to make it a ripsnorter of a day, so we were all working hard to make that happen. Flat out.

We plumped for the Sunday. The perfect day to take a drive if you're coming from further afield, like Edinburgh or Glasgow. Today was the only day the Birdie and Bramble is closed so Claude could be here to help Jeannie, and Javier could run the front of the house and use some of the Birdie's part-timers.

Foodwise Jeannie has been working on perfecting the Bakehouse menu with Claude, and their relationship has also moved on apace. They don't jump apart every time someone walks into the kitchen anymore, and with Jeannie's genius touch at baking and Claude's with everything else culinary, they are a force to be reckoned with. William and I know how fortunate we are to have the pair of them working alongside us, which we tell them regularly and they pooh pooh. Though I can tell they love it.

Hamish was working in a literal frenzy in the garden. There were green shoots sprung up everywhere, and things were coming to life much faster than we imagined.

Barclay continued to make himself available to help and was punctual and quiet, doing as he was told. Initially, Jack thought he was hallucinating when he arrived to see his normally obstreperous parent methodically digging a trough to plant seedlings. I explained his recent involvement and that since he had been included there had been not one cross word, suggesting that maybe what Jack had said to him about being out on his ear if this project didn't work had sunk in after all. Jack accepted what I told him but remained sceptical. He kept his distance, saying there was a lot of water under the bridge, and it would take time for him to believe that there wasn't some ulterior motive which, given their history, was more than fair.

Of course, we had to get the invites out and fast. There were the obvious ones, locals, friends, family and then there was De Witt's list. We hummed and hawed about how many of the hoi polloi to ask, and then decided to invite the whole damn lot. Well, why not? With this in mind, Mouse designed and printed an exquisite invitation the very same day, using her favourite painting as the backdrop.

As the days progressed, the RSVPs started to come in and Mouse began to perk up. She looked happier, one or two of her piercings had disappeared again, her makeup was less dramatic, which were all very positive signs.

The one slight hiccough was on the day we lit the old ovens for the first time. They had been cleaned out, the chimney was swept, and it was ready to roll. We all crowded into the bakehouse for the inaugural lighting; Hamish lit the kindling, the wood took without need for any further encouragement, and just as we were about to give ourselves a round of applause, the smoke came billowing straight back and blasting into our faces. Coughing and spluttering, we opened all the doors and windows and ended up in the car park confused as to what had happened. With the fire doused, a sooty Hamish got out the ladder and climbed onto the roof to discover a huge nest that had been built on the top of the chimney, completely blocking it. Deftly removing it, he placed it in a nearby tree and we tried again. This time it roared into life, the heat built and within forty-five minutes our very first loaf was ready. Jeannie was overcome with emotion when Claude told her it was the best bread he had ever tasted. It was an absolute triumph.

The last piece of the puzzle. We were good to go.

Chapter 50

Early morning on the day of the opening, I threw back the curtains.

'Overcast but not raining,' I said, as Jack opened his arms enticing me back to bed.

Going over and giving him a leisurely kiss I reluctantly wriggled free, as he complained loudly. 'We have too much to do! You will have to wait,' I said, laughing and heading off for a shower.

Within the hour we rolled up to Kelso Lodge just in time to see Clink the marquee man dragging a ginormous role of tarpaulin from the back of his truck and propping it up against the outside of the house before turning to leave.

'Is that it?' I asked.

'Aye, Hamish and Gordy said they would sort it out from here. I've two weddings this weekend,' he said, jumping back into his lorry and driving off. Staring at the gathering clouds, and the roll of tarpaulin, I looked at Jack.

'Looks like we are in the lap of the gods,' I said as Jeannie appeared from inside the house, carrying a case of wine. 'Stop, Jeannie, I want to carry this,' said Claude, running out after her in full whites,

'I'm fine, Claude, I'm fine,' she said and then spotted us. 'Morning, you two. They delivered the red wine to the house, instead of the Bakehouse,' she explained, stomping past us, beaming. We giggled at the sight of this very capable woman being trailed by a frustrated French man jumping around in her wake, determined to wrestle the wine from her.

Following them around to the walled garden, Mouse had obviously been in early to hang her pictures. As we walked in, she was still humming and hawing, chopping and changing some of the pictures over, then back again.

Jack and I stopped and marvelled at the scene. The vibrant colours, the subject matter, and vitality of the pictures were extraordinary and, in this setting, dazzling.

'Mouse, they are perfect,' I told her.

'Thanks,' she said, looking as if she hadn't slept in a week.

'It's going to be great,' I reiterated for the millionth time.

Hamish put his arm round her and squeezed. 'I'm so proud of you.'

'We all are,' added Jack.

Well, that was it, Mouse in tears, me in tears, Hamish and Jack unsure what to do, the whole thing was about to go pear-shaped when William arrived.

'What on earth?' he said, looking at the blubbing huddle before him. And then, God love him, he stopped, his hand flying up to his mouth. Standing back, he appraised his surroundings. Watching him, we all stood in silence for what felt like an age, when suddenly he turned, smiling broadly, looking at Mouse, clapping his hands.

'Bravo, Mouse! These are exquisite ... you will be the talk of the town, and not just this town, every town,' he said with tears in his eyes, walking over and giving her a kiss.

'Don't you start, or we're finished,' I said to him.

'Yeah,' Hamish said rather boisterously, which broke the ice and we all laughed and began rushing around again in preparation. The doors were opening in less than an hour.

I had arranged something special for Jack, and it was time.

261

Walking into the Hobbit house, we stopped.

'Close your eyes,' I said.

He grinned. 'What are you up to?'

'You'll see,' I said, kissing him gently on the lips.

'OK,' he said, closing his eyes tightly. Taking his hands, I opened the door and led him gently into the Bakehouse. 'Watch your step.'

The smells coming from the ovens were delicious, the substantial island was covered in trays of food already laid out for the guests. Croustades of smoked salmon and fresh dill, mini almond croissants, lined up like soldiers, perfectly cut miniature sandwiches of roast beef and mustard, crispy ham and pear, prawn and mayonnaise, and cucumber. Mini blue cheese quiches, chorizo sausage rolls, haggis scotch eggs, and much more. Baskets of loaves and platters of cheese. Jeannie had been busy, and Claude, too. There were big barrels full of ice, champagne, and elderflower cordial, two of the refectory tables were covered in crystal champagne glasses. Amidst this feast was Javier, who looked immaculate in his white shirt and black apron, talking to the front of house team, making sure they knew what was expected of them. 'Keep the fizz coming!' he said, grinning at me. We were ready to feed the five thousand, so fingers crossed someone turned up.

In each corner of the room stood a substantial fig tree, with large green waxy leaves, lending an almost tropical look to the room. Hamish had said they were very hardy and would look good and he was bang on. The walls and ceiling were a neutral stone colour, the floor a warm natural oak, the steamer deck light pendants I had sourced on eBay had been hung above the dining area and looked wonderful.

'Open your eyes,' I said.

'Wow,' he said, drinking in the scene before him.

'That's not the surprise,' I said, turning him around towards his grandmother, Flora, who came tottering in on the arm of her carer.

'Gran!' he exclaimed, going up and giving her a gentle hug.

'Jack, darling,' said the frail old lady, her face lighting up. 'Now this is a treat, this takes me back,' she continued, releasing herself from his hug and shuffling over to inspect everything.

'My, my, I spent a great deal of time in here, in the 40s, or was it the 50s?' she said. 'Anyway, it looks just wonderful. Oh, and look at that!' she added, her eyes settling on the images on the wall at the same time as Jack's. The two of them approached them, eyes wide.

Jeannie, William and I had chosen two of the original photographs of the Bakehouse in the 1940s and had them blown up and made into poster size, the quality of them superb. Stunning in black and white, they illustrated that the Bakehouse was the heart and soul of the community. A group of nearly twenty people, all gathered together, smiling, from wee children, the baker himself, farm workers, locals, the laird and his family working together, helping one another through difficult times. Sacks of flour, trays of loaves basking in the sunshine, kids dashing in and out. Flora and Jack were ecstatic, looking carefully at the faces we plucked from the past, so vividly here in front of them.

'Oh, and there's my darling James,' she exclaimed, pointing at her handsome young husband.

'Yes,' said Jack. 'And look, Gran, there you are!' He pointed to her distinctive face.

She looked at it very closely, stepped back, opened her bag and took out her glasses.

'No, no, no, that's not me,' she said.

I looked at Jack. I had hoped this larger-than-life photo

and unexpected trip down memory lane would not be too confusing – it was rather a lot to take in, and the sense of self can be somewhat distorted with age. Jack knew what I was thinking, so he gently tried to move her on.

'Now, Gran, shall we get you a drink?' he asked.

But Flora wasn't for budging. 'Wait,' she said, holding her hand up, still scrutinising the photograph as Jack and I exchanged glances, hoping she wasn't going to be upset.

'Ah yes!' she said. 'There I am!'

Bending forward we looked. And there without a shadow of a doubt was the same face with the same cheekbones, the same smile with slightly longer hair arm in arm with two other women on the left hand side of the picture.

'Oh, my goodness, so it is! Then who on earth is that?' Jack asked, referring back to the original face.

'That's Clara,' she said. 'My twin sister.'

Jack and I looked at each other. Well I never, it was all beginning to make sense.

At this point Claude marched in followed by Jeannie, resplendent in her Bakehouse apron, along with Mouse and Hamish, hands clamped together. William and Noel were both impeccably turned out in linen suits, one cream, the other black. Style gurus, I thought, as we admired them.

Walking in he nodded to everyone, walked-up to Flora, kissed her cheek 'Mother,' he said and then turned to Jack. You could hear a pin drop.

'Jack,' he said. 'I wanted to congratulate you. You've done a sterling job, nice place, nice people, it all looks very promising. Well done.'

'Thank you, and thank you for your help when I was ... away,' said Jack as he took Barclay's extended hand and shook it.

'Now, come and see this,' said Flora, slipping one arm

through Barclay's and the other through Jack's, guiding them over to see the photos on the wall. Baby steps, I thought, a lump growing in my throat.

The next time the door opened, a few well-known faces began to arrive, and it was all systems go, ensuring everyone had a glass of fizz, a napkin and a canapé, a hand-drawn map of the walled garden, showing the original layout. and how Hamish had interpreted for 2021, and of course, the exhibition catalogue which gave all details about Mouse, her background, the inspiration behind each of the paintings and the all important price list.

By the end of the first hour the Bakehouse and walled garden were jumping. There were forty or more people meandering around the garden, and more people streaming in all the time. The front of house team was doing a great job at making sure everyone was well served, topping up drinks and wandering around with trays of canapés, whilst the rest of us introduced ourselves to our guests and showed them around. I was thrilled to see Mouse engaging with people too, happily walking and talking as she wandered through the garden, engaging with them about her art, Hamish by her side chipping in facts and figures about the garden itself. They were in their element. I was delighted when Sarah and Phil arrived.

'How are things?' she said excitedly.

'Wonderful,' I mooned.

'Well, look at you,' she said, reaching out and touching my tum.

'Yes,' I said, looking at her bump, which was considerably neater. 'I can see you are going to be petite and elegant up to the day you have the baby and I'm going to be the only thing on Earth, other than the Great Wall of China, to be visible from space,' I joked as Phil called her over to see one of Mouse's pictures. Within thirty minutes, the two of them had bought one of the smaller paintings, allowing Charlie to attach the red spot, marking it as sold. The first of many as it transpired.

The weather was on our side; the sky was clear, and its bright blue made the green in the paintings pop. The warmth meant people were in no rush so they meandered around, meeting old friends and making new, slaking their thirst with chilled champagne, eating Jeannie and Claude's fresh, delicious canapés all the while discussing the paintings. As the light changed from a bright blue white to more mellow tones, the paintings evolved, revealing different depths of colour, texture and perspective.

By six we were all exhausted. It had been a long and very successful day.

The last stragglers were making their way out, a minibus arriving to take six people home as they had abandoned their cars. We waved them all off. Closing the door to the Bakehouse and locking it behind them, we looked at the damage. Empty glasses, platters, napkins balled up all over the place ... but Javier marched in with his shirt still immaculate.

'You all go and relax in the garden; I have this sorted,' he said, waving the part-timers in and setting them to work.

'Come and join us?' I asked him, as he looked like he was about to roll up his sleeves and do the washing up.

'OK. Gracias,' he said and took off his apron, following us through to the garden. By now, the solar lights Hamish had wound around the branches of the fruit trees were twinkling to life. William had lit tea lights and storm lamps, he had also set up two tables together and a scattering of chairs for us all with some glasses, two bottles of champagne in ice buckets and a bottle of elderflower cordial. We all sat down gratefully.

it had been a long day. As William popped the cork of the fizz, Jack opened the elderflower and we got ready to raise our glasses. I looked at the assembled throng: Noel and William, Mouse and Hamish, Sarah and Phil, Charlie and Tilda, Uncle Fraser and Auntie Margaret, Barclay and Flora, Jeannie and Claude, Javier and big Gordy, all chatting and laughing, gathered together to help and support one another towards this extraordinary day. And we had done it.

Hauling myself up, I cleared my throat as the tired but happy faces turned toward me.

'I just wanted to say a few words,' I said, as a clanking of glasses and a round of applause rang out. 'Firstly, I wanted to say a huge thank you to every single one of you. William for being the most supportive and understanding patient business partner a person could ever ask for and to Noel, his wonderful husband, for the never-ending support he has shown throughout the rollercoaster of the past year to William and to me.

'To Hamish for being the best gardener and cousin ever.'

'And the only one,' Uncle Fraser shouted, which got a roar of laughter.

'To you Uncle Fraser and Auntie Margaret for being there for me this past year. I know you miss Dad as much as I do, and it hasn't been easy, but you have had my back from that day to this, so I want to thank you both. To Claude and Javier for looking after the Birdie and Bramble and for supporting us all out here today with this new venture, too. Here's to the future! To Jeannie for being my surrogate mum and making the lightest scones in the history of the world. To Mouse, for being an inspiration, a wonderful friend and as of today ... a very successful and soon to be famous artist.'

Whoops and claps rang out.

'To the MacPherson Clan whose history in this house and

garden was the inspiration for us to open the Bakehouse.' Barclay patted Flora's hand, as she blushed and nodded a demure thank you.

'This last year has been such a whirlwind, so many amazing things have happened, but none quite as amazing as meeting you, Jack.' I turned to face him. 'And now I cannot imagine life without you. You have made me the happiest girl in the world,' I warbled, clearly about to lose it, as Jack took to his feet, put his arm round me and kissed me gently. Turning to the crowd, he said, 'We have news …'

'Oooooooooh,' said everyone in true panto style.

'No, I think I'll wait and tell you tomorrow.'

'Aarrrgghh noooo,' everyone shouted in unison, as a few balled-up napkin missiles came our way.

'OK, OK,' Jack said, holding his hand up and waiting for complete silence before he announced, 'Maddy and I are having a baby' and the place went wild.

Cuddles, kisses, congratulations, and happiness were showered on us.

'Do you know if it's a boy or a girl?' shouted Hamish.

'Yes, I do,' I said.

'Well, come on then, tell us,' shouted Hamish who had had quite a few. 'Is it a boy or a girl?'

I laughed and looked at Jack who beamed back at me.

'It's up to Jack, because he doesn't even know the answer to that,' I said.

'Aw, come on, Jack, man,' said Hamish. 'You must be dying to know.'

My eyes were focused only on Jack.

'Well,' he said, beaming at me, a relaxed attitude evident, his eyes ablaze. He had also had a few glasses of fizz. As his eyes locked on me, my body turned to liquid.

'Well?' I asked him.

He nodded.

'You sure?'

'Yes,' he said. 'Are we having a boy or a girl?'

'Yes,' I said.

'Which?' He looked confused. 'A boy or a girl?'

I looked at their expectant faces, all smiling, all dying to know, all utterly silent and then focused on Jack.

'We're having a boy and a girl,' I said, patting my tum, my chin wobbling, tears teetering my secret out at last. Jack looked at me, his mouth open. Sarah was momentarily confused and then the penny dropped.

'Aaarrrrggggh,' she squealed.

Flora smiled like a Cheshire cat. 'Twins!'

★ ★ ★

Acknowledgements

Well it's been a journey ... three books in two years by a woman who had never written a novel before, add to that a pandemic and it's been a rollercoaster.

Thank you to Rhea Kurien for guiding me through this last step, gently nudging me to complete my third book during what has been an extraordinary year.

Thank you to Jenny Brown, my lovely agent and advisor.

Thank you to Douglas Connon, a dear friend, voracious reader and aficionado of all things golf for keeping me on track when I lost momentum.

A huge thanks to old friend and constructive critic Sarah Alexander, a well-educated woman and fabulous sounding board.

And to the educational establishment who told me to get a job in a record shop at the age of sixteen as I would never amount to anything, I blow a loud and eternal raspberry.

And most importantly of all, a massive thank you to my long suffering husband David who calmly watched as I gnashed my teeth, bit my fingernails and raged against the machine as deadline pandemic loomed. I love you.

Printed in Great Britain
by Amazon